To: BE.

THE
IDENTITY THIEF

By C. Michael Forsyth

Chris Michael Forsey

3/4/17

THE
IDENTITY THIEF

Published by Freedom's Hammer
Greenville, S.C.

ISBN 978-0-9884780-2-2
Library of Congress Control Number:
2013950598

DEDICATION:

This book is dedicated to my father,
Chiron William Forsyth,
who taught me right from wrong.

ACKNOWLEDGEMENTS

I thank my wife Kaye for her unwavering support and my partners in crime Jordan Auslander, Jennie Franklin and John Stevens for their invaluable input. A story in the *Las Vegas Sun News* about the homeless denizens of the sewers beneath Sin City spared me from having to make a trip down there, and descriptions of the Khyber Pass in Steven E. Wilson's wonderful book *Winter in Kandahar* were equally helpful. Interviews with security experts from LifeLock provided cutting-edge information on the ploys of identity thieves – some of which will doubtless be old hat by the time you read these words!

Cover art by Mshindo I.
Proofread by Martha Moffett.
Book design and layout by URAEUS.

Chapter 1
ON THE JOB

Looking at X, one would be hard-pressed to pinpoint his ethnicity. Olive-skinned with prominent cheekbones and thick, close-cropped hair the hue of a raven's feathers, he could be, one might argue with equal conviction, Greek, Italian, Turkish, Arabic, Hispanic or Indian (either "the dot or feather kind," as a former associate once jocularly put it).

The fact that he was fluent in six languages and could convincingly fake accents of a dozen others – not to mention his mastery of a slew of regional American dialects – served him well in his vocation. Which was, of course, identity theft.

Today, X happened to be Jewish and today his name happened to be Arnold Feinberg of Great Neck, Long Island.

Dressed in a crisply pressed gray business suit, he sat in the local branch of the First Federated Bank across from an assistant manager, a lean brunette with the even features and wrinkled visage of an over-the-hill beauty queen.

"Your electronic transfer cleared last night, Mr. Feinberg," she told him and gestured toward a desk where a bald co-worker was busily stamping documents. "The check is printing out over there."

X never liked this part. The process by which information was beamed to a printer and churned out seemed interminable. Although logic dictated that it must travel at close to the speed of light, the data seemed to hover in limbo for an unnervingly long time.

Quite unwillingly, he would find himself vividly imagining FBI agents bursting through skylights, rappelling down walls from all directions and piling on him like linebackers. But he feigned nonchalance and smiled patiently.

"I'm in no hurry," he assured her in a cultured New York

accent with just a hint of a Brooklyn pedigree. It was a dialect X had mastered – exquisitely, he thought with considerable pride. "The next item on the agenda is shoe-shopping with the little woman, so time is *not* of the essence."

At last the check printed out – the figure $168,017.03 standing out in a crisp, elegant font. No G-men came crashing through the skylight. He was not tackled, handcuffed or ordered to "spread 'em."

"We'll certainly miss having you as a customer, Mr. Feinberg," the assistant manager said as she slid a document across the desk toward him. She sounded oddly sincere, although they'd met for the first time today. "Just sign here and here and we'll close the account, as you requested."

"Thank you," he replied. After he signed Feinberg's name, he stood and turned to go.

"Just a minute," the assistant manager said.

X turned slowly.

The woman looked about furtively. X could not be sure exactly at whom; it was someone behind him. He was, however, quite sure that out of the corner of his eye, he could see a younger woman at a nearby desk meet her eyes and give a knowing nod.

"I need you to accompany me to my office for a moment," she said, now wearing a blank, unreadable expression.

X looked at his Cartier watch, as if time suddenly were of the essence.

"As a matter of fact, I really do have to go ... " he began lamely.

"This will only take a minute," she said, pleasantly but authoritatively, still wearing the poker face. "I promise."

X glanced longingly at the large glass doors, gauging how quickly he could sprint to them. A burly security guard with biceps like The Rock's stood at the exit and now turned to face him.

"Fine, then," he said, turning a shade pale. She stood, and led him through a maze of desks. One co-worker looked up at X and seemed to scrutinize him; two others he caught hastily looking away.

As they approached the back office, X could feel his heart beginning to pound so hard he thought that it surely must be audible. The walls weren't glass; the door was good, old-fashioned oak. You couldn't see who or what was behind it.

Was this woman even a real bank employee? Her frozen helmet-hair suddenly reminded him of an undercover officer who once nearly snared him.

"I really, I really ..." he muttered as they reached the door, and tried to turn back. Her hand gripped his forearm and stopped him in his tracks. Wearing what was now plainly an artificial smile, she opened the door and more or less pushed him through.

The room was empty, save for a shelf full of assorted giraffe-themed knickknacks and a photo of the bank employee at the Grand Canyon with two teenage boys and an older man sporting a receding hairline. The assistant manager went to her desk, reached into a tray and plucked out a business card.

She took a pen and began to scribble on the back.

"I just wanted to be sure that you have this," she said, handing him the card.

He glanced at the front. Leslie Middleton, Assistant Manager, First Federated Bank. She'd given her name before and he'd promptly forgotten it. He flipped the card over and saw a cell phone number accompanied by the words "Call me!" And a smiley face.

When he looked up she was blushing profusely.

"If you need anything, be sure to contact me," she said with a coy smile.

"I'll definitely do that if something ... comes up," he replied warmly.

As he turned to go, his heart rate returning to normal, he noticed the jar of lollipops on her desk.

"May I?"

"Help yourself."

He dipped his hand into the jar and plucked out a lemon-flavored lollipop. Lemon had always been his favorite.

Chapter 2
THE MARK

Swiping Feinberg's identity had been monumentally easy. The real Feinberg, a rising exec at an advertising firm, had applied for a mortgage online and was blitzed by offers from numerous banks and brokers. What he had no way of knowing was that one company, Worldwide Bank, was bogus and its Web site existed solely as a device for collecting personal data from unsuspecting customers.

Feinberg had to provide his mother's maiden name, his date and place of birth, and his Social Security number. He also set up a password, which was Amber. (This, incidentally, was not his wife's name, nor his daughter's. Perhaps it was a former paramour for whom he still carried a flame.) In any event, Feinberg made the lazy, all-too-common error of choosing the same password he'd used for all his personal accounts. Plus he provided the numbers of all his savings, checking, money market and brokerage accounts.

Feinberg had received an apologetic email stating that he'd been turned down for the loan, a minor blow to his ego, but no real inconvenience since he had plenty of other banks to choose from. Within a couple of days, he'd forgotten he ever heard of Worldwide Bank. But by then, of course, all the raw material needed to fabricate Feinberg's doppelganger had been obtained.

Taking the Long Island Railroad back to Manhattan that afternoon, X congratulated himself on a job well done and phoned ahead to Samantha, his partner in crime and erstwhile girlfriend.

"Any hitches?" she asked.

"Smooth as a baby's bottom," he assured her, while perusing *Bloomberg* on his iPad to see how their stateside investments were performing.

"Hurry back. I've got a surprise for you."

X frowned. He did not like surprises. Indeed, he preferred events to unfold like clockwork according to a meticulously conceived plan of his own design.

Knowing this preference all too well, Samantha hurriedly added, "It's good news. You won't believe what our Homeland Security – "

"Sounds like pillow talk, Sam," he broke in.

"Pillow talk" was their codeword for a topic that should not be discussed over the phone and almost exclusively referred to a criminal enterprise.

"Okay, okay. Get your ass home quick. I'm getting wet just thinking about this thing."

X grinned, pleased by the dueling promises of a major score and afternoon delight. Returning to his iPad, he thought *Life is good.*

Mind you, X did not think of himself as an identity thief. Indeed, he bristled at the term – sometimes making the point that a person's identity cannot be stolen.

"Why, it makes about as much sense to speak about stealing a soul," he once observed. He would instead refer to "borrowing" the identities of his marks, a term he preferred to "victim." Among his cohorts, he described himself as a "professional imposter" and took tremendous pride in his chameleon-like ability to alter his appearance and speech patterns.

"An imposter," X lectured Samantha on more than one occasion when waxing philosophical, "practices the highest level of acting. The performance has to be absolutely flawless, because the penalty for failure isn't a bad review, it's a stint in Attica." He sometimes spoke of his "craft" with a kind of reverence one might expect from a long-in–the-tooth member of the Barrymore clan rattling on about the theater.

Of course, X boasted no such impressive lineage. He could be maddeningly cagey when discussing his past with his accomplices. His place of birth, true name and ethnic background were details he never divulged. But, while spooning in the blissful afterglow of his first roll in the hay with Samantha three years ago, he once revealed this much: His immigrant mother had worked as a maid for a series of rich families, and on not one but two occasions she'd been taken advantage of – once in a pantry, once on a freshly mopped kitchen floor.

So he felt he was striking a blow for all those who cleaned the toilets of the hoi polloi, "the little people who drive their limousines and trim their hedges," as he put it. Because he limited his practice to targets who boasted a net worth in excess of $500,000, he felt that he was redistributing wealth.

"We're like Robin Hood and his Merry Men," he once declared, when trying to persuade a reluctant geek in a computer repair department into turning over a disk bearing a copy of a certain celebrity's My Documents file.

X resided in a loft in lower Manhattan leased to "Mel Gallo," a name X rather fancied. There existed, as one might guess, a real Mel Gallo, who had been unfortunate enough to pass X in a crowded New Jersey restaurant 11 months earlier. This fellow patron's wallet contained several RFID-enabled credit cards and a Veteran's Administration ID card. A radio frequency identification chip on these cards allows data such as the bank name and account number – and the vet's Social Security number – to be read a short distance away.

This makes transactions smoother than with cards that rely on magnetic strips. It also allowed the identity thief's handy-dandy little scanner to pick up the information four feet away from the real Mel Gallo.

Honestly, it was little more than an updated form of good old-fashioned "shoulder-surfing" – standing next to an old lady at a checkout line and memorizing her name, address, and bank information as she scribbled out a check (to the annoyance of the growing line behind her). But X found this much more dignified and hoped to get a good deal of mileage from the little gizmo before more people wised up and turned to the new, electronically shielded wallets.

The apartment was on the fifth floor, accessed by an old-fashioned elevator that rattled unnervingly as it crawled up. But X, who was a bit claustrophobic, preferred to trot up the stairwell, eerily lit though it was.

Their digs were far from luxurious, surprisingly Spartan one might even say, because they were prepared to skip town at a moment's notice – bags were packed in a closet. A genuine Miro obtained a year earlier in an auction-house scam was one of their few extravagances, along with a few choice pieces of antique furniture.

No, rather than invest in pricey furnishings, designer clothes or luxury autos, they stashed most of their funds in the Cayman Islands, while rolling the dice with some small change on Wall Street. One associate of X's, a retired flimflam man in his late 80s, scolded him that this frugal approach was folly.

"Spend it while you've got it," the wizened old Irishman advised between puffs on a cigar. "That way, if you end up in jail, at least you'll have memories of having lived like a king."

But X had no more intention of winding up in prison than becoming Emperor of Japan. He was, so he thought, far cleverer than any lawman.

As soon as he opened the door, Samantha, blond and voluptuous to the verge of being pleasantly plump, rolled away from the computer where she did the majority of her work, hopped off the swivel chair and wrapped her fleshy arms around him.

"Where have you been?"

"The trains were slow."

She sniffed his collar.

"You didn't stop off at some old girlfriend's, did you?"

He sighed. "Yes, I confess. Jessica Alba and I spent 20 minutes knocking boots. And I have to say, she's not all she's cracked up to be. So a three-way is out."

She smacked his shoulder with mock anger and they kissed.

When not accusing her partner of infidelity, Samantha had the perky manner of a morning news personality. She projected sufficient warmth to easily convince people to surrender the most personal information over the phone. When she called potential targets posing as a representative of the IRS and said, "I have to verify to whom I'm speaking. What is your Social Security number?" they'd typically comply without hesitation.

Although her flair for dialects was by no means as impressive as X's, she could pull off regional accents well enough to sound like your next-door neighbor, whether she was calling Boston or Mississippi. Even when she posed as a debt collector, homeowners would readily spill their entrails. When talking to a man, her voice would become so sweet even the gruffest old curmudgeon would melt.

Apart from phone work, Samantha spent most of her time at the computer, creating impeccable dummy Web pages, and deluging the Internet with emails sent to potential marks – phishing as it was dubbed by authorities.

Perhaps due in part to her sedentary "job," she was 15 pounds overweight and insecure about it. She tended to become hysterical if X eyed the legs of a pretty girl on the street. She once pouted for a day when he opined that J.Lo had a nice butt, as if this were somehow a veiled commentary on her own derriere.

Yet – and X would never admit this to a soul – there came a certain security in having a woman that not every young stud was banging down doors to bang.

"Okay, okay," X demanded. "What's got you so fired up you blab over the phone like some kind of newbie."

"Take a look at this," she said, eagerly leading him to the computer terminal. "You'll never believe who we hooked in the Homeland Security hustle."

Many low-level identity thieves relied on dumpster diving – retrieving documents that victims had failed to shred, such as bank statements, preapproved credit card applications and deposit slips. Although this remained a staple of their trade, X and Samantha used far more sophisticated techniques for gathering information. And they typically kept their hands clean, employing a trio of underlings – interns, X called them fondly.

One intern's duty was to make dental appointments around town and sit in the waiting room innocently Twittering and answering emails. While doing so, he would "sniff" for a poorly secured network; medical offices rarely had much security. Once the office computers were accessed, a treasure trove of patient Social Security numbers, addresses and other information was ripe for the taking. X often used the info to file tax returns in the patient's name, collecting an average $6,000 a pop on refunds from Uncle Sam.

Another intern's assignment was to hang out at the big bookstores and wait for some poor soul to log onto the free WiFi on what marks believed to be the store's network. They were, of course, on X's lookalike network, and those who used the time to pay bills online later found their accounts drained dry.

One very fruitful scam was to send out *en masse* (sometimes as many as 300,000 in one wave) emails ostensibly from the mark's bank, warning that there had been a security breach and asking for verification of personal bank account information. A hyperlink imbedded in the email, when clicked upon, whisked the victim to what appeared to be the bank's Web site. The spoofed sites, as they were called in the trade, looked entirely authentic because Samantha loaded them with official-looking logos ripped off from the real bank's Web site.

In a lucrative variation of this scheme, Samantha would phone, claiming to be from the state superior court, politely but firmly warning people that they'd shirked jury duty. To avoid fine or arrest for contempt of court, the marks must cooperate by immediately turning over personal information such as their Social Security number.

In one of X's most lucrative operations, he ripped off the identities of inmates whom he contacted under the guise of a lawyer working pro bono on their court cases. Through correspondence, he gleaned enough personal data to apply for student loans using the inmates' identities. X assumed more than 50 aliases to rake in about $250,000 in federal student grants and loans over a three-year period.

In the opinion of X, this particular operation was a victimless crime. At the most he had sullied the reputation of murderers, rapists and other criminals who could hardly be too concerned about their good names.

But it was the follow-up hustle that really filled him with self-admiration. A paid-off clerk at the FBI fingerprint office intercepted a request for one of the inmates' fingerprints. He substituted X's prints, which Samantha had emailed to him in a PDF file. The switched prints, along with a few forged documents, helped X to assume the identity of the criminal. He walked right into a court building and waltzed out with $90,000 in assets the authorities couldn't prove the guy had embezzled and had intended to return.

This, X preached to his crew, was "poetic justice."

In their latest gambit, initiated just last week, about 3,000 emails had been sent to resident aliens from Muslim nations, as well as to visitors who'd recently had their visas approved. A sternly worded letter ostensibly from the Department of Homeland Security warned them that they were being investigated for possible links to Al-Qaeda. They were directed to a Web site where they were asked to provide detailed information about their assets, financial transactions, charitable donations, etc.

"Have I got a live one for you," Samantha declared, gleefully steering him toward the computer screen. Her voice was giddy and her face was flushed. Getting Samantha to achieve orgasm in bed was an exhausting chore but the intense thrill she got from larceny was almost scary. She pointed triumphantly to the screen as a name materialized.

"Ali Nazeer," she read. "He's a filthy rich Kuwaiti playboy who visits the States once in a blue moon. When he does, he blows through money like there's no tomorrow. Luxury cars, yachts, jewelry and fur coats for his wives, concubines, girlfriends, hos and whoever. He also gambles recklessly and has a history of making enormous wire transfers to cover his losses."

X smiled. This was right up his alley: The target was clearly an asshole who richly deserved to be parted from his riches, or at least a significant portion of them.

Samantha continued. "Here's the sweet part, X. Virtually no one in the country knows what Mr. Moneybags looks like. He's been written up in all the London and European tabloids, but he's notoriously camera shy."

She clicked to another window, revealing a page from the *London Sun* crammed with screeching headlines all vying for attention. One large headline read, "Harem Scarem: Arab Playboy Adds Movie Scream Queen to His Stable." The photo showed a bosomy British starlet who, as far as X could glean from his quick glance at the article, had dumped her rock star boyfriend for Nazeer. The curvaceous crumpet stood arm in arm with a turbaned man whose back was to the camera as he directed her attention to his Arabian stallion.

"You see, just pictures of her, never his face," Sam went on. "The last publicly available photograph of him, which I got after a lot of Googling, was taken when he was a student at Kuwait University at the age of 19." She held it up. "Look like anyone we know?"

The group photo, taken outside of what appeared to be a dormitory, was fuzzy, but with the large somber dark eyes, heavy brows and prominent nose, he could easily have been X as a teen. Nevertheless, X mockingly protested.

"Oh, come on – is my schnoz really that big?"

"Trust me, it is."

X grinned. For starters, that would make forging a passport and an international driver's license a cinch.

"Well, you've got my attention," he said. "What's his net worth?"

"$6.2 billion."

"Did you say *billion*?"

"Billion."

"You're kidding me."

"No, his father was some kind of shipping tycoon whose specialty was building yachts for the royal family. Ali was the sole heir. And he's managed to burn through only about a third of it since his old man kicked the bucket seven years ago. Which makes him a skinflint by international playboy standards, I guess."

X did some quick math in his head (that was another of his gifts). Assuming that they didn't rob Nazeer blind, desirable though that might be, but managed to bilk him of even 1 percent of his fortune, that would still be a cool $60 million.

He hugged her and as her big bosom crushed against him, he wasn't surprised to find that she had what his female Generation Y intern had once somewhat provocatively termed "a titty boner". (X didn't much go in for such vulgar slang).

He could hardly blame her for being aroused; the thought of a rip-off of this magnitude made even the usually cool-as-ice X lightheaded. Sam had always been a good "catcher," grifter lingo for the person who finds a mark. But this time she had outdone herself.

"You know what that means?" he exclaimed. "We've hit the jackpot, Honey Hips. One last score and we're retired and living in Sri Lanka."

This was a private joke of course. Sometimes they'd say Madagascar, sometimes Nepal, sometimes Outer Mongolia. In actuality, they both knew they enjoyed the game, needed the game, too much to give it up. But they talked this way every time they struck what appeared to be the mother lode.

"Guess I'm going to have to brush up on my Arabic – and grow a beard," he said.

A few moments later, forgoing the formality of fully undressing, they were doing the horizontal mambo on the scuffed hardwood floor, X with his trousers around his ankles and Samantha with her dress hoisted up to her waist and thong hauled to one side. Samantha insisted on being called names for the duration of the act – not that he simply talk dirty, but that he lambaste her as a "dirty slut" and other increasingly filthy and demeaning epithets as she approached the peak of passion.

Perhaps Samantha wanted to be punished, X sometimes mused afterward. But what did he know? He was no psychoanalyst. In any event, this night's frenzied lovemaking session was one of their most intense in months, fueled by the promise of the vast riches awaiting them.

Chapter 3
THE SETUP

Over the next few weeks, based on personal data Ali Nazeer had so graciously and unwittingly provided, they went to work recreating key personal documents including a passport, international driver's license and two credit cards. Among the pieces of information the real Nazeer had revealed in their phishing expedition were his driver's license number and his passport number. An associate of X's – you would probably call him an accomplice but X thought of him as a subcontractor – provided the identity thief with a blank Kuwaiti passport purchased from a contact at the embassy for a price of $2,000.

X viewed this as an investment. Beginning with an authentic blank passport, it was child's play to forge either a paper or plastic passport, even to duplicate a hologram-protected image. "When filled out correctly, a blank passport is impossible to detect," X lectured the interns more than once.

X was amply equipped to carry out the task himself, but for a job this big – with so much money on the line and no room for error – he felt it was worth it to farm the work out to a specialist. X knew at once whom he wanted for the job: An ancient Italian master named D'Amato who worked out of a room above a pizza parlor in Little Italy. He had started out making funny money during the Depression, apprenticing under a counterfeiter who churned out bogus $5 bills.

D'Amato had promised X the passport would be ready by 5 p.m. that Friday. X arrived an hour early because he loved to watch the old man work. Bent, gray and wrinkled as a prune, D'Amato was a master craftsman. It was like watching some old-world violin repairman tune a Stradivarius.

X watched, fascinated, as D'Amato fed a blank passport into a laser printer. The most common error of amateurs, X knew, was to print out a blank stolen passport in the wrong typeface. D'Amato would make no such errors.

"Patience is the key," the old man informed X for the perhaps the 20th time.

The trickiest part was to recreate the official government seal, the inkless stamp that leaves an embossed image on paper.

X watched with fascination as the old man placed an old vinyl record – A Tony Bennett LP – over a passport marked with a real seal, then heating the record with an iron, took an imprint. He then pressed the record onto the bogus passport – and when he withdrew it, a perfect duplicate of the seal appeared, raised and all.

"Most of these young wannabe scratchers out there today have never even held a vinyl record, let alone know how to do anything like this," D'Amato grumbled. "Without their Macs, they'd be helpless."

X loved to hear about such tricks of the trade.

"In the old days, we would cut a fresh potato in half and use it to transfer a stamp from one passport to another," D'Amato said. "Today most young folks put all their faith in computers. THIS is perfect." He kissed his handiwork for emphasis.

The duplicate of Ali Nazeer's 2007 passport didn't require the insertion of an RFID chip – it was made before the widespread use of electronic passports. All that was needed was a magnetic stripe and bar code.

It made X a bit sad to think that in this high-tech era, with paperless identification such as retinal scans growing in popularity, D'Amato would soon be obsolete and would probably be puttering around in his daughter's garden in a few years. On the other hand, X expected that the trend would be a boon to identity thieves such as himself. He and his colleagues were already using their wireless scanners to read e-passports at close range – electronically pickpocketing airport passengers of their passport information.

In any event, Al Nazeer's real passport had been issued long enough ago that the old-school approach was just what the doctor ordered.

D'Amato handed X the dummy Al Nazeer passport and the genuine Kuwaiti one he'd used as a model. Except for the names, passport number and salient data – which X double-checked for accuracy – the fake travel document was indistinguishable from the real McCoy.

"Great work as usual, Tony," he said, handing over an envelope stuffed with cash.

X was satisfied with the result. There are more than a dozen different versions of the United States passport alone in circulation. It would take a bona fide passport scholar to be able to detect the difference between a real and a fake Kuwaiti passport.

The mark, X was able to ascertain by running a game on a Kuwaiti airline staffer, wasn't scheduled to visit America again for another two months. That gave them nearly 60 days for X to impersonate him, and hopefully, suck up his money like a vacuum cleaner.

To get a fuller picture of Al Nazeer, Samantha phoned his credit card company fraud prevention number, claiming to be the fat cat's executive secretary. Informing the customer service representative that her boss was concerned that there was suspicious activity on the account, she requested detailed records of the credit-card use for the past six months. Samantha asked that the material be Fedexed overnight to the front desk of Manhattan's exclusive Mayflower Hotel where Mr. Nazeer was staying. The concerned customer service rep agreed to oblige.

X, who'd checked in as Nazeer, collected the documents the next day. He called back and reassured the credit-card rep that all the charges were legit – and provided updated information on how to contact him if any new suspicious activity cropped up.

The credit-card statements spoke volumes.

The Kuwaiti was a gourmand with a weakness for French cuisine. He golfed; he tipped lavishly. He had an Internet account he used to keep in daily contact with business associates and frequently gambled online. He had a penchant for Western call girls and, apparently, great confidence in his own stamina because he generally paid for two at a time. Although he was a bon vivant, he was a teetotaler; no champagne or wine had been ordered by room service.

"It amazes me how these Arabs can be so uptight when it comes to booze, but are such big fans of whores and strippers," Samantha observed. "Remember those 9/11 hijackers; how they spent their last night on Earth getting lap dances at a titty bar?"

"Never underestimate the appeal of a pair of big of American hooters," X said, tweaking her right nipple playfully.

Within two weeks, X had Ali Nazeer's driver's license, passport, and the numbers of his bank accounts in New York, London, Dubai and Riyadh. More than enough to execute their plan.

Chapter 4
THE PLAYBOY

In most identity-theft rings, the culprit who actually exposes himself to risk by purchasing goods under the stolen name is a peon at the bottom of the pecking order – akin to a drug mule who transports contraband stuffed up … well, you know where. But X took pride in his ability to play almost any role. He would rarely trust anyone else in the crew to be the inside man. Besides, of course, in this case he had the advantage of that fortunate resemblance.

D'Amato's passport did the trick. X used it to fly to England, then back to the States five days later. (Ali Nazeer's U.S. visa, thanks to a bogus letter to the State Department, had been rerouted to X's P.O. box.) He strode through McCarren International Airport outside Las Vegas without so much as a raised eyebrow from the officer at the immigration desk.

X arrived at the Giza Hotel and Casino in a sleek white limo rented on one of Al Nazeer's credit cards. Although rather hirsute, his attempt at growing a respectable beard in time had not been successful. The result was by no means as long and flowing as the role demanded, but instead resembled a scraggly cross between that of Yasser Arafat and Shaggy from *Scooby Doo*. So he'd shaved and simply applied a pricey but extremely convincing theatrical beard. He wore a turban with a business suit; full Arab regalia would draw undue attention, he decided.

He came accompanied by two swarthy lugs with a combined weight of 520 pounds, who carted in his six suitcases, giving the bellhops fierce "Don't even think about it" looks when they raced to the curb to help.

When casting these roles, X chose a pair of brothers, Bahador and Babak, who looked the part, although they were Egyptian. Their day jobs were at a car wash and the only camel they'd ever seen was on a cigarette carton. Since theirs were nonspeaking roles, this didn't trouble X very much.

Even in a city whose name is virtually synonymous with garishness, the Giza stood out. It was housed in a giant bronze pyramid that climbed 350 feet into the desert sky and was crowned with the world's brightest beam of light: a laser light beam that, the hotel's brochures boasted, could be seen 62 miles up in space. A replica of the Great Pyramid of Giza built to approximately three-quarters scale, the hotel was an enormous 36-story marvel of engineering that "rivals the original," PR materials claimed. That assertion was somewhat preposterous to X's way of thinking.

The spectacular lobby was a recreation of an actual temple dedicated to Osiris, featuring four colossal statues of the god. Tours were available of a replica of King Tut's tomb, also on the premises. A placard advertised a floor show in the Cleopatra Room, featuring half-naked belly dancers. The comedian Carrot Top would also be performing five nights a week.

Despite the huge throng of people of all nationalities, shapes and sizes surging through the lobby, X and his entourage didn't need to stand in line. There were at least a dozen reception clerks at the ready and one signaled to Ali and his men to approach. The clerk, a rail-thin woman with an obscure accent that would baffle most Americans, but which X instantly identified as Armenian, asked for his reservation number. When he provided it, his name popped up on her screen almost instantly. She gawked as if he were a movie star.

"It is certainly the greatest honor to serve you, sir," the desk clerk announced. "We have you in the Pharaoh Suite. I'm certain you'll enjoy it. Have you stayed with us before?"

"No." X had made sure of that, for obvious reasons.

"And you've reserved a second suite?"

"My wives and their servants will be arriving in a few days," X informed her in a cultured British accent with just the slightest hint of Mideast, subtle as a desert breeze. The real Nazeer, X had learned thorough his research, had attended boarding school in Great Britain and spoke the King's English better than Prince Charles.

"Certainly. There is an adjoining suite we can open up for your use when they arrive. To complete the check-in process I just need to see a photo ID, plus a credit card for incidentals."

He produced his passport and a forged platinum MasterCard.

X had learned not to stare at a clerk who was perusing personal documents – to do so might give the impression that he had some doubt about whether their authenticity would be accepted. He babbled small talk in Arabic to his henchmen.

Always a stickler for detail, he had boned up on his Arabic and had, for the occasion, perfected a Kuwaiti accent with the help of language CDs.

"Hold on one moment," said the clerk, whose hair was in such a tight bun that her skin was pulled back like a Beverly Hills housewife after plastic surgery. She picked up the phone and whispered into it. She nodded, said "Yes, yes, yes," and then hung up. She smiled pleasantly at the faux Arab playboy and there was an awkward silence as she evidently waited for someone to emerge from the back office.

X became aware that a trickle of perspiration was running down his forehead. Whether he was sweating because this was the biggest score he'd ever pursued or simply because he was unused to wearing a turban, he wasn't sure.

A door swung open and a manager scurried out, a skinny fellow with a wispy yellow comb-over and bifocals.

"Mr. Nazeer, I want to personally extend my welcome on behalf of the entire staff of the Giza," the man gushed. "If there is anything at all that you need, I am at your complete disposal. The concierge will be more than happy to assist you in finding entertainment around town. And if there is anything special you desire, please do not hesitate to call me directly."

"You are most gracious," X said, with a bow, while thinking, *I guess I'll be shelling out more in tips than I bargained for.*

The upper floors of the hotel were accessed via "inclinators." Since the pyramid's outside walls were all at a 39-degree angle, at each of the four corners there was a slanted shaft that carried an elevator car up and down. X, as noted earlier, had more than a trace of claustrophobia – and the fact that the car traveled at such a peculiar angle didn't help much. Again, small beads of sweat rolled down his forehead. A blue-haired lady was staring at him, he noted.

"Are you okay?" his bodyguard Bahador whispered in English. X nodded.

There was a young couple crowded in beside him. The dad held a squirming toddler of about two years of age in his arms. The child gazed at the turbaned man with open fascination. X, never very fond of children, nevertheless gave what he deemed to be an avuncular smile. To his dismay, the little boy reached and took firm hold of his beard.

X grabbed the boy's hand and tried to wrest it away, but found to his horror that the tyke had a death grip on the costume-shop whiskers. The beard was supposed to be immune to water and wind, but it wouldn't take much force to yank it off and that was just what was about to happen.

Babak pushed toward him in the crowded elevator, raising an arm as if he intended to bat the toddler away.

"Taylor!" the father shouted in dismay and quickly dislodged the boy's fingers.

"I am so sorry," the young man said, obviously mortified.

"Think nothing of it, my son," X said, in as beneficent a tone he could muster. He gave a little chuckle and tickled the tot under the chin, prompting the little boy to begin bawling like a banshee.

*   *   *

The Pharaoh Suite was advertised as soundproof and as promised, when the door slammed shut, the racket from the casino fell silent. The suite more than lived up to its name – in fact, the Sultan Suite might have been more apt, for the accommodations would suit an Oriental despot.

The 1,500-square-foot suite (for which a non-high-roller would pay a hefty $5,000 per night) featured Egyptian-style wardrobes decorated with hieroglyphics beside a 120-inch-screen plasma TV. The headboard of the king-size bed sported a cartouche of Cleopatra, and a replica fresco depicting the discovery of King Tut's tomb hung on the wall. The spa tub could accommodate up to 12 people. (A certain rap impresario and his groupies had indulged in an orgy therein, according to a tabloid report). Even the commode was luxurious; the seat was gold-encrusted and decorated with gemstones.

Not necessarily practical, though certainly impressive, X thought. *This is going to be a truly epic gig.*

The window wall, which looked out on the Strip, sloped inward. It offered a spectacular view of Sin City's famed boulevard and X opened the window, admitting a rush of dry desert air.

A change in city policy had taken place six months or so before the Giza went up. Before then, per fire department regulations, windows in Las Vegas could open only a few inches. Apparently, there'd been a period when people threw themselves from Las Vegas hotel room windows after betting the farm and losing it. Others had taken the chicken's way out after being filled with guilt in the wake of an adulterous indiscretion. However the "What happens in Vegas stays in Vegas" campaign must have sufficiently reduced the problem to put visitors at ease and the law had been changed.

The first order of business was to establish credit with the casino, which was comparatively easy, and X did so in the business office. All it entailed was a personalized check, his international driver's license and his credit card, along with his very impressive banking references. The casino was all too eager to enable him to gamble. He was, in the parlance of the industry, a "whale" – a hugely rich, big-time loser.

With a $100,000 credit line, he promptly plunked down 10 grand on the roulette wheel and lost. The casino bosses were no doubt pleased.

Ordinarily, when attempting to rip off a casino, he would work with a partner who countered X's losing bets with winning ones – betting on black if he bet on red, etc. After a few days of this, they would skip town with his partner's winnings and stiff the casino bank on the debt owed – by someone whose identity they'd stolen. It was a risky gambit since casino security was always on the lookout for that scam.

But now, since they were bent on draining Al Nazeer's account rather than ripping off the casino, there was no need for a counterbalancing partner (sometimes called a "blow"). This time, the hustle was simple, elegant really, X thought proudly. As Nazeer, he would be seen gambling and losing big. He would require a transfer from his bank. He would wire $2 million to the casino's business office, which X would then promptly wire to his own offshore account.

X did not like gambling. Chance was something he detested. Whether he lost money – which he dreaded – or gained it, he preferred that it be the result of his own ingenuity.

Yet, as distasteful as games of chance were to X, he had to put on a convincing show. He spent a brief but busy time on the gaming floor because he knew that multiple cameras would be watching him. Heavily disguised though he was, he was leery about having his image captured. He played several losing hands of blackjack at a table with a $1,000 limit. But no game afforded him an opportunity to lose bigger, quicker than roulette, so he played that until he'd lost another 20 grand. After four hours of laboring on the casino floor, he retired to the Pharaoh Suite.

X soaked in the hot tub, smoking a Cuban. X appreciated such fine things. The warmth of water swirling about the tub was making him horny. He picked up his cell phone and called Samantha, with vague aspirations of phone sex.

"Where are you?" she demanded.

Even without seeing her, he could tell she was pouting. She definitely deserved a vacation but letting the blonde tag along would surely have raised a few red flags.

"I'm in the Jacuzzi, Honey Hips. Naked," he said.

"Have a great time jerking off."

"No, I think I'll have a couple of hookers sent up. I've got Ali's reputation to maintain, remember. Would five be overkill?"

"You better not, if you want to keep your balls."

"Party pooper."

"I've got access to garden shears, remember."

"Well, how about a full body massage?"

"Only if she's over 80."

"How about a man?"

"Maybe."

"Okay. I'll ask for a male masseur, Scout's honor."

This was, in fact, a white lie – a concept that, you might not be surprised to learn, X interpreted broadly. He had no intention whatsoever of having a male masseur. The thought of a man's hands on his naked body was enough to make him puke. Even a manly clap on the back made him uneasy. No, he would certainly express a preference for a female masseuse. X had no hidden, libidinous agenda. He simply knew Samantha too well to be perfectly candid. She would fret all day and call on the hour.

A short time later he called downstairs to schedule a massage and after being put on hold for a surprisingly long time, he was told, apologetically, that one would not be available until the following evening. He was only slightly disappointed.

*   *   *

The next day he gambled equally badly and by mid-afternoon, $90,000 blown, he was ready to make his move.

X sat in the casino bank, located within the lobby, listening patiently as the manager spoke on the phone with a party at Al Nazeer's bank in London.

"He wishes to make a wire transfer in the amount of $2 million," the manager was saying.

There was a pause as someone spoke on the other line.

X glanced around the bank at customers of all races and virtually every nationality on Earth – a United Nations of suckers who refused to believe the house always wins. A young man with orange hair, seated behind a desk, appeared to be staring at him. As soon as they made eye contact, the redhead looked quickly down at a stack of papers on his desk. X felt a wave of paranoia wash over him.

"The funds will be available in 24 hours, sir."

X had hoped the transfer could be expedited. But he said, "That's quite all right."

He got up, took a quick look at the red-haired man, who now seemed oblivious to his presence, and left.

Chapter 5
THE GAME

That evening, at the invitation of a Texas agribusiness tycoon, he played a few hands of poker with four other high-rollers in a chamber called the Nefertiti Room set aside for such private gatherings. Mahogany paneled, with a 19th century map of Egypt lining the wall, it resembled a meeting room of the Royal Geological Society in the Jules Verne era. X had almost begged out, but knew that it would be in his egotistical alter ego's character to accept the challenge.

In time the conversation turned to politics and X was asked to offer an opinion about the current crisis in the Mideast. X waved his hand dismissively, flashing three diamond rings purchased on one of Nazeer's credit cards for a total of $18,000.

"I leave those problems to the royal family – that's their headache," he said. "Politics bore me."

"Here, here," the Texan agreed. "As long as the candidates I bankroll do right by farmers."

Farmers. The guy doesn't look like he knew what part of a cow to milk, X thought.

A plump man with a full white beard that made him look for all the world like Father Christmas was not content to leave it at that. The player, who had identified himself as Mr. Jones, a Wall Street financier, lowered his cards and leaned forward.

"So, when you hear that a busload of your countrymen have been blown up by terrorists, it doesn't bother you?" Mr. Jones said, taking a puffing on a pipe.

X didn't take the bait.

"I am neutral," he said. "As you Texans say, I do not have a dog in that fight. And as we say in the Middle East, I do not have a camel in that race."

That earned him a round of laughs. Thankfully, another player changed the topic.

"Hey, do they still allow you to have as many wives as you please over there?"

X nodded. "The Holy Koran says we may have four."

"How many do you have?" the oilman inquired.

"I have only three: Jasmine, Akilah and Malika," rattling off real names he'd committed to memory, foreseeing just such an eventuality. He felt as if he were being tested in some way. The thought flashed through his mind that if he were to get up from the table and make a dash for the door, the quartet of players would be able to tackle him.

But this time, the pipe-smoker came to the rescue.

"My hat's off to you. I don't know how you do it," Mr. Jones said. "I have just the one and she drives me to drink."

"They do bicker about everything," X conceded.

"That's why I'll never marry again," the Texan said with a chuckle.

X's full house was beaten by Mr. Jones's four of a kind.

"Luck is not with me tonight," he said, flinging cards on the table. He reminded himself not to sound so much like Omar Sharif in *Lawrence of Arabia.*

Chapter 6
NO HAPPY ENDING?

When X got back to his suite, he was drenched in sweat, his clothes were rank with cigar smoke and his neck muscles were tense from playing the role for an hour. His massage appointment couldn't have come at a better time.

The "bodyguards," who'd accompanied him everywhere up to this point, had been given the night off. When the doorbell rang, he donned the lush white robe provided by the hotel and opened the door himself.

The masseuse strode in, a leggy, light-skinned African-American in a tight miniskirt that put her high, round rump on spectacular display. She looked about 25 and stood taller than him, thanks in part to stiletto heels that gave her an extra two inches. She would have been out of his league had he not been a wealthy Arab playboy. Now she was most definitely in his league, a thought X found tantalizing.

An aroma wafted in with her – but it was merely soap, he realized. She'd showered recently and, unbidden, the image of her stark naked and scrubbing down entered his mind.

"My name is Stacy." She stuck out her hand in an incongruently professional manner and X took it.

"Come right in," X said, so taken by the shapely miss that his accent didn't kick in right away.

"What kind of massage are you interested in, Mr. Nazeer? We offer Swedish, Shiatsu, deep tissue, full body."

"What is full body?" he asked, although he knew the answer perfectly well.

"That is a very sensual message that reaches all areas of the body."

"That sounds … quite appealing."

"We can use the bed."

He led her through the luxurious suite to the bedroom, with its emperor-size mattress large enough to accommodate four people.

"I'm going to step into the next room," she said. "Please, undress completely and lie facedown. Here's a towel."

X stripped except for his turban, neatly folded his clothes and placed them over a chair, then lay face down on the table, the warm towel covering his hindquarters.

He was going to miss being Nazeer, he realized. The thought of returning to his old existence – holed up in that apartment in New York – suddenly seemed dismal. Of course, with the money they earned from this endeavor, he could live like a prince anywhere in the world.

X lay prone as the lithe young thing oiled his shoulders and worked her way to his lower back.

It wasn't the most expert massage he'd ever had; X was something of an aficionado. But her hands were soft and surprisingly strong. The stress X always felt when called upon to pretend to be someone he was not for extended periods began to ebb. She had lit some scented candles and placed a CD of New Age music in the room's player.

"Where are you from?" she asked him in a breathy little voice.

"A place you have probably never heard of. Al Jahra, in Kuwait."

"Is that in South America?" she leaned into him, kneading one buttock at a time.

American high schools are getting worse and worse, he thought. *You'd have thought the gigantic turban would be a clue.*

"It is in the Middle East."

"Oh. What kind of work do you do?"

"I'm in business. I invest," he said.

"Cool, cool," she remarked, now massaging his inner thighs.

X felt something stirring. Her fingers, working his abductor muscles, would come tantalizingly close to his genitals, and then dance away.

"My daddy is in business. He owns a garage," Stacy said.

X wished she would just shut up. Although lying was second nature to him, the effort of having to speak was something he could do without right now.

"Where are you from, young lady?" he inquired, trying to get his mind off his rising manhood.

"I'm from Georgia. It gets mighty hot there too."

He was drifting off to sleep, lulled by the bland conversation, hypnotic music and cloying scent that acted as yet another sedative.

It then occurred to him that her accent was not authentically Georgian. Why was she talking with a phony southern accent? An ordinary solid citizen might not be too concerned by this – after all, how many showgirls in Las Vegas recreated themselves, leaving behind pasts as runaways or battered wives? There were perhaps a thousand reasons why she would be something other than what she claimed to be. But X could not afford to take any such chances.

He listened more closely as she rambled on.

No, the dialect was all wrong. It was definitely from the West Coast. Though she threw in some southern expressions like "y'all" from time to time, she sounded as if she'd picked up bits and pieces of redneck patois from reruns of *Hee Haw.*

She's an undercover cop. The sting that he had been dreading for years was actually taking place.

"Now I'm going to leave you for a few minutes. Just go on ahead and keep your eyes closed and relax, sweetie."

Yeah, right! She was supposed to lull him to sleep, so that her partners could slip in and arrest him, naked and half-asleep, with no threat of resistance. X knew he had to do something quick.

He rolled over and caught her wrist. He pointed to the bulge under the towel.

"What about, how do you say, 'a happy ending?' "

The girl's eyes betrayed her – was that a flash of panic? Obviously, respectable massage therapists did not stoop to hand jobs, but they were accustomed to such requests and knew how to field them.

"I'm sorry, sweetie. We don't do that." And she blushed.

He laughed like a man whose whims are never refused. "Oh come now, do not be shy. Name your price. Shall we say $5,000?"

Now the undercover cop – if that was what she was – might feel trapped. To turn down an offer so generous after creating such a flirty, sexy persona could be seen as out of character.

"Well, okay, sweetie. Let me just powder my nose first."

The girl turned her back. As she headed toward the bathroom, X silently arose from the bed, tiptoed up behind her and clapped a hand over her mouth.

"Don't move. I have a gun," he whispered in her ears.

X was bluffing about the gun; he abhorred firearms and regarded any con man who toted a handgun an amateurish embarrassment to the trade. He was not ordinarily a violent man, but desperate times called for desperate measures.

He pushed her onto the king-size bed, grabbed an errant sock and stuffed it in her mouth. He quickly whipped the belt out of his silk bathrobe on the bed and used it to hogtie her, face down. His hand slid under her blouse and slid up and down her torso, searching for a wire. Sure enough, there was a tiny microphone and transmitter taped to her creamy brown lower back.

Stacy, though he doubted that was her name, began to make muffled protests.

He tried to cover the noise by saying loud enough for any mike to pick up, "That's it. That's it. That feels fantastic. Your mouth feels so good."

The undercover cop rolled her eyes in fury.

The good news was there must not be any hidden cameras, otherwise her partners would have burst through the doors and busted him already.

X crept up to the front door of the suite and peered through the peephole. He was 90 percent sure he would see two or three armed cops outside, backup waiting for a verbal signal from the undercover policewoman to move in. What he saw instead made him gasp. There was not one or two or even six. There had to be 10 FBI agents crowded in the hall, decked out in body armor and "Fritz" helmets, and toting MP5s.

WTF? Yes, he'd arrived at the hotel with a couple of bodyguards, but the raiding party looked like it was prepared to shoot it out with the private militia of a Colombian drug lord.

Well, strolling out the front door isn't an option, he thought.

X quickly hauled on his pants and shirt, and raced to the door to the adjoining suite. He always packed a lock-picking kit with him for just such occasions. But as he knelt he heard shuffling from the other room that told him G-men were on the other side. This was no avenue of escape – more than likely the other suite housed the command post of the FBI team, including their recording equipment.

The "masseuse" continued to let out muffled protestations, which did sound for all the world as if her mouth was working magic on a male member. But he knew this stalling tactic had only bought him a matter of seconds. Assuming they were listening in, they would not want to burst in on the female agent and humiliate her in the act of fellatio. On the other hand, they wouldn't allow the supposed love act to go on for more than maybe two minutes before some cowboy decided it was time to kick down the door.

He had to get out of the suite, but how?

He raced to the slanting window. X had beaten a hasty retreat through more than one window in his day. During his stint pulling the classic Lost Puppy scam door to door, when the deal went sour he'd often used the bathroom window as an egress. But those were the first or second floors of homes. This was the 25th story.

He futzed around for a moment, trying to recall how the slanted windows slid open, before succeeding. He poked his head out and looked at the wall sloping down 250 feet to the cement.

I should have booked a lower floor, he thought.

From the ground, the pyramid walls looked like perfectly smooth black glass, but upon closer inspection, X saw that there were subtle ridges where the giant blocks of glass met. The ridges looked just deep enough to accommodate human fingers and toes – perhaps. About 14 feet away another window was open. Tantalizingly close.

X, whose mountaineering skills were meager, hesitated. If he slipped he'd go sliding down and slam into the pavement below as surely as if the angle was 90 degrees instead of 39. But X could NOT go to prison. The image of a concrete prison cell was more terrifying at that moment than that of his body as a heap of broken bones at the foot of the pyramid. He could imagine himself as the smallest guy in the cell receiving the unwanted attentions of some tattooed gangbanger.

That unpleasant image propelled the identity thief into action. He began to climb out the window. He did not, fortunately, have much fear of heights. In fact, in his boyhood, the rooftop of the mansion where his mother worked as a maid had been one of his places of refuge.

"Stacy" managed another muffled protest – perhaps warning him of his folly.

"Yes, I'm almost there," he groaned as he slithered out.

X's fingers and toes fought for purchase on the tiny ridges as he inched his way toward the other window. The ridges were slighter than he'd thought – no more than a few centimeters deep. Another thing he hadn't factored in was how windy it was up here. It felt as if a sudden gust might at any second yank him from his precarious position. Those 14 feet looked awfully far away now. X resisted the temptation to shut his eyes.

That's it, he thought, *that's it. Keep going. Not far now.*

A loud noise from his suite – a door being kicked in – startled X and he lost his grip. Suddenly, he was cascading down the pyramid like a child sledding on ice. He was too scared even to shriek. Now he did shut his eyes, although the image that filled his mind – his body smashing into the pavement and splattering like a tomato – didn't much put his mind at ease. He slid down at least 30 feet – down a full three stories – picking up speed as he descended. Then, miraculously, X skidded across another open window. His hands caught the metal window ledge and he gripped it for dear life.

X dangled for a couple of seconds, letting out a deep sigh of relief. *I can't believe I'm alive,* he thought.

Using all his upper body strength, the identity thief hauled himself up. X clambered in through the window with difficulty and rapidly slid it shut.

By now the agents had burst into the Pharaoh Suite and were rampaging through it. One peered out the window, scanning for any open ones and spotting a few to the side, above and below. Fortunately for X, he'd closed the one he entered in the nick of time.

X crawled on his hands and knees through the stranger's room. *Damn, the shower is running. Someone is in here.* X hopped like a rabbit into the closet and cowered there, peering through the crack between the double doors.

A middle-aged couple, dressed in Giza bathrobes, emerged from the bathroom. *Oh, no,* he thought. *They'll head straight for the closet for their clothes.* X balled his fist, ready to strike. The guy was only a little bigger than X, but had a rugged build that worried him. X was no fighter; hadn't struck a blow since middle school. He tried to concoct a story that would innocently explain his presence, but everything that came to mind seemed ridiculous. A tech checking out a WiFi outage?

But fortune was on X's side. Instead of approaching the closet, the couple headed for the room door. They were going down to the pool, X realized.

If he continued to be blessed by such serendipity, he had a good chance of getting out of this in one piece.

"Jon, your wallet," the wife said.

"Oh, yeah."

Through the crevice, X watched as the man turned back and took a bulging wallet from the night table. He strode toward the closet. X glanced down and much to his dismay saw that in the far right of the closet sat a squat little room safe.

The husband reached the closet 10 seconds later and yanked open the right door. He flicked the light switch and the closet remained dark.

"Bulb's blown. Can't see a thing. I'll just stuff it under the sofa cushion."

"You know I hate when you do that."

"I don't trust these things anyway," the husband said grumpily.

"Jon … "

"Okay, okay! Can barely see the numbers."

The husband punched in a four-digit code, opened the safe and stuck in his wallet.

A moment later, the room door slammed shut. X, crouching in the left corner of the closet with the light bulb in his hand, breathed again.

He exited the closet and headed straight for the bedroom. He hurriedly ripped off the turban and false beard and stuffed them in a night table drawer. The man's black shoes fit fine; the sleeves of the jacket were a bit short. X rolled up them up.

Learning a hotel safe's code by recognizing the distinct tone of each key as it's punched in was a trick he'd learned ages ago. He popped open the safe and retrieved hubby's wallet from its hiding place. Jon Preston, the Arizona driver's license read. Also in the wallet was an official-looking badge. Tucson Police Department.

Christ almighty, the guy is a cop!

There was $400 cash and assorted credit cards. X stuffed the wallet in his pants pocket. There was a holstered .45 in the night table. Even in a state of panic, X was not tempted to take it. He found a cell phone plugged in and hurriedly punched in Samantha's number. On the third ring she answered.

"Sam, remember to pick up my medicine," he told her.

"What, why?" she demanded.

"Can't talk now," he shot back and hung up.

That was another code phrase. Within 15 minutes, Sam would have vanished from the apartment. The operation had blown up in X's face and it felt as if his world was crashing down on him, but he had an ace in the hole: Steven Holdenbrook.

Steven Holdenbrook was X's ultimate creation. An identity so perfect, so complete, that X could step into it and disappear forever. In a parking garage of the Trump Casino, walking distance away, was a green Ferrari. In the glove compartment lay stashed $100,000 cash and documents authenticating his identity as Steven Holdenbrook. X thought of that car, always parked near a "jobsite," as his lifeboat. If he could get there he would be safe. Of course, that left the minor task of first getting out of this building.

He looked out the peephole and, seeing no one in the hall, ventured out.

X pressed the button for the inclinator, and stood trying not to tremble while he waited. The agents must still be checking out the floors above, he thought. They never could have imagined he made it down three stories. But they'd be down here any second.

The inclinator arrived and though it was crowded, X pushed his way in – earning him a look of chagrin from a porky occupant in a Michael Moore baseball cap and his equally chunky bride, who couldn't spare much space. He maneuvered to the back. Just as the glass doors whooshed shut, X saw a half dozen agents emerge from a stairwell into the hall.

X ducked down so that he was concealed behind the obese pair and the inclinator continued its descent. From his vantage point looking down through the glass he could see dozens of agents swarming through the casino.

What in blue blazes is going on?

He was a small-time con man. Okay, maybe a big-time one, this was no occasion for false modesty. What could possibly make him so important to the Justice Department? Whatever hopes he had nursed of simply walking out through the front door were dashed.

X crossed the casino floor, where an unusual number of uniformed security guards as well as men his practiced eye identified as undercover security personnel were also roaming. He approached a beefy, mustachioed security guard.

"What's going on?" X demanded in as tough a Southwestern voice as he could muster.

"What do you mean?"

"Come on, all this heat."

"I can't tell you anything, sir."

X flashed the Tucson police badge.

"Hey, I'm a cop, cut me some slack."

The guard leaned down and whispered confidentially, "Department of Homeland Security operation. There's some kind of terrorist loose. A high-value target." He didn't look bright enough to know precisely what "high-value target" meant.

X felt his blood run cold. Some kind of terrorist. So THAT explained the Gestapo-type raid.

What exactly was going on now came to him in a rush. Ali Nazeer's carefree-playboy persona was merely a ruse. He was actually some jihadist Scarlet Pimpernel. X couldn't believe his ill fortune. What were the odds, of all the thousands of potential marks that came into his sights in a year, that he would have chosen this one!

"What does he look like?"

The guard looked around, then showed him a black and white printout of X's bearded face and turbaned head caught earlier that day by a security camera.

"I'll be on the lookout," X said, trying hard not to stagger as they parted company. "I'll keep it on the down low."

Chapter 7
ON THE LAM

X drifted into the casino, plopped down at a slot machine and started mechanically feeding in dollar bills. If Nazeer was a terror suspect there were agents at every exit. Worse still, he also knew that agents must be glued to monitors in the security station, where images were being beamed back from cameras trained at every foot of the casino floor, offering multiple angles on every gambler. He couldn't sit there indefinitely.

Suddenly aware that someone had sidled up beside him, X almost jumped out of his skin.

"Cocktail, sir?" asked a smiling waitress holding a tray of drinks. The strongest drink imaginable would seem in order, under the circumstances.

He nodded. "Scotch on the rocks."

In the periphery of his vision, he saw men moving through the casino, methodically checking out aisle after aisle, like a pack of wolves sniffing out prey. It would be only a matter of minutes, or perhaps seconds. The inclinators were frozen, he noted – the lawmen had shut them down.

The waitress was back with the drink in under a minute. X gulped it down and sadly, it did little to steady his nerves. *Even heroin might not.*

A voice came over the loudspeaker, crackling and barely audible over the din of the one-armed bandits: "Tours are beginning of King Tut's tomb in five minutes."

Hurrying to the lobby, X joined the tour group, which included a couple struggling to ride herd over four excited kids, a trio of middle-aged women and five Japanese tourists. As they entered the dark series of chambers, X felt a momentary relief. The place was as cool, dark and tranquil as, well, a tomb. He felt as if he had magically escaped to another place and time.

"In November 1922, the British archaeologist Howard Carter discovered beneath the Valley of the Kings the long-lost tomb of King Tutankhamun," the youthful male tour guide intoned in a reedy tenor, as they clattered across the stone floor into the first chamber. Melodramatic prerecorded music accompanied his spiel.

"He had to break through four doors to get to the burial chamber. In the first was the greatest collection of Egyptian antiquities ever discovered. This is a replica of the first chamber and many of the artifacts."

As X's eyes grew accustomed to the light, details of the room emerged, including statues of strange animals and gods, many of them painted gold.

"On your left is a statue of the god Ptah. This golden vase is in the shape of an ibex and beside it is an alabaster jar in the form of a lion," the guide was saying.

"Beyond this antechamber, breaking through another wall," continued the guide, "the archaeologists found a smaller room filled with equally magnificent treasures.

"Finally Carter broke through a fourth sealed door into the holiest of holies, the burial chamber of King Tut." With a dramatic gesture, the geeky youth flung open a heavy door.

In the center of the fourth room, a huge yellow sarcophagus stood on a dais. Inside was a remarkably convincing replica of the anthropoid coffin X had seen a dozen times on covers of magazines like National Geographic.

"The lid of the coffin itself is carved in high relief with an image of the dead king as the god Osiris," the guide went on. "His arms, crossed on the chest, clutch the twin symbols of kingship, the scepter and the flail. The divine cobra of Lower Egypt and the vulture goddess of Upper Egypt, rise from the king's forehead.

"Attached to the mummy were more than 100 small items placed in accordance with the famous Book of the Dead to ensure the king's safe passage into the afterlife.

"In the next room, we'll see replicas of some of those items."

As they passed through the doorway into the next room, X was almost curious about what they'd see.

Not a bad tour, really. He'd been very fond of field trips to museums in grade school, with the wondrous though fleeting escape they offered.

X spied a quartet of agents entering from the far side of the chamber. He ducked behind a column, and then doubled back, making his way quickly to the start of the exhibit.

Well, hello.

Two more agents stood guarding the entrance, their backs to him. *Just dandy.* He turned again, hurried back into the faux tomb – and there he saw his one and only chance.

With some effort X pushed aside the lid of King Tut's coffin; thankfully, it was made of some kind of Styrofoam, not stone. To his relief, the designers of the exhibit had been insufficiently fixated on authenticity to include a real mummy. He climbed in and gingerly slid the lid back in place.

As the darkness settled in around him, X's claustrophobia flared up. It felt as if he had been buried alive. *Is this thing airtight,* he wondered, panic rising. He lay there in silence, listening to the footsteps of the tour group retreat. How long was he going to have to stay here? Hours?

Perhaps not so long. He heard gruff male voices nearby.

"Check out everything. Malloy swears he saw him sneak in with a tour group."

FBI agents might not be rocket scientists, but how long could it be before they thought of looking in the coffin? X had to act and act quickly. The identity thief slipped the purloined cell phone out of his pocket and called the hotel's front desk.

"Can you transfer me to security?" he whispered. When he got casino security, he asked to speak with the chief.

"Chief Royton here."

"This is Agent Malloy," he said in a low voice, trying not to whisper. (He was a gifted mimic, but had only heard Malloy utter one sentence). "We've ascertained that the suspect has some kind of dirty bomb," he said. "We have to get everyone out right now."

"I can't authorize the evacuation," Chief Royton said, aghast. "I'd need permission from the manager."

"Remember what happened on 9/11, when companies ordered employees back to their desks. Do you want that on your conscience? Order the evacuation – now," X demanded sharply.

"All right. All right."

X waited in the darkness, listening to the footsteps of agents on the stone floor. Two sets of footfalls approached the coffin.

"Larry, give me a hand with this."

"You've got to be kidding me."

"I'm serious. Remember the perp we caught hiding in a washing machine?"

X was almost relieved to be caught – anything to get out of this suffocating box. The lid began to move above him and a shaft of light poured in.

Then a voice boomed over the speaker: "All guests and employees of the Giza Hotel and Casino. We ask that you please exit the building in a calm and orderly manner."

"What the heck?" said one of the agents.

He heard their footsteps clattering as they dashed from the chamber. X climbed out of the coffin and hurried through the dark chamber and out to the lobby. He joined the throng of people flooding toward the exit.

Despite the call for calm, most of the guests and casino workers were savvy enough to know this was an emergency. A fire at the least. X was shoulder to shoulder with topless showgirls, gamblers with drinks still in their hands and a few guests still in their underwear.

As X neared the door, he saw a pair of guards who looked as if they might have played professional football in their younger days. They were trying to check people as they passed through, but the crowd was shoving so hard it was impossible to see everyone's face.

He was so certain he'd be nabbed, he nearly shut his eyes again. But the crowd pushed him past the agents into the street.

"Nobody else gets out," he heard a voice shout. He could hear a howl of protest from inside the casino as the doors were shut behind him.

Chapter 8
THE DEN OF INIQUITY

Adopting what he hoped was an air of nonchalance, X boarded a moving sidewalk headed toward to the monorail station. The Giza was one of three hotels connected by monorail service, and to the best of X's recollection from his quick glance at the brochure, there were trains arriving every three minutes. The sidewalk moved so slowly X was tempted to race-walk on it. But of course he didn't dare do anything but stand perfectly still and stare directly ahead, like a horse in blinders.

The monorail station was just 50 feet away now.

Yes, yes, he thought. It was beginning to look as if he might actually make it out of this colossal shit storm. But just outside the station, he spied two dark-suited men talking discreetly into their lapels.

"Oh, no," X moaned. He hadn't meant to say it aloud; a fellow beside him gave a funny look.

He plucked the cell phone out of his jacket pocket, "accidentally" dropped it, then knelt to pick it up, obscuring his face. As fellow pedestrians jostled by him, he stood, pivoted and, stepping off the moving sidewalk, began walking back in the direction from which he'd come.

"Hey!" The voice behind him was deep and authoritative.

X turned, beginning to raise his hands. *Huh?* There was no one there. Then he looked down to see a dwarf with enormous heart-shaped spectacles and an Uncle Sam top hat. The wee fellow handed him a flyer.

"Come check out the Pink Panther," the *Lord of the Rings* escapee said cheerfully, in that incongruously deep voice. "Two for one drink specials."

The flyer bore the image of a curvaceous cartoon blonde

bending to smooch the famed celluloid feline. X glanced around surreptitiously. *Well, any port in a storm.*

*   *   *

Along the sidewalk an FBI van crept, equipped with two portable millimeter wave scanners similar to the kind used at airports to screen passengers. The machines afforded the viewer of the subject fully nude, leaving nothing to the imagination.

The two agents inside the unmarked white van ignored passing women, children and old folks, concentrating on males with Al Nazeer's reported height of 5-foot-8.

The younger agent drew his partner's attention to the glowing image on his screen.

"Look at what that guy with all the dreadlocks is packing."

"A weapon?"

"Yeah, a Magnum. His johnson's got to be nine inches soft."

The older agent sighed. "I'd sell my soul to be Jamaican for just one *day.*"

The other agent tilted his head. "Isn't it a little crooked, though?"

*   *   *

At the temporary command center Mark Normand Jr., agent in charge of the manhunt, was fuming. Though just a hair over 5-foot-6, the Chicago native had a booming voice that would put Nick Fury to shame.

"How did we lose control of the subject in the first place?" he demanded. "Having to rely on a girl with a wire? Are we living in 1985?"

"We don't know, sir," said Agent Malloy, who sported a high red pompadour (yes, he's the fellow from the casino bank). "We had enough cameras planted in that suite to cover the Super Bowl – including a pinhole over the bed. And 11 microphones."

"And he dry-cleaned the place – managed to find them all?"

"No, the signal was jammed. We still don't know how."

"You had no backup?"

"Across the street, on the 24th floor in the Bloomberg Building, we had a laser microphone directed at his window."

This nifty surveillance device works by picking up sound vibrations at a distance. The mike beams an invisible infrared laser at the windowpane while a photo transistor picks up the reflection. The vibrations from the speaker's voice create tiny differences in the distance traveled by the light from second to second as it bounces back. These fluctuations are detected by an interferometer, and electronic hardware linked to an audio amplifier converts the signal back into sound.

That sound, Normand knew from experience, would probably stink.

"We got a conversation between Nazeer and his bodyguards," Malloy was saying as he held up a digital player.

"The idiots killed in the car chase?"

"Yes, sir. We're still trying to ID them."

"Well, get a translator in here."

"It's in English."

"So they knew that we were listening in."

Malloy nodded and flipped a switch.

Although the recording had been digitally enhanced by computer whizzes, it was difficult to make out the words, just as Normand anticipated. The voices were so distorted and synthetic, it might have been three Stephen Hawkings talking.

"Where are you two spending your night off?" the first voice said.

"We want to see Wayne Newton," replied a second voice.

"Don't you know he's retired?"

"That's so disappointing. The man is such a big legend. Maybe Celine Dion?"

"Yes, yes. That *Titanic* song still makes me sad," a third voice chimed in.

"Leonardo DiCaprio is such a good actor," the second voice said. "I'm glad he's making a comeback."

Normand and Malloy looked at each other for a moment.

"They're talking in code obviously," said Normand.

Agent Malloy nodded. "Wayne Newton, that must be The

Chief, Abdul Gamel. "

"Retired, that's dead."

"The Chief is dead?"

Normand shook his head. "No way. They must be using elliptical communication. Everything mean's the opposite. He's telling them that The Chief is alive."

"And who is Celine Dion?"

"Dr. Zawari, maybe, his second in command."

"The *Titanic* could mean a big catastrophe, major loss of life. "

Norman nodded grimly. "A WMD."

"Or if it's the opposite, maybe it means something wonderful is going to happen."

Normand frowned at this attempt at humor.

A knock came at the office door.

"It's Agent Kingsmith."

"Come in."

Agent Traci Kingsmith, whose foray into undercover work as Stacy the masseuse had been less than a smashing success, came into the office bearing a printout. She now wore a gray pantsuit and had scrubbed off the makeup; she looked a paragon of professionalism.

"You didn't have to change right away," Malloy said with a mischievous grin that made his freckled face resemble Howdy Doody's.

Traci gave him a "We are not amused" glare that wiped the smile off his face.

"We have the facial recognition analysis," she said, handing Normand the printout.

As soon as Ali Nazeer had escaped the Pharaoh Suite, the surveillance team had commandeered the hotel's cameras and the incoming signal was processed live by facial recognition software. Such software, which organizes digital video footage into a searchable database, had been around for more than 10 years. As far back as 2001, police had used a program called FaceIt to scan the Super Bowl XXXV crowd for known terrorists. It hadn't turned up any, but identified 19 poor saps with pending warrants who, sadly, didn't get to see the halftime show.

"He shaved the beard," Traci told her boss, pointing to the

close-up of X at the slot machine. "That's why the program didn't identify him immediately. He would never have gotten out of the building otherwise."

"That was some fast work – not a nick on him," marveled Agent Malloy. "He ought to be doing Gillette commercials."

Normand shoved the printout back into Traci's hand. "Distribute the picture, get it to everyone."

"Not the media?"

"Including the media," Normand snapped. "Maybe Geraldo will have better luck than our people."

*　　　*　　　*

The Pink Panther was the biggest gentleman's club on the strip, boasting 50 topless dancers. From the exterior, it looked as huge as a Wal-Mart. Inside, marble stairs led to a semicircular front desk where X paid the $25 cover charge and ducked into the inner sanctum through an ornate metal door.

His nostrils were immediately assaulted by the dueling aromas of cigarettes and perfume. X hadn't set foot in a strip club in years. He did not frequent such establishments, where women used their charms to empty the wallets of suckers with flattery and unspoken promises of intimacy. Strippers were con artists, to his way of thinking, and he considered himself a purveyor, not a consumer of flimflammery.

However, for someone attempting to pull a disappearing act, The Pink Panther was all you could hope for. The establishment was jam-packed, dark and noisy, with rock music alternating with hip-hop blasting over man-size speakers. On six stages curvaceous cuties swung on poles and enthusiastically shook their tails. These were Venuses of all ethnicities, heights, sizes, natural boobs or synthetic – a beauty to suit whatever one's favorite flavor.

Flashing neon lights poured down on the stages, three bars and scores of tiny drink tables covered with dainty pink tablecloths. X gazed out across over an ocean of bare-breasted temptresses writhing in the laps of patrons, while dozens of other vixens, clad in lingerie, roamed like famished sharks in search of cash-laden prey.

As he entered the club, he passed a drunken man being

led out by three buddies, in what X immediately recognized as the aftermath of a raucous bachelor party. X deliberately bumped into the foursome and slipped the Tucson cop's cell phone into the besotted bridegroom's pocket. It was only a matter of time before the identity thief's pursuers used it to track him down. X was by no means an expert on police manhunts, but he knew that much from the movies.

He sank onto a stool at the bar and ordered an $8 Heineken. Like his alter ego, the notorious Al Nazeer, X was a teetotaler. Not for religious reasons; although raised a Catholic, X hadn't seen the inside of a church in more than a decade. It was simply that he preferred to be in control at all times. So he nursed his "greenie" – as beer connoisseurs call the brand – and consumed a modest sip every few moments. On a TV over the nearest bar, CNN was reporting a late-breaking story. The sound was either muted or completely overwhelmed by the eardrum-busting music, but the words were close-captioned at the bottom of the screen.

"A spokesman for the Department of Homeland Security has announced that it is close to capturing Ali Nazeer, described as the No. 2 man in the Jihadist Brotherhood, one of the world's most dangerous terrorist organizations."

His own face, apparently lifted from a casino surveillance camera, filled the screen, and X winced. Fortunately, none of his fellow patrons were paying attention to the TV. All eyes were fixed on a comely dancer on stage, as she spun around a pole upside down with the grace of an Olympic gymnast.

He read on.

"For years the Kuwaiti national posed as an international playboy, authorities allege, while secretly pursuing a double life as a terrorist leader.

"He allegedly funded a string of audacious attacks such as the raid on the Afghan army barracks in Kandahar as well as last year's bombing of Mount Rushmore, which as we all know, resulted in the destruction of Teddy Roosevelt's nose. A reward of $5 million is being offered for information leading to his capture."

This just gets better and better, X thought grimly.

Onto the stage strutted a pale dancer with silicone breasts and a waist-long head of curly red hair that looked suspiciously like a wig. Nature had endowed her with the most perfect ass X had ever beheld, a pair of succulent ripe melons. It appeared to have a life of its own from the way it moved left, right, up and down to the thumping beat. The redhead planted her legs wide apart, bent over at the waist and stuck her magnificent, milk-white rear end in the air, then gleefully smacked it. Looking backward between her legs, she caught him gawking and winked.

X turned away in embarrassment. On CNN, the anchor continued: "In a related story, Abdul Gamel, leader of the Warriors of Allah terror network and known as The Chief – identified by the Director of the CIA as Osama Bin Laden's 'puppeteer' – has released a new video. In it he defends his declaration of a *fatwa* – a death warrant against all Americans."

A bearded man – who surprisingly resembled an older version of Sean Connery in his dubious performance as an Arab desert warrior (Scottish brogue and all) in *The Wind and the Lion* – appeared on the screen. Beneath his stern visage words crawled, translating his Arabic:

"America makes no distinction between soldiers and civilians. The only nation to use an atomic bomb was the U.S., which inflicted a holocaust on the innocent people of Hiroshima. They are the true terrorists. So, no, we will not limit our targets. The *fatwa* includes all those who help the Jewish occupiers of Palestine and the killers of Muslims."

X shook his head. *You belong in a loony bin, old fellow,* he thought.

As the song ended, X turned to watch the red-haired dancer put her top back on, then gingerly walk down from the stage in precariously high heels. As he spun on the barstool, he spotted three agents entering the club. They attempted to look casual, but their stern demeanor and the fact that they were peering into the dark recesses of the bar instead of the stages where half-naked girls were strutting their stuff made it easy for X to peg them as law enforcement.

And of course he couldn't help noticing that all three were sporting sunglasses – rather peculiar, given the darkness of the establishment. They were oddly thick, like goggles, and it occurred to X that they could be some kind of new streamlined night-vision lenses. He had to hide – fast.

X reached up and tucked a $5 tip in the passing redhead's G-string. She grinned broadly. "$20 for a table dance, $30 for a lap."

It sounded a bit steep, but X was inexperienced in such matters, and furthermore didn't really have time to negotiate.

"A lap."

"Good choice. We're gonna have some FUN!"

X watched her flaming hair bounce as she guided him to a purple leather chair and pushed him gently into it.

The girl unfastened her bra and straddled him, her double D's wobbling impressively in front of him. Her flesh was dotted with freckles, he noted upon closer inspection. Maybe she was a genuine redhead.

Out of the corner of his eyes X could see the first of the trio approaching and presumed that his own face was just as visible. With infrared night-vision goggles, his features would probably be distinct. He had to get the girl closer to him, to hide completely.

"What's your name?" he asked, as casually as he could.

The girl leaned in to whisper into his ear. Her erect nipples grazed his chest and his face vanished into her flowing orange hair.

"Party. What's yours?" You had to hand it to her: the moniker was something of a novelty.

"Steve."

"Where do you hail from, Steve?"

"South Carolina," he replied, having already adopted the appropriate drawl. "You?"

"Wisconsin."

This time, at least, the accent matched the purported place of origin.

Peeking through the girl's hair, he could see the agents moving through the crowd, discreetly probing the darkened bar with tiny flashlights. Every time Party started to lean away from him, presumably to give him a better view of her silicone-enhanced breasts, X would renew the conversation, luring her in closer.

"Have you been dancing long?" he asked.

"Three years. I quit for a few months when I found Jesus and did some waitressing, but this place is in my blood."

"I'm sure it pays better."

"So true," she said. "Speaking of a whole lot of loot, did you hear about that huge reward they're offering for that motherfucker?"

"Beg pardon?"

"That rag-head terrorist who's loose in Vegas."

"Oh yeah, saw something about that on TV," he said weakly.

"With that money, wow – I could like produce a movie and star in it," she said, a dreamy look in her eyes, "You know, like Drew Barrymore."

He nodded. "Yes, I could see you as maybe one of those teachers who turns an inner-city school around."

"Wow, you're like reading my mind." Then, growing thoughtful, she added, "But honestly, I would turn that guy in even if there was no reward. My uncle was killed in Afghanistan. We all have to do our part. I would personally cut off that creep's balls if I had the chance."

"Your patriotism is truly admirable," X remarked.

On the TV screen, the words "This just in" appeared under a computer-generated image of X – without a beard.

The redhead expanded on her point. "I don't mean with scissors. I mean with garden shears. No, a bolt cutter."

"Outstanding," X whispered, turning paler by the minute.

The song – "Bad Influence" by Pink – abruptly ended.

"Want another?" Party asked.

"You bet." X dug into the policeman's wallet for another $20.

The redhead swiveled around in his lap so that her pert round buttocks were perched on his groin. The position, fortunately, put the TV out of her line of sight.

But his face was exposed again. X could see the broad-shouldered, square-jawed Agent No. 2 just feet away. To his alarm, the fugitive saw that the lawman was turning in his direction. X leaned forward and kissed the exotic dancer between the shoulder blades, so that his face disappeared from the agent's view.

"You're sweet," she giggled.

"I love your perfume," he whispered with all the enthusiasm

he could muster.

She giggled again and, as a raunchy rap tune by 50 Cent poured out of the speakers, she began to gyrate her thong-clad rump vigorously in his lap. Despite himself, X found he was swiftly growing hard for the second time that day. He disliked the feeling of losing control over his own body. He tried to fight it off, but resistance was futile, as the Borg liked to say.

"Whoa, you've got a big dick for a guy with such small hands," Party cooed appreciatively.

"Thanks – I think," he whispered in her ear, keeping his face nestled in that red mane. "You've got a really ..." he groped for the appropriate adjective, "impressive little caboose on you."

"Oh, not so little," she giggled. "Not with all the pizza I eat."

*   *   *

At the command center, Normand stood in a sprawling room surrounded by walls of giant video monitors, with incoming data and images flashing up on the screen from all 360 degrees.

"I'm getting a headache," he groaned. "Who designed this display? I swear to God, I'm going to have an epileptic fit in a minute."

"The IT people based it on the Bourne movies," said an aide manning one of 12 consoles.

"Remind me to ask our friends at the CIA to terminate that producer."

Traci Kingsmith pointed to one of the giant screens, filled by the face of a fat, grinning Asian man.

"We're getting human and/or electronic intel from every building and street within a two-mile perimeter. That's coming in from a strip club a half mile from the hotel. We commandeered the club's surveillance cameras and the feed is being digitally enhanced and run through the facial recognition program."

Male faces, some leering, some blank, some with eyes fluttering in passion flashed on and off the screen.

A nearby screen displayed a feed from three mini-cameras built into the penlights borne by the three agents on site and also run through the automated video analysis software. The video was much shakier and more indistinct, as the cameras probed the dark recesses of the club. Murky (and somewhat disturbing) images of breasts, thongs and dollar bills emerged and vanished into the gloom.

"Do we have live mikes in there?" Normand asked.

"Coming from the agents' communicators," Traci replied. "The system is searching for key words now."

The program analyzed complex sounds by using advanced psychoacoustic modeling (the science behind how humans distinguish and understand the meaning of sound). Cutting through even levels of ambient noise, it would not only pick out key words like "bomb" or "Allah" but even subtle vocal changes that suggested anger or fear.

An agent wearing headphones yanked them off excitedly and pointed to the computer monitor at his station.

"Mr. Normand, look. On the screen the phrase "has great artillery" was flashing in big white letters.

Normand sighed. "That's '50s slang. It means boobs. The guy must be 80."

"Three cheers for Viagra!" said Malloy, coming up behind the boss. "We've identified the cell phone Nazeer used to contact New York. We'll have the point of origin pinpointed within four minutes."

"Now that's more like it. Any word on the New York cell?"

"A team raided it 12 minutes ago. Just missed them."

Normand buried his face in his hand.

"I guess I picked the wrong week to quit cocaine."

When he removed his hand he saw that Traci was staring at him.

"It's from *Airplane,*" he assured her.

"Yes, I know, I'm just surprised that … never mind, sir."

*   *   *

In the bowels of the Pink Panther, Party was squirming to the thumping beat.

"Damn," she moaned. "It feels like a broomstick back there. Hey, are you going commando, Steve?" X remembered that he indeed hadn't had time to don any underwear and grunted in the affirmative.

She giggled again. "Naughty, naughty!"

Unexpectedly, Party bent forward at the waist, arching backward into him. Under other circumstances, X would have no objection, but now his face was exposed again – and, he observed with some dismay, Agent No. 3 was approaching.

X knew from the prominently displayed warning sign at the entrance that touching a dancer with his hands was a no-no, but risking a screech was necessary. He gently touched Party's arms and pulled her back until her shoulder blades mashed against his chest.. He buried his face in her mass of curly hair, so deep he could smell shampoo. So it wasn't a wig.

Through the red locks, X could see first the pants leg and then the whole body of the third agent. The giant of a man – who looked as if he could easily hurl X through a plate-glass window – stood stock still, slowly turning his head to survey the crowd.

Meanwhile the redhead was enthusiastically clenching her buns together.

"You're making me so goddamn horny," she claimed.

"I'm glad you enjoy your work," he gasped.

"Seriously, you're exactly my type."

He wondered what type that was – a full wallet?

Out of the corner of his eye, X saw the third agent striding straight at him. The big man was no more than four feet away when he abruptly stopped, put his finger to his earpiece and nodded. He spoke into his lapel and then, much to the identity thief's relief, he and his fellow agents retreated from the club as stealthily as they'd entered it.

Nine blocks away, the taxi carrying the bachelor-party quartet was being pulled over and surrounded by dozens of lawmen. The four occupants howled in drunken protest as they were dragged out and tossed to the ground. One of the agents roughly frisked the groom-to-be and arose brandishing the stolen cell phone.

"Where did you just come from?" the agent demanded, rolling the guy over and, shoving the muzzle of a shotgun up to the guy's nostrils. The terrified bridegroom looked at him blankly for a moment, then sputtered, "The Pink Panther."

The agent barked into a walkie talkie: "Units five and six, get back to the club, immediately. I repeat, get back to the club."

The car bearing the agents from the club, who were speeding toward the scene and had traveled four blocks, made a screeching U-turn.

Meanwhile, the dancer bounced up and down on X with gusto, like a teenybopper testing out a new pogo stick. X was biting his lower lip and fighting back the urge to climax. Fortuitously, at that moment the song wound down and the redhead looked over her shoulder expectantly. "Another dance?" she murmured.

X had held $100 in reserve.

"I want you to do something for me," he whispered.

"If you want any extras, you need to take me into a VIP room," she said with a lascivious grin. "Oh, Steve, baby, I'm really gonna rock your world."

What exactly comprised an "extra" X would never know. He waved one of the Ben Franklins in front of her greedy lime-green eyes.

"Is there another way out of here?" he asked. She hesitated, but the easy money was irresistible and she snatched it from his fingers.

"Sometimes a girl will get stalked by one of the ATMs. Y'know some loser who blows all his money on you – no offense meant – "

"None taken."

"And who falls in 'love' and wants to date you. There's a back exit in the dressing room so we can sneak out without getting hassled."

Before surrendering his last C note – leaving the stolen wallet empty – he whispered: "And there's one more thing."

Two minutes later, just as the agents burst into the club, Party bolted to her feet and screamed at the top of her lungs, "Raid!"

Pandemonium erupted in the den of inequity, with panicked

half-naked girls darting in all directions like cockroaches surprised by a kitchen light. Plastered customers stumbled to their feet, knocking over chairs. Perhaps few of them knew what a "raid" might constitute in the post-burlesque-show era – but obviously, it couldn't be a good thing.

X had already snuck into the dressing room, where a skinny blonde sat with a pair of jeans around her ankles, attempting to pull them off. She hadn't applied her makeup yet and had the despondent demeanor of a teenage runaway.

"What the hell are you doing in here?' the girl demanded, covering her bra-clad bosom with surprising modesty and showing a mouthful of braces. "You're not allowed back here, dude."

"All hell has broken loose out there," he informed her. "The place is crawling with cops. I don't know about you, but I'm getting the hell out of here."

The girl cocked her head and listened to the shouts emanating from the club, then hurriedly yanked up her jeans and began buttoning them. Maybe she was 16, maybe 17, but there was no doubt she was underage.

X charged past the dancer, flung open the door and slipped out. He looked left and right and then – resisting the urge to run – hurried down the narrow alleyway. In about 30 seconds, he knew, a dozen scantily clad babes were about to spill out of the secret exit. That might certainly tend to draw attention to the egress.

As he burned the corner, he spied a roadblock up ahead. At least 15 agents, some in suits and others in flak jackets, were sprinting full throttle in the direction of the club.

Oh darn it all, X thought, ducking back.

There was a truck parked next to a dingy pawn shop. X dropped to his belly and rolled underneath it. He could hear the clippity clop of heavy government-issue brogans headed his way. *Well, end of the road,* X thought. He'd had a nice run of it, but they'd ferret him out in short order.

Then he noticed it: A manhole cover. It would be only a matter of seconds before the agents reached the corner. X lurched for the manhole cover. It was heavy as lead, but an adrenaline rush gave him the strength to pry it off. He descended into the sewer and hauled the cover back over his head.

The fumes – so potent they were almost visible – were overpowering. X nearly passed out on the way down the ladder. But to retreat would mean a prison cell if not a bullet in the brain. So he pressed on, deeper and deeper into the abyss. His claustrophobia kicked in as he climbed, rung after rung, down the narrow shaft into Stygian darkness. He was perspiring profusely – unusual for a man of whom his colleagues often joked, "He's not human enough to sweat." Finally, he splashed down into a waist-deep pool of fetid, bacteria-laden wastewater.

God knows what diseases I'm going to pick up, thought X, who was normally the type to wash his hands eight to 10 times a day.

Chapter 9
NOTES FROM UNDERGROUND

FBI special agent Traci Kingsmith, AKA Stacy the masseuse, sat at the conference table in the makeshift command center set up at the Giza Hotel as her superior Mark Normand pounded the conference table in fury.

"You're telling me we have satellites that can read the label on a Coke bottle, but we can't locate one man we had in our sights three hours ago," the potbellied, graying Bureau man grumbled.

"Let me explain," said an NSA specialist. He punched a button and a satellite photo showing the roof of the Pink Panther appeared on a screen at the front of the room. "When the subject exited the back entrance, he passed through a dark alley. There wasn't enough light for a good image. We're having the image enhanced as we speak.

"Las Vegas is more than 84,000 square miles – that's a lot of ground to cover, even with the manpower at our disposal."

The multiagency taskforce working on the manhunt also included the Department of Homeland Security, the CIA and the Defense Intelligence Agency, in addition to at least four outfits Traci had never heard of. "Swimming in alphabet soup" is how one of her colleagues termed such sessions.

"Un-fucking believable," fumed Normand, who headed the task force.

Traci saw an opening and took it.

"Maybe that's our problem. Maybe he's not above ground."

"Are you suggesting that he's in the sewer?" said the CIA man dubiously. "Like in *The Fugitive?*"

"I didn't kill my wife," joked red-haired FBI agent Malloy, quoting Harrison Ford.

"I don't care," the Defense Intelligence Agency rep quoted Tommy Lee Jones.

Everyone laughed.

The female agent pulled out a chart from her carrying case and expanded on her theory.

"It's technically a storm drain system," she said. "There are more than 350 miles of flood channels under the city. And it's largely habitable, although I wouldn't want to build a summer house down there. According to some estimates, as many as 700 'tunnel people' call it home."

A tall woman, close to six feet, with a rapid, clipped manner of speaking, Traci was a graduate of Rutgers, cum laude, and her research skills had been among the attributes that had impressed Bureau recruiters. Traci was fluent in Spanish, French, Italian, German, Arabic and Pashto. The first four of these she had actually learned before she entered college.

Her parents were of modest means. Her father was an Episcopal minister who'd served 20 years as a missionary in China and her mom was a school librarian. They were firm believers in education as a means to climb the social ladder. From the age of five, her father introduced her to foreign languages through books and audio tapes. And beginning with Spanish, she learned one every two years.

She was brilliant enough that the burdensome Rutgers tuition was paid for by a basketball scholarship. Traci was a gifted athlete and continued to maintain a state of fitness through running, weight training and kickboxing. Traci was a black belt in kung fu – one of the reasons she was so furious she'd allowed herself to be overcome by the relatively shrimpy Ali Nazeer. She was justly proud of her figure, her long, lean legs and high, taut buttocks.

Yet, truth be told, the agent had not had a date in eight months nor sex in a year. She was, as her friends put it, "very, very picky." To be considered boyfriend material, the suitor had to be African-American, a church-goer, exceed her height (5 feet 10 ½ inches to be exact) and have an income exceeding her own.

Some potential boyfriends were intimidated. Though some would, in a gentlemanly manner, retreat from the field saying, "You're too good for me," the fact was men tended to find her brittle and high-strung.

Traci pointed to the map. "If he's down there, he could go

beneath our perimeter and reach Lake Mead in a matter of hours."

An agent appeared in the doorway. "The computer-enhanced image of the alley is back, sir. It shows the subject approaching this dark truck, and going under it."

"The truck was searched, wasn't it?"

"Our men went through it with a fine-toothed comb," confirmed the representative from Homeland Security.

"Call up the image of the alley as it looks now," said Traci. Normand nodded and up popped an enlarged image of the alley on the conference room screen.

"Here is the alley with the truck gone," she said.

Where the truck had been, only a manhole and a flattened soda can remained.

Normand swiveled his chair slowly until he faced Mr. Homeland Security.

"No one noticed that there was a goddamned *MANHOLE COVER* at the scene?" he growled. "Did it need a big orange 'Down here' arrow on it?"

The Homeland Security man looked as if he wanted to pull a vanishing act himself. Traci gave herself the pleasure of flashing a quick, smug smile. Then she came to his rescue.

"There was a lot of confusion at the scene," Traci said. "In that kind of pandemonium ... "

"That's nice. Bring me the heads of the clowns who searched the truck," snapped Normand. He addressed Traci, to her delight. "So we send a party down there."

"I would suggest 10 eight-man teams,' Traci said.

At the far end of the table, a white-bearded man who'd been introduced only as Mr. Jones puffed thoughtfully on a pipe. Exactly what organization he worked for was something of a mystery. Traci had been told "That information is strictly need to know."

"It's vital that he be taken alive," Mr. Jones declared. "The information he has about terrorist networks – the Jihadist Brotherhood and the Warriors of Allah in particular – is invaluable."

Normand nodded. "Understood."

Traci cleared her throat. "Sir, I want to lead the search team."

Her boss hesitated.

"After what happened I think I'm owed a little payback," she said.

Traci was certain she heard a low snicker from her colleague Malloy but ignored it.

Normand pounded the table. "It's your show. Let's roll."

Traci shot out of her seat. As the crowd poured out of the room, Agent Malloy whispered to her, "Your feminine wiles came through again. This is going to be a real feather in your cap – if you catch the guy."

Traci usually ignored the redhead but couldn't resist saying, "By the way, Malloy, I thought you told me your sister was an ophthalmologist. Don't forget to get her out of lockup when her interrogation is over. She'll get cold in that G-string."

Malloy stood there, trying to think of a comeback, but by the time he did the room was clear.

*   *   *

X hadn't the vaguest clue where he was. The tunnel, about eight feet high and five feet wide, was as dark as the inside of a womb. His hands groped the sides of the tunnel and found them slick with slimy algae. He recoiled in disgust but he forced himself to slide along them for support, for to fall into that foul water was unthinkable.

He sloshed through the now knee-deep water, through which floated plastic bags, Styrofoam cups and crushed beer cans. It was like wading through the digestive tract of some garbage-eating sci-fi monstrosity.

It reeks like a week-old corpse down here, he thought, clapping his left hand over his nose while the right clung to the tunnel wall.

X had expected it to be hot but the temperature was actually at least 30 degrees colder than above ground, and the fugitive felt goose bumps rising on his arms. The stream, though shallow, roared like a mountain river. Occasionally from far above, X could also hear the rush of traffic and the occasional rattle of manhole covers.

Retrieving his getaway car and the clean identity of Steve Holdenbrook was, of course, now a lost cause. But X had a plan. He had a friend – all right an acquaintance, for X had no friends as an ordinary person would understand the term – who operated a legal brothel about 50 miles outside Vegas. If X could make it there, he could probably find a temporary refuge.

X's face encountered a spider web that stretched the breadth of the tunnel and he brushed it away in revulsion. *The bug that made that thing must be the size of a raccoon*, he thought, wiping lingering strands from his cheeks.

It was slow going. About 100 feet later, he felt a punch to the rib cage as he slammed into a protruding lateral pipe. X lost his footing and – horror of horrors – fell to his hands and knees in the water. He scrambled to his feet, screaming in disgust and fury. He hated germs, he hated dirt.

Why is this happening to me? It isn't fair!

"Yuck, yuck, yuck!" His voice echoed through the tunnel and he cursed himself for his stupidity. Hardly the time for loud complaints.

X trudged on.

About 150 yards farther down the tunnel, X came to a juncture where a sewer drain, 15 feet above, above cast a parallelogram-shaped beam of light, unveiling graffiti scrawls and arcane official markings reminiscent of hieroglyphics. The sudden illumination also revealed cockroaches scuttling over the walls, while crawfish the size of trout wallowed in the green-brown water. Compared to that loathsome sight, the dark was almost comforting.

In the distance X heard approaching voices. Reluctantly, he abandoned the oasis of light and broke into a run, splashing in the opposite direction.

Traci and a team of eight heavily armed agents were at this point no more than 500 yards to the east. There were 10 such teams pouring into the tunnels from various ports of entry. The searchers were outfitted with masks, hazmat suits and rubber waders that reached to their waists. Traci's high-intensity LED flashlight illuminated rats swishing through the water, on top of which floated a child's doll, a basketball and a moldy, torn-up sneaker.

Though theoretically protected from biohazards, the overall repulsiveness of the place brought Traci nearly to the point of retching. Only her pride prevented her from ripping off her mask and puking in full view of the otherwise all-male crew.

Pulaski, an expert from the city's Streets and Sanitation Division who looked a bit like Tony Soprano, guided them, pausing now and then to consult a map. They had reached yet another fork and had to decide which way to go.

"We're just under Bonanza Road now," the beer-bellied guide informed her, panting from the effort of their descent. "That way leads east, that's west."

Traci flashed her light down one corridor, then the other. Each was equally dismal, each equally forbidding.

"We split up," she decided.

"That cuts us to four," protested a husky male subordinate.

"I can divide, Agent Greavy," she said sharply.

X sloshed down a snaking tunnel, guided by blind instinct. To his alarm he saw two pinpricks of light appear suddenly in the distance. As the far-off flashlights swiveled in his direction, he crouched down, barely ducking the beams in time. Then, with no other option, he lay flat, head underwater. After holding his breath as long as he could – close to a minute – he surfaced, gasping for breath. The lights were gone.

He struggled to his feet and staggered on.

Traci walked alongside the husky male agent, who was just a few years older than herself.

"So, are you married or what?" Greavy asked casually.

She couldn't believe she was being hit on, decked out in full hazmat attire, mired in crappy water and in the midst of the most intense manhunt the city had ever seen.

"That's not appropriate," she responded sternly.

"Just making small talk. Yeesh, excuuuuse me."

The talk at headquarters was that Traci was a lesbian, a theory G-men could not resist frequently putting to the test.

"Hey, what happened at the Giza?" the agent blundered on. "You wouldn't believe some of the rumors floating around. Some people are even saying you gave the guy a– "

"Shh! I see something," she whispered.

X emerged from a narrow tunnel and suddenly a bright

beam of light shone in his face. He cowered from it like a vampire avoiding sunlight. Then he raised his hands quickly.

I beat the odds making it this far, he thought.

A hoarse voice came from behind the glare. "Are you from the city?"

X didn't skip a beat. "Yes," he said, lowering his hands. "What are you doing here?" He pumped as much authoritative bass into his voice as he could summon. "This area is off limits."

"Hunting rats," the stranger said. "I sell the pelts for women's winter hats."

"I see," X said. Then paused and added, "That can't be true."

"No. But then again, you're not from the city, now are you?"

The stranger directed the flashlight at himself and X saw that he was a wrinkled, 70-something man wearing the tattered remnants of a priest's garb, including a stained white collar.

"Are you lost?" the old man inquired.

"I bet your pardon?"

"It looks like you've lost your way, son."

"Yes, yes," he said. "I'm a reporter for the *Las Vegas Sun.* We're doing a report on life beneath – "

The old man raised his hand, stopping X mid-babble. The priest could see right through his line of bullshit.

"Come follow me," he said, gesturing with a crooked, yellow-nailed finger.

X hesitated. The old geezer was clearly nuts. The question was how nuts. He could be some kind of serial killer, preying on the derelicts who supposedly haunted this loathsome place. An old movie called *C.H.U.D.* (Cannibalistic Humanoid Underground Dwellers) came to mind and he briefly imagined his bones being gnawed on by rats while the creepy cleric dined on his kidneys.

"Come quickly," the priest whispered.

Well, beggars can't be choosers, X thought and stepped toward the light.

A moment later they were hunched over, wading through a five-foot-tall tunnel, ankle-deep in thick, soupy sludge.

"You actually live down here?" X asked, astounded.

"I minister to the people of this place," the old man said. "The homeless, the hopeless who find themselves here."

X had heard rumors that beneath some cities drug addicts and lunatics dwelled in the sewers and subway tunnels, but had always dismissed them as urban legends.

"There are about 40 people in my little flock. Men, women, children."

"And the church pays you to do this?"

X knew that Catholic priests weren't paid much. But even the bundle raked in by evangelical preachers at mega-churches – whom X had long admired as the greatest scam artists of them all – wasn't enough to entice any sane person to work in this hellhole.

The priest chuckled.

"The church lost track of me long ago," he said. "I wasn't excommunicated; I simply fell off the radar."

That makes a little more sense, X thought. *So I'm talking to a fallen angel.*

"I came here to gamble. The roulette wheel was my poison. I gambled away church funds, to the tune of $43,207. This is home for me now."

He pointed his beam at a corner where four big pipes formed a rectangle. A bed hung suspended from wires about four feet from the floor. It was composed of couch cushions and a rotten wooden door; a stack of old *National Geographics* served as a pillow. On the walls were pictures that X recognized vaguely from his days as a Catholic schoolboy as saints. That was St. Francis over there, wasn't it?

"It's not much but it keeps you dry at night," the priest said of his accommodations.

Night, day, is there any difference down here? X wondered. This made even the most barren monastic cell look like digs at the Ritz Carlton.

"How long have you been down here?" he asked.

The old priest stroked his beard and thought for a moment. "Now, let's see. Three ... four ... five years now."

X shook his head in disbelief.

"Have a seat," the priest said, pointing at a battered car seat upholstered in what had once been fine Corinthian leather. How the chair ended up down here was anyone's guess. X pondered the mystery as he sat down. He knew he should keep moving, but he was physically and mentally spent. He had vaguely hoped the old man might be able to hide him somewhere, but right now he only longed for a few moments' rest.

"Care for some crackers?" the old man asked, retrieving a cellophane-wrapped package from a tin on the bed.

X was indeed hungry, but he had a feeling those crackers dated from the Eisenhower administration. "Not just yet," he said.

"Are you Catholic?" the priest asked.

X had not set foot in a church of any stripe in 15 years.

"Well, not practicing. I was raised as one."

"I can hear your confession, if you wish. "

"Excuse me?"

"It still counts, if that's what you're wondering. As I said, I was never defrocked, deserving of that as I may be."

"I ... I don't really have anything to say."

The priest smiled wryly.

"So you've led a blameless life, have you, me boy?" he said in a mock Irish brogue, the kind an old movie priest might employ.

Is this guy some kind of mind reader? X could only presume that his desperate appearance suggested criminal behavior.

"Thanks, but I don't have time."

"It may be later than you think," said the old man. "Listen, son, you can keep running from who you are. But sooner or later you have to choose which life to lead."

The old man was creeping X out now. The priest continued, "Find something beyond yourself to live for – before it's too late."

In the distance, X heard multiple feet splashing through water. And although it meant the enemy was at hand, it was almost a relief to be rescued from the conversation.

"Listen, I've got to get out of here. The truth is I'm – I'm being hunted."

"I suspected that a little bit."

"Please, which tunnel should I take?"

The priest chewed that over for about 30 seconds then pointed.

"Go 75 yards down here, then where it forks, take the tunnel to the left. Another 50 yards or so, take a right. Another 20 feet and you'll find a narrow tunnel on the left. It's an abandoned shaft. I don't think it's even on the maps."

"Left. Right. Left. Got it," X said. "Thank you. Thank you, father."

"Bless you my son." The priest said. "May the Lord give you a chance to redeem yourself."

X began to back away, then the old man said, "Wait." He handed the identity thief his flashlight, handle first.

"You need a light to guide you," the priest said.

X backed away, turned, then bolted into the tunnel.

Traci and her party were closing in on a moving figure – identified with the help of an infra-red sensor that picked up body heat. Another team was covering the only escape path, so the target was cornered. Her heart beat faster in anticipation of finally nailing their quarry.

Normally Traci was cool as a cucumber; some co-workers even called her "cold." But after that humiliating episode in the hotel room ... well, this was personal. She had, of course, been given a "safe word" to use if she got in a jam. But, believing she could handle the situation, she had hesitated to ask for help a second too long and had ended up hogtied on this little creep's bed. Now it was payback time.

"Over there!" one of her men shouted. They turned the corner and saw a human figure. Guns flew out of holsters as if they were a posse of Wild West gunslingers.

"FBI, don't make a move!" Traci hollered, pointing her Glock 17 at a shadowy figure just a few yards from her.

"Don't shoot! Please don't shoot!" a female voice responded.

Four beams from the search party's flashlights converged, shining with the intensity of stadium lights on what turned out to be a five-member family in filthy rags. All had hollow, haunted eyes that winced from the light. They looked like a cross between the Joads from *The Grapes of Wrath* and a tribe of hitherto undiscovered Neanderthals. Behind them tottered a makeshift cardboard dwelling.

Miscellaneous belongings ranging from jugs of water to a rusted tricycle were piled five feet high in shopping carts. The youngest child, clutching a one-eyed teddy bear even dirtier than she was, appeared to be no more than three. They surely needed rescue from their predicament; a visit from Social Services or some other agency seemed in order, but that wasn't Traci's concern at the moment.

"Sorry to scare you," she said. "Have you seen a man pass this way?"

The small, ghostly waif pointed silently.

X was crawling now, through a flooded tunnel that narrowed at an alarming pace, until it could barely accommodate his shoulders. His head was just above the stinking water. Why had he listened to that crackpot? He was going to drown like a rat.

"I'm beginning to doubt my career choice," he whispered to himself.

Then a faint light appeared in the distance. As he surged on, the light grew brighter and brighter, like the arrival of an archangel. It was an outlet. He felt a gentle breeze and plowed ahead, hoping against hope, toward the light.

If I get out of this … If I get out of this … I'm going to go into another area of crime entirely. Carjacking, perhaps.

But soon, to his horror, he saw that a rusted iron gate blocked his passage. The bars were thick as a man's wrist and spaced no more than four inches apart. A toddler couldn't squeeze through. X stopped and began to laugh at the Good Lord's sadistic joke. His mad cackle echoed through the tunnel.

Going back was not an option, so he crawled forward, wriggling on his belly like a snake now. As he got closer, he saw that the grate was ajar. He pushed tentatively, and the grate swung open, creaking like the door of Dracula's castle.

X slid out of the drainpipe and found himself in an open-air channel. Bulrush grass poked up from the stream and cinderblocks cluttered the bottom. The concrete walls of the ditch had to be 20 feet high and fenced, with barbed wire crowning the top. But after what he'd been through, that seemed hardly formidable. After about 50 yards he found a ladder and, hand over hand, he pulled himself up the rungs.

Miraculously, he found he was miles outside the city, which he could see, a hazy monument, in the distance. It was raining cats and dogs. But the thorough drenching was welcome after the mire of the sewer.

X shed his filthy clothes. He yearned mightily to burn them. Instead, he stretched them over a cactus and when most of the muck was washed off, he wrung them out. If he could make it to a highway, he could hitchhike, get far from here.

X began to walk, stiffly at first, and then with hope, toward the roar of the Interstate.

Chapter 10
WHEELS WITHIN WHEELS

X stood by the side of a highway surrounded by a bleak desert landscape Goya could have painted. Although he'd cleaned up to what he deemed a reasonable degree, and looked less like a zombie bum, a dozen cars zoomed passed. He thought of that old Rutger Hauer movie *The Hitcher*, and couldn't really blame them.

Finally, after about half an hour, a battered yellow pickup pulled over. It bore two occupants, the driver a chrome-dome with a long, straggly gray John Brown beard and alarmingly thick glasses, the passenger a wiry man who could be his kid brother, sporting a baseball cap and a thick handlebar moustache.

"Whereabouts you headed?" X asked after they'd been on the road a few minutes. This time his voice had its normal, mid-Atlantic inflection. He couldn't muster the energy -- nor was there really any need – for any bogus accent. He had introduced himself as Jack and the brothers didn't probe for details.

"Groom Lake," replied Don, the bearded one.

"Fishing?" X suggested.

The brothers guffawed in stereo.

"I guess you've never heard of Area 51," said Earl, the wiry one. X dimly recalled having read about such a place in a supermarket tabloid while standing in the checkout line.

"It's some kind of secret military base, isn't it?"

Don now adopted an officious tone. "Jack, we're researchers with the Ohio Institute for Unexplained Phenomenon. We're investigating reports of new UFO activity on the base."

He pronounced it "you foe."

"UFOs?"

"You've heard of the Roswell incident?"

X shook his head. The bearded man responded with the bewilderment as if the hitchhiker had said he'd never heard of

Corn Flakes.

"In 1947, near Roswell, New Mexico, a UFO crashed. Air Force investigators visited the site and announced that it was a flying saucer. It was reported in newspapers coast to coast. But just a couple of days later, the Air Force retracted the story and claimed it was just a weather balloon. The story goes that alien remains were retrieved from the wreck."

Earl chimed in. "It's also widely agreed that the Air Force recovered alien technology from the wreckage and took it to Area 51. Our scientists used reverse engineering to develop the Stealth Bomber, the Star Wars missile defense system and a lot of weaponry that's never been declassified. Possibly even a time-travel device."

X nodded. "Why, it only stands to reason," he said encouragingly.

He might have known no sane person would pick up a male hitchhiker these days. *Well, at least they seem harmless. Not more than a 10 percent chance I'll wind up in a dozen different garbage bags along the highway.*

"When it comes to the federal government, you've got to understand that every word they tell the public is a lie – including 'and' and 'the,' " Don continued. "It's wheels within wheels, lies within lies, riddles inside of riddles. Heck, there are so many secret agencies today, they keep secrets from one another – the left hand doesn't know what the right hand is doing and one group ends up foiling the plans another group has had in the works for decades."

Earl added, "When that happens they call it a 'Wilderness of Mirrors.' If things go rhino and everyone ends up shooting each other, a team is sent in to cauterize the scene – liquidate all the compromised assets.

"They call it the 9 mm pension plan. All the documentation on the botched mission goes to a place at CIA headquarters called the Pit where it's dumped into an enormous shredder, then burned. You know there are agencies not even other agencies know about? One is – "

Earl interjected, "The most secret of all is called the Secret Committee. It's so secret the President doesn't even know about it. They say it's been around since the American Revolution and it's tied up with the French Foreign Legion."

He wrapped his index and middle fingers around each other to emphasize this closeness. "Politicians pretend to hate France, but that's just a cover. We're like that."

"It's like the Kennedy assassination," Don said, warming to the topic. "Did you know the real reason was that the CIA wanted to keep him from revealing the truth about extraterrestrials?"

"Didn't know that," X said.

"JFK was about to reveal the presence of aliens on Earth in his speech that day in Dallas," Earl said, digging a crumpled newspaper clipping out of his pocket. "See, I have it right here."

The source of the article was unclear, but the byline was "Mike Foster," which sounded like a pseudonym to X. He scanned the article quickly and saw that it included an excerpt from the undelivered speech. "Citizens of the Earth, we are not alone," it began dramatically and continued in a distinctly Kennedyesque style and cadence X recognized from documentaries. The source of the article was an upcoming book titled *Killing the Messenger* by one Professor Merrick.

"Here's the spooky part," Earl said in a hushed voice, turning fully back to look at the passenger. "You try to find the book on Amazon and it isn't there. You Google this expert Merrick and there's absolutely no trace of him."

Don nodded gravely. "It's like the guy has been erased. Poof."

X had a feeling that the historian's lack of any footprint suggested something else entirely. But he'd gone 48 hours without sleep and had no interest in debating the subject.

"The world sure is full of mysterious stuff," he agreed and leaned back.

As his rescuers launched into a feverish discussion of the role of the Illuminati and the presence of their symbols in monuments like the Statue of Liberty, he drifted off into an uneasy sleep, descending into a dream world populated by bulbous-headed E.T.s, a buoyant JFK with a bullet-hole in his forehead and the spiraling concentric circles of an impossible gyroscope, wheels within wheels within wheels.

*　*　*

"Go, go, go! Floor it!" Earl was hollering at the top of his lungs. X's eyes flew open and he braced himself as the pickup tore down the road at better than 90 m.p.h.

The whir of chopper blades flooded his eardrums and he looked out the window. Overhead, a pair of sleek black helicopters hovered like hummingbirds. A huge, ugly machine gun projected out of the open door of one.

"The Men in Black," Earl gasped more in awe than fear.

"Like in the movie?" said X, trying to determine if he was still dreaming.

"The helicopters aren't in stealth mode. I can hear them," said Don.

The chase lasted only a moment or two before the driver hit the brakes, nearly sending X through the windshield, and the pickup screeched to a stop about 20 yards in front of a roadblock. About two dozen men in body armor toting assault rifles stood in front of a trio of jet-black Humvees.

"Get out of the vehicle," a voice roared over a bullhorn.

"Jesus Christ, they're going to kill us," Earl said. Tears were pouring down his face. "We know too much."

"Don't panic, man," Don said, though his tremulous voice suggested he was doing just that. "They'll blank out our memories, that's all. Come on."

The brothers climbed out of the cab, arms raised, walked a couple of yards and prostrated themselves on the baking road. Men raced over and quickly cuffed them, and then dragged them away. Don kept whimpering that he didn't want *all* his memories erased, not the ones of childhood or "my first time."

X got out of the car, hands raised. As he strode toward the roadblock, he began formulating in his mind the story he would tell. He was an identity thief, yes, but merely a pawn in a vast organization. And he would certainly be willing to cooperate if given a guarantee of immunity. X already had a name in mind, Jared Spinrad, age 35, from St. Louis.

As he walked toward the row of guns pointed at him like a firing squad, one of the gleaming black helicopters whooshed down in front of him.

"On your knees, NOW!" a voice boomed through another bullhorn, this one from the aircraft. He obliged, still holding his hands up high.

Six black-clad men brandishing weapons that resembled M-16s but a bit fancier poured out of the chopper and ran toward him. *What is it with all this black?* X thought. *If it's to make them inconspicuous, it's not doing the trick.*

A female figure climbed out last, a black woman with an FBI cap and flak jacket, holding the bullhorn. As she approached, he recognized the agent who'd posed as Stacy the masseuse.

A smile came to X's lips. "Fancy meeting you here."

Traci didn't return his smile as she put down the bullhorn and cuffed him. Her boss Normand had moaned when she requisitioned a military-type drone aircraft to be on the lookout in this area, but it had paid off. Seeing this SOB face-down on the asphalt was giving her so much satisfaction, she almost DID smile.

"Ouch. Easy there," X said as the cuffs bit into his wrists. "Now listen, sweetheart, there's been a big mistake and I can clear everything up in about two minutes."

"My name isn't sweetheart, you terrorist, baby-killing son of a bitch."

She drew something metallic from her holster – not a gun, X could see. A taser.

"Hey, that isn't necessary, " he cried. "I'm surrendering."

The zap hurt like hell. It felt for a moment as if he was on fire. He collapsed backward. While he was still on the ground, one of the men rolled him onto his belly. From head to toe, his body shook uncontrollably as another goon rolled up his sleeve and stuck a hypodermic needle in his arm.

.

Chapter 11
RENDITION

When X awoke he found himself wrapped in a blanket in what he quickly recognized as the cargo hold of an airplane. His hands were still secured behind his back with handcuffs and his ankles were shackled as well.

Well, this is an unpleasant surprise.

A man clad in black from his cap to steel-toed boots sat on a bench a few yards away, a huge .44 Magnum holstered at his side, his nose buried in a copy of the *Sports Illustrated* swimsuit issue

"Where are we going?" X said hoarsely.

"That's for us to know and you to find out," the guard said without looking up and without a trace of playfulness.

"Can I have a pillow and some peanuts?" X requested. "What's the in-flight movie?"

His attempt at levity didn't merit even the slightest snicker from his guardian.

X had heard of the process. Newspapers called it "rendition" didn't they? He was undoubtedly bound for some gulag the CIA kept under wraps in countries like Egypt or Saudi Arabia where torture – or as the U.S. media delicately called it "enhanced interrogation techniques" – was legal.

"Listen, I gotta to talk to your commanding officer, ASAP." He deliberately spoke in a pronounced Brooklyn accent, to leave no doubt in his captor's mind that he was as American as a Nathan's hotdog.

The guard neither replied nor tore his attention from page 41 – which is to be excused since it featured a slice of Australian cheesecake who resembled a young Cindy Crawford.

"There's been a big mistake. I am not Ali Nazeer." Still no response.

"I'm a U.S. citizen!' he practically screamed.

Now the guard rose and quietly approached him. He crouched in front of X, wearing an expression so savage it would have suited a Viking berserker. His blond eyebrows were nearly invisible and his eyes the color of ice, adding to the frightfulness of his appearance.

"Open your mouth," he instructed, drawing his sidearm.

"Now wait a minute."

"I said open your fucking mouth."

X parted his lips an inch and the guard shoved the muzzle past his teeth and so far down his throat he began to gag.

"Don't open your damned trap again with that bullshit," his minder growled. "Say it again and you're going to get your head blown off. Where you're going, we have people inside, listening. Say that shit again, and you're dead meat. Nod if you understand me."

Shaking like a sapling in an earthquake, X nodded.

"Now I'm going to sit over there and relax. I strongly suggest you shut the fuck up for the rest of flight."

He withdrew the Dirty Harry weapon, wiped it on his pants and holstered it, then resumed his former position, calmly thumbing through the magazine.

Under the circumstances, X elected not to attempt small talk for the remainder of the flight.

*   *   *

It was hours – X had no idea how many – before the plane touched down. Long enough to cross the Atlantic and then some, the identity thief thought. A pair of brawny men, similarly clad in black (apparently the look this season) came back to the hold and blindfolded him.

He felt a rush of heat as the door to the cargo hold glided open and he was led down a steep ramp, shuffling in the leg irons. The prisoner was shoved unceremoniously into the back of a truck. The vehicle roared to life noisily, and then rumbled along.

How long he sat on that metal bench in the back of the truck he couldn't tell. Perhaps three hours. His wrists ached and he was starving. He couldn't remember the last time he ate or drank.

"Could someone loosen these handcuffs, please?" he said.

There was no reply.

"Okay, how about some water?"

Again, no answer.

"Can you turn on the radio? I'd like to hear the latest from Lady Gaga."

Finally the truck stopped.

"Get out," ordered a gruff voice that exuded all the friendliness of a grizzly bear. With difficulty he rose, hunched over and climbed out of the vehicle. He was marched in the leg irons, shuffling across a courtyard of some kind.

A buzzer sounded and metal doors clanged open. Complete cacophony assaulted X as he was hustled in. There were American voices barking orders, Arabic ones uttering prayers.

Jesus, I really have been rendered!

He was familiar enough with Arab dialects to know they spanned the Middle East. There were Yemini, Iraqis, Saudis, and Jordanians. There were Afghanis too, Iranians and Pakistanis represented. When they finally took the blindfold off him, along with the cuffs, his eyes stung from bright fluorescent lights and he shielded his pupils.

He stood in a small room with grim, gray cinderblock walls. Somewhat ominously, he noted, there were dark red stains on the concrete floor. A female soldier with prominent breasts, a 6-foot-5 giant and a younger guy with bad acne faced him. The men sported buzz cuts; the woman a short, butch-looking hairdo. All wore what looked like Marine uniforms with the nametags and rank insignia missing. *Not a good sign,* X thought.

"Strip, son – right down to your birthday suit," ordered the big guy, with a deep Mississippi accent. There was nothing avuncular about the "son." He came off like a KKK cretin snarling "boy."

X took off his now ragged jacket and shirt and dropped them to the floor. He hesitated when he got to the pants. When he escaped the hotel suite, he hadn't had time to don underwear. Despite a life of crime that extended to his early teens, X had never been arrested and never strip-searched. Never been naked in front of a clothed person since early childhood. He avoided eye contact with the female soldier, who made no effort to turn away, evincing neither interest nor embarrassment. Like she'd been through this a thousand times, which X supposed she had. Reluctantly, he dropped his trousers and stepped out of them, placing his hands over his genitals.

Without his clothes he felt vulnerable as a newborn baby. More than that, he felt stripped of all identity.

"Open your mouth," Giant Redneck said. X obliged. The Southerner's thick, gloved fingers probed his mouth roughly, lifting his tongue and peering under it with a penlight. He stood back and nodded to Big Tits, who smirked at X.

"Turn around," she ordered. She, too, was wearing yellow latex gloves.

"Now wait … " X began.

"Shut up," Big Redneck commanded. "You heard her."

X sighed and turned around, fearing what was coming next.

"Bend over," Big Tits barked, in a sadistic tone that more properly befitted an audition for a low-budget women in prison movie.

X hesitated. "Wait," he said. "Just wait a second."

"The lady said bend the fuck over, turd," Pizza Face snarled. He was from the north, somewhere in New Jersey. "Or am I gonna have to bend you the fuck over?"

X leaned forward.

"Clap your hands on your ass," the female soldier said. He obeyed.

"Spread your ass cheeks. Wider … wider."

X wanted to kill her.

"Ugh," she spat in disgust. "You've got the hairiest asshole I've ever seen."

Pizza Face guffawed. "Fucking Chewbacca!"

Giant Redneck's deep laugh was unnervingly similar to a mule's.

Being stripped by a woman was supposed to humiliate him, X knew that much from *Time* magazine. Muslim men were supposedly so uptight that to be nude in the presence of an American woman would be abhorrent. He remembered reading how one poor detainee at a Guantanamo Bay had been "tortured" by a CIA agent who kept rubbing her chest in his nose. Poor devil, X had thought at the time.

X didn't share the Muslim view. Frankly, he preferred that the woman was conducting the cavity search – if that hillbilly was doing it, it would be like something out of *Deliverance*. Still, this was hardly tea with the queen.

He let go of his butt cheeks and started to rise.

"Get back down," the woman said. "I'll tell you when to stop cracking a smile. Spread wider." X sighed. *When this piece of work leaves the service, she could make a mint as a dominatrix.*

"Come on, this ain't your first rodeo," Giant Redneck rumbled. "We know you towel-heads hump each other every chance you get, fuck the Koran."

He braced himself for the insertion of a finger. *It's not a dick, it's not a dick, it's not a dick,* he told himself. His heart was palpitating and he felt like throwing up.

The finger didn't come. Only a flashlight illuminated his alimentary canal. After what seemed like an inordinate amount of time, Big Tits told him to stand up and turn around.

"Lift up your nut sack."

X sighed and hoisted his testicles. *Okay, it's just like being at a doctor's office, getting a hernia test,* he told himself.

"Jesus Christ, are you getting a goddamn hard-on?" the female soldier demanded in patently false alarm.

"No," X stammered, reddening.

"Don't give me that shit. Yes, you fucking are. You're disgusting," she said, turning to Giant Redneck. "Sarge, this sack of shit towel-head is flashing me. The fucking pervert!"

The big Southerner got so close to X he could smell tobacco on the soldier's breath. X drew brief satisfaction from the thought the brute would probably die from lung cancer, a tracheotomy hole in his Li'l Abner neck.

"Are you insulting a United States Marine, son?" Giant Redneck growled.

"Look, I'm not, not," X sputtered. "This is ridiculous – "

"Now he's calling me a liar," Big Tits complained, aghast, crossing her arms and pouting.

Without warning, Giant Redneck kicked him in the family

jewels with his steel-toed boots.

X crumpled to the floor, his eyes welling with tears. The pain was simply unbelievable.

"Chris, get the pooch," Giant Redneck said.

"Now we're talking," Pizza Face said with a wide grin. He disappeared into an adjoining room and after a moment, X heard feverish barking. He wasn't especially afraid of dogs, but facing one nude was another story.

The female soldier stood with her arms folded, looking on approvingly. "This is so going to be fun," she declared. "Best entertainment we've had since karaoke night."

"Your 'Oops, I Did It Again' really kicked ass," Giant Redneck was thoughtful enough to mention.

"Thanks."

Pizza Face reappeared leading a huge black mastiff by a leash. *Where the hell did they even get that thing?* the identity thief wondered. The creature looked like something you'd find guarding the gates of hell; all that was missing were two extra heads. He scuttled back on his rear end as Pizza Face led the beast on a leash toward him.

"Go on, boy, sniff out the terrorist," Pizza Face said encouragingly. The dog began to snarl and pull toward the prisoner. The giant canine began to bark – a deep, Hound of the Baskervilles bellow.

X cowered in the corner of the room, desperately trying to shield his reproductive organs from the snapping jaws of the hellhound.

"Hey, hey, guys, come on," he said. "This is taking it a little far, isn't it?"

"Listen to him trying to sound like an American," Big Tits said and spat on the floor contemptuously, the wad missing X by millimeters. "Must watch a lot of American Idol on TV."

"Talk in fucking Arabic," Giant Redneck growled. "Say another word in English and you won't believe what happens next."

"We oughta let Rambo here rape his monkey ass," Pizza Face suggested, letting out some of the leash and allowing the monstrous dog to bound to within half a foot of the prisoner.

"Yeah, don't they fuck their camels?" Big Tits said and chortled.

"Go on, Rambo, bite his little teeny wiener off," Pizza Face commanded.

X was in the fetal position now, his face tucked between his knees and his hands covering his genitals. Rambo's snout was so close he could feel its breath on his body. His intellect told him there was no way American soldiers, even if given license to ignore the Geneva Conventions, were going to stand by while a dog emasculated him. But the ancient fear of being eaten took over and he was shaking in terror.

"Get your hands off your dick," Pizza Face yelled. "Stop trying to protect it. It's gone, dude, live with it. It's history. Mr. Winkie's going bye-bye. You're gonna be a unit."

Eunuch, idiot.

"He said get your hands off your dick," Giant Redneck roared. "My partner wants to get another look at what you're packing. Weren't you trying to show off your weak little wee-wee just a minute ago?"

Tears began to roll down X's cheeks. Jesus, he hadn't cried since he was 10. He hoped they wouldn't notice, but no such luck.

"Awww, look. Mr. Terrorist Big Shot is crying. He's crying like a little bitch," Giant Redneck said. He signaled to Pizza Face to pull back the dog.

"You're pathetic, you know that?" the big man said with disgust. "I guess you're pretty tough when it comes to blowing unarmed babies to kingdom come. But stick a gun in your face and you show your true colors – yellow."

"You said it, dude," Pizza Face echoed. They traded high fives.

"Get on your knees, puke face," Giant Redneck commanded.

X crawled to his knees, grateful for the dog's retreat.

"Now apologize to Madison for flashing her," the Marine said, crossing his arms.

"I'm sorry," X said. *Okay, maybe this little exercise in performance art is winding down.*

Giant Redneck and Pizza Face exchanged puzzled glances

that were obviously fake.

"Excuse me? What was that?" the Southerner said, cupping a hand over his ear.

X could scarcely think at this point.

"I'm sorry, ma'am," he tried.

"In Arabic, dumbshit."

He repeated the words in Arabic.

"That's more like it," Giant Redneck said.

And with one sweeping kick he sent X sprawling.

*   *   *

X was outfitted with an orange prison jumpsuit and ill-fitting white army-issue skivvies a size too small – which, as he later, learned, was quite a privilege. Some of the prisoners were forced to wear pink panties for weeks after their arrival.

He was tossed into a windowless, cement-walled cell, no more than 12 square feet. A naked light bulb hung from the middle of the ceiling; there was a steel toilet and a bunk bed. On the bottom bunk a boy of about 17, sporting peach fuzz on his cheeks, lay reading the Koran.

The teen jumped up, excitedly.

"At last a companion. I was going mad with loneliness."

"Aloha," X sighed.

"Asar Gulzar of Kabul," his cellmate said in Arabic, with an accent that X recognized as Afghani.

The teen scrutinized at his face. "Are you truly Ali Nazeer? There have been rumors whispered that you had arrived here."

X was in no mood to argue. He nodded.

"It is an honor to meet you, sir. Come, come, you may have my bunk."

"I couldn't –" X responded in Arabic.

But the young man insisted and led X to the lower bunk, where he collapsed.

"So you are the great Ali Nazeer," Asar said admiringly. "You have become a legend here; everyone has heard how you eluded the Americans in their own country for so long."

"You get TV here?" X replied, surprised that his exploits

were already the stuff of legend.

Asar laughed. "No, but a boy was brought in yesterday who told us the whole story. You are truly a brave warrior in the Jihad."

X tried to think of something that would shut the guy up for a while.

"All praise belongs to Allah," he said. "It is only he who gives me strength."

"Indeed, indeed," agreed Asar. "Would you like some taffy? I have a small tin."

X nodded and the boy shared with him. It was chewy but sweet and, as the first food to enter his mouth since a handful of peanuts in the Pink Panther what seemed eons ago, much appreciated.

"I have been doing my part for the Jihad as well," Asar said. "Nothing so grand as you, of course. I shouldn't even mention it."

"Please, tell me," X begged. Although, of course, he didn't have the slightest interest.

The teen puffed out his chest proudly. "For two years I was the driver for The Chief. Every day I was by his side."

"You are very young to have been given such responsibility," X said. *Allowing this juvenile delinquent to think I AM Ali Nazeer might play to my advantage.*

"I learned to drive a tractor on my uncle's farm when I was 12," Asar explained. "I drove a cab in Kabul for three years. After that you can either drive like a racing car driver or you've been killed in an accident."

As X anticipated, Asar was not shy about detailing his exploits serving The Chief. On one occasion, so he claimed, the driver rescued the terrorist honcho from Mossad agents who were on his trail by taking a shortcut through a crowded market.

"It was just like something you'd see in a James Bond movie," Asar reminisced fondly. "Merchants were pushing their carts out of the way, melons were rolling. The Chief awarded me a medallion. I would show it to you but the Americans took it from me when I arrived."

Asar asked X about his own reception and X told him about his mistreatment at the hands of the U.S. soldiers.

"The Americans are real pigs," Asar declared, angrily. X

could hardly argue with him.

"Their etiquette could use some fine-tuning," he conceded.

*   *   *

Over the following days, X was allowed to mingle with fellow prisoners in the exercise yard. They hailed from all over the Middle East: the Gaza Strip, Yemen, even a contingent from Indonesia and a thin, jet-black brother from Somalia.

"This is the hero who made fools of the Americans," Asar would proudly introduce him. "We have become great friends."

They spent their time in the cell reading each other passages from the Koran. X had never even thumbed through it before – nor had he gotten past Noah in the Bible for that matter. His religious knowledge consisted of what he dimly recalled from coloring books he read in a Sunday school his mother had dragged him to. Before his imprisonment was over, X would end up knowing many verses from the Islamic holy book by heart.

At night, they lay on their bunks and chatted. Asar proved to be the talkative type and very curious. He asked specifics about X's operations in Kuwait. X told him that such information was top secret and Asar nodded gravely. Asar, a former street urchin whose father abandoned the family when he was eight, was intrigued that X came from a wealthy family and wanted to know all about what it was like growing up in the lap of luxury.

X had no clue what life was like for some Richie Rich in Kuwait, but since he knew Asar didn't either, he felt free to confabulate. He described in detail his father's mansion and the beautiful silk dresses his mother and sisters wore; the life-sized marble statues; the Olympic-size swimming pool with a waterfall gushing down into it from the landscaped hillside.

Asar oohed and aahed, and X embellished further and further, inventing a palatial estate worthy of an Oriental despot. The physical descriptions came mostly from old movies he used to watch with his mother, like "The Prince of Baghdad." It was the only time he remembered her being at peace, the two of them lost together in a fantasy world.

Each night "Ali Nazeer" regaled the teen with tales of family trips around the world to hot spots like Paris and Beijing, playing with the children of rich and famous movie stars and jet setters. He became Asar's Scheherazade.

X had to admit it was fun creating this blissful imaginary childhood so different from his own. The rich, powerful father, the doting, educated mother reading Dickens and Shakespeare to him and his loving sibling at bedtime.

Asar would ask him to repeat stories, and X did, fleshing them out with more minute details as he did. Some were funny. He told anecdotes about maids and gardeners who misunderstood orders – plagiarized from homophone-challenged Amelia Bedelia – that made the teen roar with laugher.

A week passed before "Ali Nazeer" was escorted from his cell for his first interrogation.

"Be strong, my brother," Asar told him, clapping him on the back.

"We'll have him back in a jiffy," one of the guards said cheerfully. "You'll be amazed how quick your hero breaks."

X was marched down a long corridor with barred cells on either side. It looked like one of those old black and white movies about Alcatraz except that rather than Jimmy Cagney or George Raft, the residents were bearded, swarthy men, two or three to a cell. Some were prostrate in prayer, others were scribbling on pads. Some saluted him; a few even bowed reverently.

"Allah will protect you, brother," one called.

Unfortunately, the identity thief didn't believe in Allah (or hold much stock in the god of the Hebrews either).

He was shoved into a small, barren room at the end of the hall. X was not pleased to see that Pizza Face, Giant Redneck and Big Tits were all in attendance. This time they were joined by a clean-cut young man in natty, wire-rimmed glasses that must have cost $600, a blue blazer, yellow sweater and fraternity tie. He looked as if he was home for the holidays from an exclusive prep school.

"I give him about eight minutes," Pizza Face snickered.

"Five," said Big Tits.

"It's a bet." They shook hands.

He was stripped again, and hung by his wrists with ropes from a hook on the ceiling. The Yuppie, who had been silent up until now, stepped forward and spoke in a calm voice, barely above a whisper.

"Now let me tell you the game plan for today, Mr. Nazeer," he said. "I am going to ask you questions and you're going to answer them. Any time you don't answer, this gentleman will do something to you that's not very nice."

He pointed to an ugly-looking cattle prod in the hands of Giant Redneck. This time X was ready for them. He would not be intimidated, he would not be crushed.

"You can't torture me," X said smugly. "We watch CNN, you know. I know your leaders have forbidden it."

The Yuppie laughed and the soldiers followed suit.

"That's right, dude." he said. "All that went out with the Bush administration. You have absolutely nothing at all to worry your little head about." He nodded to the Giant Redneck, who poked X in the testicles with the cattle prod.

Volts lanced through his gonads and X screamed in agony. It was hard to believe he'd ever be able to reproduce.

Okay, he thought. *Hold out for a minute to make it believable, then tell them the most credible lie you can muster.*

"Now whereabouts can we find The Chief?" the Yuppie asked pleasantly, as if asking the directions to the nearest Starbucks.

X shook his head. Giant Redneck zapped his private parts again.

To hell with holding out a minute.

"All right, all right," he sputtered. "He's in Afghanistan, near the village of – "

The Yuppie imitated a game-show buzzer. "Wrong answer. We know he's crossed over into Pakistan."

Another electrical assault on his testicles.

"I have to, I have to go the bathroom," X moaned.

"He's stalling," Pizza Face warned the Yuppie in his nasal New Jersey accent.

"You can drain the old dragon on the floor," the Yuppie offered. "You have our permission."

Big tits snickered.

"Go ahead, I told you to piss yourself," the Yuppie said more sternly. Now it was a command.

Finally X let go. If he was worried about his dignity, that ship had sailed. A yellow stream shot from his dangling organ onto the concrete floor. *This psycho prep-school brat from hell probably did worse plenty of times after keg parties back in college*, he told himself, if it was any consolation.

"Look at what that filthy sand nigger did," Giant Redneck said, shaking his head. "He messed up the floor. They just mopped it yesterday."

The Yuppie clucked his teeth. "Well, here we clean up our own messes. We don't want to create extra work for the staff." He nodded to the Marines.

They unhooked X's hands. The Giant Redneck dragged him across the floor by the nape of the neck and stuck his face in the pool of piss. Big Tits planted a boot on his backside to hold him in place. Pizza face tossed him his underwear.

"Now wipe up that fucking piss," the Redneck said.

"Next time we'll make you lick it up, ass eater," Pizza Face put in.

X sighed and began to scrub up the yellow pool. He felt the urge to weep again, but steeled himself this time. He refused to give them the satisfaction.

"You're going to break, bro," the Yuppie informed him. "Maybe after we pump you full of babble juice so strong it leaves your brain fried. Maybe after we show you snapshots of some street thugs partying in your wife's tush. Sooner or later, you'll talk. So why not cut to the chase?

"Now I'm going to ask you one last time, Ali. Where is The Chief? Work with me here, dude."

"I don't know," X said, in his most convincing voice, what he always thought of has his "honest" voice. "As Allah is my master, I do not know."

"You are one lying Arab bastard," the Yuppie hissed. "You are so going to get your clock cleaned." He nodded to Giant Redneck, who seized a fistful of X's hair. He dragged the prisoner out of the room into the corridor, where fellow detainees flocked to the bars of their cells to see what was going on.

X could see Asar clutching the bars, looking on as if it were his father being abused.

"In front of all your homies here, you're going to swear to Allah that you don't know where The Chief is," the Yuppie demanded, raising his voice for the first time. "No, dudes and dudette, I'm getting a brainstorm here. Swear on the freaking Koran."

X vaguely recalled accounts of how at Guantanamo Bay the Koran was abused in interrogations back in the Bush days, but had chalked them up to Arab propaganda.

The Yuppie snatched the Koran from Asar's hand and said, "Enjoy the show."

Giant Redneck and Pizza Face hoisted X up to his feet and the Yuppie waved the Islamic holy book in his face, "Put his hand on it."

Big Tits grabbed the prisoner's hand and forced it onto the book.

"Swear you don't know where The Chief is," the Yuppie demanded.

"I swear on the Holy Koran that I do not know the hiding place of The Chief."

"Bullshit. Bullshit!" the Yuppie exclaimed, turning blue in the face and flying into a fury that looked almost genuine. "Make him eat the freaking thing."

There came howls of protest from the cells and prisoners began banging objects on the bars. The din only added to X's torment.

Big Tits tore out four pages from the book with obvious relish and stuffed them in his mouth, knocking a filling out of his mouth in the process.

"Eat it," the Yuppie snarled. "You're going to eat your beloved Koran and shit it out. That's right, Ali, you're going to turn Mohammed's words into doo-doo. "

Giant Redneck pulled his sidearm from its holster and pressed up against X's temple.

"Do it, camel jockey!" he barked in X's ear. "Do it right now, or we'll splatter your brains on the floor."

The Muslim prisoners booed in fury. They shook their cages like furious baboons.

"Infidels!"

"Cursed American dogs!"

"May Allah give you strength, Ali!"

"It is better to die with honor than to live on in shame!"

The Yuppie paced back and forth. "Let him go," he said after a moment.

"Ali Nazeer" collapsed to his knees, the leaves of paper clenched between his teeth.

"I'm going to count to three, you freaking sand monkey," the Yuppie said quietly. "And if you aren't chomping down on your good book by then, I swear to Christ himself – the *real* God, by the way – I'm going to give the order to shoot."

X had had enough. He was 99 percent sure they weren't going to shoot him. Besides, what would happen to him if he defiled the Koran in front of that pack of fanatics? Surely he'd be beaten to death in the exercise yard within a day.

So "Ali Nazeer" stood up, and spat out the pages. He grabbed his dick and waved it at the Yuppie.

"Eat this, you sick cunt," he shouted. Then, for the benefit of his fellow prisoners, he repeated the colorful insult in Arabic.

From the row of cells, the roars of his fellow prisoners were deafening.

"You see," Asar called to the guards, triumphantly. "To threaten a brave man with death is like promising water to a duck."

While X tried to make sense of that, his fellow prisoners chanted a phrase meaning, X knew, "one who is praiseworthy in the eyes of Allah."

Strangely enough, the admiration of these strange men – with whom he had nothing in common and whose philosophy he despised – uplifted him. Perhaps it was because it had been so long since anyone had shown him admiration. He felt like he was a seven-year-old child again, getting applause for the winning a spelling bee, his mother in the audience.

I'd forgotten about that.

His moment of glory was short-lived, though. He was gang-tackled by the Marines and hauled back to his cell.

Chapter 12
I AM ALI NAZEER!

Another few weeks dragged on. Now, without the Koran, X and his cellmate were forced to converse even more. The nightly tales became more vividly detailed and intricately embroidered, to the point that X almost convinced himself he really had been raised with love in the lap of luxury. They also conversed about their current lives, and inevitably, women. Asar had a girlfriend in the small town in Afghanistan where he'd been born, a neighbor's daughter who had been promised to him at birth.

"I have composed a poem for her," Asar said diffidently. "Would you like to read it?"

"Read it to me," X said.

The teen took a sheet of paper from under his mattress, cleared his throat and began:

"Your voice is like a babbling brook,
Sweet and gentle,
When you speak,
I hear the harps of angels."

He was praising her voice, X realized, because in all likelihood the girl was veiled and the teen had never actually seen her face. Still, it was touching. Hard to keep in mind that the boy was a stone killer who would murder him in a New York minute if he knew his true identity.

X could not share with the boy the names of the many American women he'd bedded. Nor could he say he'd slept with them, of course – intercourse outside marriage was contrary to Islam. The call girls, the barmaids, the grifters, the occasional housewife who pegged him for a con artist and jumped his bones nevertheless because she found it exciting. So he talked about Ali Nazeer's third and youngest wife, Jasmine. She was the upstanding daughter of an iman, according to the backstory he concocted – a woman who was wise, virtuous and obedient.

"If I told her to put her hand in fire, she would do it without question," X said and the boy nodded reverently.

One night before they went to sleep, Asar announced that he had something to say.

"Your friendship has meant so much to me," the teen said solemnly. "I thank Allah for bringing you into my life."

X hated to admit it, but he felt the same way (except for the Allah part). He didn't know how he would survive the cruelty and monotony of this place without the relentlessly cheerful and optimistic young man. It was puzzling, because he'd never felt the need for company before. Never.

"It is written, 'Without companionship even paradise would be boring,' " he told Asar. In preparation for his role as Ali Nazeer, he had boned up on Middle Eastern culture by perusing a list of Arab proverbs he'd found on the Internet. It was coming in handy.

It was not only with Asar that X forged a bond. Now a hero to his fellow prisoners, he was surrounded by followers who hung on his every word.

They told him stories of their suffering in wars and mistreatment by their captors. They asked for his help in settling disputes. They sought his advice about how to deal with problems at home – pushy mother-in-laws, rebellious sons. One asked him how to handle a black-sheep cousin who refused to do his manly duty and volunteer to be a suicide bomber. He was an unemployed ne'er-do-well who could, in the frustrated prisoner's view, at least do that much for the family name.

"In time Allah will speak to him and he will do the right thing," X replied sagely. "Only he can choose his destiny."

X tried, as in that case, to affect Solomonlike wisdom, while actually saying next to nothing. Usually he borrowed from that indispensable list of aphorisms, plagerized fortune cookies or adapted quotes from kung fu movies.

The only area he steered clear of was religious matters. Men debating finer points of the Koran would come to him for his opinion, and he would modestly say they should turn to someone more qualified to resolve the argument, because he was no expert.

Putting it mildly, since the only thing he knew about the Koran were the verses he and Asar had read to each other and the dubious contentions of a former partner who'd gone straight in the joint and joined the Nation of Islam.

As his legion of followers grew in number, X began to feel a sense of pride at their high regard. Holding court under the blazing sun, he would momentarily forget that he was NOT Ali Nazeer, not a heroic defender of Islam. His beard had come in, and he looked the part as well.

One morning he was strolling about the exercise yard when a dark, skinny Egyptian named Amir clapped him on the back.

"Everyone in the prison has heard how you stood up to the Americans and word has spread to the outside world as well," Amir informed him. "We are all so proud of you. We know you will not let us down, or Muslim people around the world down."

X looked at him quizzically. Amir leaned in.

"They say you are to be interrogated again today," he whispered conspiratorially. "The real deal. A torturer brought in from Iraq, a true sadist who used to work for Al Amn Al-Khas, Saddam's secret police. The word is that at his hands, a man either breaks or dies."

And Amir was just warming up. "He's a European, some say he was trained by the KGB in the art of pain. They call him The Monster."

X was screwed and he knew it. Because this time his tormentors wouldn't stop until they got the information out of him. And he didn't know anything. Which meant there was a real possibility he would be tortured to death.

*   *   *

Sure enough, two hours later, X hung upside down from his ankles, looking like a crucified, inverted Jesus, in a dimly lit, barren room.

This time, at least, he wasn't naked; he'd been allowed to keep those over-tight jockey shorts. Nevertheless, it was freezing and he shivered as he hung waiting interminably. He was determined to give this torturer extraordinaire nothing; to spit in his face.

"I am Ali Nazeer, leader of the Jihadist Brotherhood. I fear nothing but Allah," he told himself. The real Ali Nazeer would not cry or buckle and neither would he. He said it again and again, a mantra.

The door opened and a fat man entered, his face shrouded in darkness. He was wheeling a cart, which squeaked unnervingly. The cart entered a pool of light and X saw that it was loaded with implements of torture. Some were recognizable as relics of the Spanish Inquisition; others more modern like pliers, an adjustable wrench, dental tools and a cattle prod. It was like some kind of dessert cart from hell.

This master torturer must have passed the cell block, giving other detainees food for thought about what they, too, would face.

This went far beyond water-boarding (delicately described as a "harsh interrogation technique" by the American press). X had heard tales from other prisoners of torturers breaking chemical lights and pouring the phosphoric liquid on detainees; splashing ice-cold water on naked prisoners; beating detainees with a broom handle and a chair; sodomizing a prisoner with a chemical light five times and then a plunger for a change of pace. And sure enough, among the items on display on the table was a foot-long, studded dildo that looked like it was designed to satisfy a mare.

That is going in me, X realized. *I'm going to be raped with it.*

The Monster picked something from the table. X couldn't see which of the items it was but he lost it.

To hell with the goddamned Jihadist Brotherhood!

"Look, please, I'm not Nazeer," he jabbered in Arabic. "This is all a mistake. Please, please, please. You've got to listen to me. Please, I'll do anything, just stop, please. Just wait."

The man put a finger to his lips and, pressed a button on the object in his hand. A recording of high-pitched screams erupted from it. X would have perhaps preferred a manlier yell as an imitation of his cries, but under the circumstances, he was relieved that the sounds weren't coming from his own mouth.

The man stepped into the light and X, even upside down; eyes blurry from tears, recognized him at once. It was the pipe-smoking Santa Claus from the Giza Hotel and Casino. Mr. Jones.

"Who are you?" he asked hoarsely, daring to speak in English now for the first time in weeks.

"You can keep calling me Mr. Jones," the man said. "I suppose the million-dollar question is who are you?"

It took a moment for the import of the question to sink in. And now, for the first time in more than a decade, X uttered his real name.

"Oh, yes. Born in Washington, D.C.," Mr. Jones said. He proceeded to rattle off the identity thief's date and exact time of birth, his mother's name, her mother's maiden name, his Social Security number, his home addresses dating back seven years and a litany of other personal details, as he unstrapped X and gently lowered him to the ground.

The guy's done his homework; he would make a class A identity thief, X thought.

"I wonder what role your mother's suicide played in the formation of your pathology," Mr. Jones pondered aloud.

For a man considered a cipher by even his closest associates, it was as if X had suddenly become transparent. Although Mr. Jones gave him back his numbered orange jumpsuit, X felt more naked than he had ever been before in his life.

"You know ... who I am," X gasped. "For how long?"

"Since you checked into the Giza."

"You've got to be kidding me."

"We knew you couldn't be Ali Nazeer. Because this is Ali Nazeer."

Mr. Jones handed X an 8 by 10 photograph showing a man who looked eerily like himself lying on a slab, a half circle of bloody bullet holes in his chest. Two dots in the right place and you'd have a smiley face.

"He was killed in a raid in Pakistan eight weeks ago – not long before you decided to step into his shoes."

X shook with righteous indignation.

"You bastards have let me be hunted like an animal and tortured, knowing that I'm innocent."

"Well, innocent may not be exactly the right word, now is it, young fellow?" Mr. Jones said, lighting his pipe.

X could only respond with a hostile glare.

"Personally, I have no respect for identity thieves," Mr. Jones said. "A fellow who has the testicular fortitude to knock over a bank with a .357 Magnum in his hands, yes. But you – stealing from old ladies, taking the names of dead babies. Tut tut. Not exactly the stuff that would make you a folk hero like Dillinger. You seem to enjoy being treated as folk hero by your peers though, Mr. Nazeer."

X wasn't in the mood to be lectured.

"What is this all about? What do you want?"

"We need you to infiltrate the stronghold of The Chief – as his ally, Ali Nazeer."

X guffawed so loudly that pain shot through his ribs. He wasn't one to follow international affairs, but he'd seen enough cable news in passing and heard enough reverent jabber from Asar to know who The Chief was. The head of the Warriors of Allah, and grand wizard of the loosely organized alliance of terrorist outfits to which the Jihadist Brotherhood belonged. He was the mastermind who, it had been learned in recent years, was the boss of Osama bin Laden and a rogue's gallery of other terrorist bigwigs.

"So all that rough stuff, in front of the prisoners ... " he asked.

"A charade. You're a hero to them now. There is no question about your loyalty, your dedication to the cause. Your courage, your piety."

X shook his head. "Not interested."

"Interested or not, that's exactly what you're going to do."

"So I have no choice?"

"Certainly you have a choice. Play ball or get shot attempting to escape."

"I'm an American citizen. I have rights."

"You're a man who doesn't exist. You've gone to such lengths to erase your true identity that if you disappear off the face of this Earth, no one will miss you."

X knew this to be true.

"Let's say I go along with this harebrained scheme of yours. What do I get out of it, other than, of course not being shot in the back?"

"A full presidential pardon. The 50 or so counts of grand larceny the attorney general has on his desk just go away. As a cherry on top, your charming girlfriend Samantha Adamson will also be pardoned. The authorities are hot on her tail, you know."

X hadn't thought of Samantha in weeks, he realized with some shame – a rare emotion for him. He needn't have lost any sleep over this. As it happened, his partner in crime had made it to Brazil, where she took up with a soccer player. Because the jock was a fitness freak and twisted her arm into jogging, she'd even lost weight and was now a size 2.

X sighed with resignation.

"What am I expected to do – kill The Chief? I'm no assassin.'

"No, you're going to do what you do best – rob him blind."

CHAPTER 13
The Secret Committee

The organization to which Mr. Jones belongs has a storied past, although it's a story few will ever hear. Originally known as the Committee of Secret Correspondence, it dates back to the American Revolution, when it was helmed by none other than our versatile founding father Ben Franklin.

Under its auspices, Franklin established a secret navy that distributed gunpowder and supplies to pirates paid to disrupt the British Navy. He coordinated the activities of secret agents, gathered information on enemy war plans and secured clandestine funding from nations that were ostensibly friends of England.

These field agents were equipped, *à la* TV's *Wild Wild West*, with nifty gadgets of Franklin's own design, such as a boot with a hidden compartment storing lock picks that could defeat even the most skillfully designed locks of the time and an opiate strong enough to make the user immune to torture.

The author of *Poor Richard's Almanac* also concocted misinformation and propaganda distributed by Committee operatives. The fearsome Hessian mercenaries fighting for the Redcoats had become a growing menace to the Continental Army. Ben forged a letter from a German prince to the commander of his mercenaries ordering the officer to leave his wounded for dead rather than have them unfit to serve their prince. The Committee also saw that a bogus news article detailing the horrible deaths of Hessian soldiers at the hands of the American Indians found it way their homeland. Thanks to the campaign of lies, the demoralized Hessians soon withdrew from the war.

Most of the papers from this time were so sensitive that they were destroyed. Officially, the Committee was disbanded soon after the British surrender, but in fact it continued its work secretly, often in concert with America's greatest Revolutionary War ally, France.

During the war of 1812, the Committee joined forces with agents of Napoleon to engineer the U.S. invasion of Canada, and to undermine the relationship between Britain and Indian tribes. In the First World War, Committee operatives worked hand in glove with the French Foreign Legion to defeat the Turks and Germans in North Africa.

In the early years of World War II, when the United States was officially neutral and long before the OSS got into the act, the Committee teamed up with the French Resistance. The secret partnership also came into play, with varying degrees of success in trouble spots like Vietnam, where Committee spies aided the Frenchies in their fight against the Communists long before America's official foray into the war. In Haiti, French and American spies joined forces to quietly dispatch a dictator without bloodshed.

It should be noted that the Committee's efforts were unknown to the CIA, the Secretary of State and even to the President himself. Funding came not from Congress, but from monies raised from various enterprises – those notorious pirates in the early years, and even more unsavory characters in the present. The upside of this is that not a single dollar of U.S. taxpayers' money went toward the Committee's work.

None of this did Mr. Jones share with X. He told him only that the Committee was so secretive that only two other people in the prison were aware of the mission.

"How are we even supposed to find The Chief?" X demanded. "The CIA, the Marines, everyone else has been hunting him for years."

"Ah, that's where your young cellmate comes in."

"Asar? The Chief's driver?"

"The only man in U.S. custody who knows The Chief's whereabouts. It's no accident that you were placed in his cell and given an opportunity to earn his trust."

"So the plan is…"

"You and he escape from jail and he leads you to The Chief's hiding place."

"We fake a jailbreak."

"No, you're going to really escape. As I said, other than two people in this prison under my command, no one knows you are working for the Committee. Not the Colonel in charge, not the Marines, not the CIA interrogators."

"Well, I'm clearly not as gifted a planner as you, but wouldn't it be easier to tell them?"

Mr. Jones shook his head. "Unfortunately, the prison is lousy with moles. Warriors of Allah moles."

X found that hard to swallow. "What, posing as Marine guards? As janitors and cooks?"

"The Warriors of Allah has been putting people in place, deep-cover operatives, for years, long before 9/11. They're masters at creating false identities."

"Gee, you can't trust anyone these days."

Mr. Jones seemed genuinely amused by that; his blue eyes twinkled. He drew a paper out of his vest pocket and handed it to the identity thief.

"Here are the plans. Read them, memorize them, then I'm afraid I'm going to have to destroy them."

X perused the plans, trying to ignore the increasingly loud and frequent screams emanating from the digital recorder.

They were to crawl through a narrow ventilation shaft from the isolated ward of the prison hospital out onto a rooftop, run across it without being seen and drop through a hatch into a building that housed equipment being used to remodel what had once been the old commandant's quarters, turning it into a chapel. There they were to borrow tools and use them to dig a 16-foot tunnel under the prison fence.

"You've got to be joking," X protested. "Sixteen feet? How long is that supposed to take?"

"According to our calculations, three weeks, working hours nightly. You'll have proper tools, remember. Not sharpened spoons."

"Nightly? You mean we're supposed to make that trip through the air shaft, like *Mission Impossible*, and over that rooftop every night for nearly a month without ever being spotted?"

"Precisely!" said Mr. Jones, pointing his pipe at X for emphasis.

All X knew about prison breaks was what he'd seen in old World War II movies like *The Great Escape*. Perhaps if he were humble enough to believe he'd ever be pinched, he would have read up on the subject. This didn't sound particularly feasible. But he saw a bigger problem and brought it to Mr. Jones's attention.

"How are we supposed to get into the infirmary?" he demanded.

Mr. Jones gave a smile that made X uneasy.

"Ah, yes, how indeed," he said. "This is the really creative part of the plan, the part an ingenious mind like yours is sure to appreciate."

He took from the cart a black plastic container about the size of an eyeglass case. He opened it, revealing a hypodermic needle.

"What the fuck is that?" X demanded.

The bearded man held up the needle and grinned.

"Yersinia pestis," he revealed. "Also known as Pasteurella pestis. AKA plague bacillus."

X shook his head in disbelief. "As in the Bubonic Plague?"

Mr. Jones nodded, still wearing the benign smile. X stepped back, folding his arms.

"You expect me to let you inject me with Black Plague germs? If that's your plan, you'd better just hang me back on those chains. I'd be better off. In fact, hell, I'll hook myself up."

The spymaster chuckled. "It's a genetically engineered variety our lab boys cooked up. We call them the Ben Franklin Department. Don't ask me to explain the science of it, but in a nutshell, you have all the symptoms of the plague and your blood will test positive for it, but the bug is designed to die out after 72 hours. After that your temperature will continue to run high for a few weeks, but you'll be fit as a fiddle. You'll have to fake feeling too weak to move. Make believe is your strong suit, isn't it?"

X was picturing Black Death bacterium swimming like salmon through his bloodstream, and continued to shake his head. "No, no, no, no," he kept muttering.

"You'll infect your cellmate, and you'll both begin to experience the symptoms: swollen lymph glands in your armpits, groin and neck, chills, fever. You'll vomit up blood fairly continuously for a while and there'll be blood in your piss as well. You'll cough a good bit and most dramatically, little black dots will appear all over your body. You'll suffer some real delirium, although, as I said, after a few days you'll have to go on faking that in front of the medical staff."

X's distrust of Mr. Jones was quickly blossoming into hatred. The old man delivered this news with obvious relish.

"I suppose it would be too simple to just give us the flu," the identity thief said without any attempt to disguise his bitterness.

Mr. Jones opened a bottle of alcohol and dipped a cotton ball in it.

"We need something that will get you into the special isolation room and keep you there. For obvious reasons, the room has its own ventilation and the shaft leads to precisely where you need to be."

He stepped toward X, with the needle in one hand and the cotton swab in the other. X stepped back.

"Now, don't be a baby," Mr. Jones said. "You know there's no alternative. It's either this or I leave you to the CIA interrogators. You'll be tortured – excuse me, subjected to harsh interrogation techniques – for weeks or months, given rougher and rougher treatment because you refuse to break, since of course, you have nothing to give them.

"Then, your mind and body broken, you'll be deep-sixed and forgotten in some holding center until the War on Terror is over – a few decades from now. Or, you somehow manage to convince someone of who you really are, in which case you go to prison stateside until we have flying cars."

X stared at the rotund, white-bearded man, trying to his make his Santa-like appearance jibe with his heartless words.

"You make a compelling case," he said finally, raising his arm.

"No, no," Mr. Jones said, pushing down his arm, "not there."

X smirked and turned around. "In the butt? Why am I not surprised? How appropriate."

"Bottom of your feet, between your toes, if you don't mind," the elderly spook said. "I'm afraid you'll be searched before the symptoms kick in and we can't have any obvious marks on you."

X sighed and lifted up his right foot, like a horse being shod.

Chapter 14
WELCOME TO THE TEAM

Mr. Jones – whose real name was Arnold Fiorella, by the way – didn't always want to be a spy. Indeed, he attended divinity school with every intention of being ordained a priest. But during the '70s, when the intelligence community was ravaged by the corrupt influence of politicians, all the way up to the White House, he saw the need to restore American spies to the role they'd played in World War II. Back then, the OSS matched wits with Hitler's spymasters, and secret agents were knights without armor, championing the cause of liberty. So he joined the CIA and within a year was recruited by the Committee.

Mr. Jones still considered his current calling God's work. When the second President Bush was chided for using the incendiary word "crusade" to describe the war on Islamofacism, Mr. Jones solemnly told his colleagues the Commander in Chief was right the first time.

"This is a holy war, make no mistake about it," he said in the musty, mahogany-paneled meeting hall in Philadelphia where Committee chiefs had gathered since the Revolution. "A clash of civilizations doesn't begin to cover it. This is Good versus Evil."

Mr. Jones was a vastly talented spymaster. He was especially adept at black flag recruitments – convincing people to surrender their country's secrets to what they believed was a friendly nation. How many Jewish intelligence officers in Argentina had he flipped into double agents by convincing them their handler was Israeli?

Despite his rather broad puritanical streak, he made liberal use of "ladies" as they were called – to lure officials into compromising situations. Photographs of such "honey traps" provided Jones with biographic leverage (known to the uninitiated as blackmail material) to control the subject. Mr. Jones pulled the strings of such hapless souls so deftly that his nickname on the Committee became The Puppet Master and later Geppetto.

*   *   *

Back in his cell, wearing a few obligatory bruises the spymaster had apologetically applied to his cheek, eyebrow and lower lip, X lay on his bunk. Though he'd feigned a limp when lurching into the cell, there was nothing fake about his mental exhaustion. His eyes were shut, and he said nothing, but his cellmate didn't take the hint.

Asar rambled on effusively, "I knew they couldn't break you! Those infidels know nothing about the strength of spirit Allah confers on his warriors, those who have surrendered to him."

"You bet," X said in English.

Asar laughed heartily. "I know what that means. I heard it in a Tom Cruise movie."

X rolled over on his belly. Was he already beginning to feel ill, or was it his imagination? Surely the microbes couldn't work that fast. Or could the genetically engineered medical miracles do anything their creators wanted?

"I can't wait until they come for me," Asar declared, thumping his chest. "I will spit in their faces, just as you have done. You are my inspiration, Ali. It is an honor to share the company of one such as you."

*   *   *

FBI agent Traci Kingsmith walked across the prison yard, escorted by a pair of Marines, uncomfortably aware of the stares of prisoners in orange jumpsuits milling about the exercise yard. It was obvious they hadn't seen a woman in a long time, certainly not one without a burqa.

Jesus, is there no prohibition against undressing a woman with your eyes in your culture?

Why she had been excused from her duties in the middle of her lunch break by her boss Mr. Normand and flown halfway around the world she could not imagine. She'd simply been told that it was a matter of national security and she was to pack only necessities. Until she boarded the small jet – a Cessna 560 Citation V – she was not even told by the pilot where they were bound. He and the co-pilot were the only other souls on board and they didn't utter a single word to her except to tell her to buckle her seatbelt before takeoff and unbuckle it after landing.

Now, with her escorts, she strode toward a drab, windowless, flat-roofed cinderblock building in the center of Abd Al-Rahman Prison in Afghanistan. It was one of a dozen squat buildings surrounded by a double line of 12-foot high chain-link fences. Each fence was topped with rusted razor wire.

There were four guard towers, one at each corner of the compound. Machine gun muzzles protruded from the covered platforms. She and her silent escorts approached the two-story building – the only one with windows, albeit tiny ones. Two Marine guards toting M-4 carbine assault rifles stood on either side of a metal door. A hand-painted sign above the entrance identified this as the Administration Building. After Traci's escort gave one of the guards her papers, he pushed a button at the right side of the door and a buzzer sounded so loudly she almost jumped. The door swung open and they were admitted.

They marched down a long, sterile hall lined with closed doors. Then the agent was ushered into a small room that, suspiciously, had nothing but the word "office" on the plaque beside it.

When Traci saw Mr. Jones behind the desk, she was not bewildered, more pissed off, really.

"I might have known you had something to do with this," she snapped. "What agency do you work for?"

Mr. Jones lit his pipe. "Have a seat."

Traci didn't move. "Are you going to answer my question?"

He smiled enigmatically.

"Then I'm out of here," she declared, and turned.

"The only thing I'm at liberty to say is that I have the authority to have you shot before you set foot outside the gates."

He said it calmly and without overt menace, but with enough iron in his tone to leave her no doubt whatsoever that he was speaking the truth. She turned slowly. He gestured to the chair, and she sat, her ankles crossed in a ladylike manner with her hands in her lap.

"Congratulations on your capture in Nevada," he said. "Very

impressive."

"Thank you," she replied icily.

"I should tell you, however, that the man you took into custody is not Ali Nazeer."

"The hell he isn't."

And so Mr. Jones told her of Nazeer's death, of X's true identity, of the mission, and with every fresh revelation, she shook her head with incredulity.

"Why wasn't I informed that the man we spent hundreds of man hours and millions of dollars pursuing was a fake?" she said. "A two-bit hustler."

"No one in the FBI was informed, nor in the Department of Homeland Security."

"You've got to be joking. We were all on a wild goose chase? Why weren't we in the loop?"

"There are plants in all of those agencies. Muslim Americans – and perhaps even some non-Muslims – who are deep-cover operatives of the Warriors of Allah."

"In the CIA? Homeland Security? Come on!"

"You probably know that 9/11 caught our nation with its pants down. Our intelligence agencies had only a handful of Arabic-speaking agents and we had to go on a recruiting spree. Well, while we were busy catching up, our enemies were busy planting moles. In fact they planted many of their moles years *before* the attack."

Okay, that makes a crazy kind of sense, she thought.

"Well, wouldn't it be more prudent to use one of our own agents? Why would you want to use an untrained, unscrupulous – to put it mildly – civilian on a sensitive mission like this?"

"As I said, the U.S. Intelligence community is riddled with moles. And how many CIA agents just happen to be dead ringers for Ali Nazeer? When this 'Ali Nazeer' suddenly surfaced a few weeks after the real one was eliminated, well, it presented a once-in-a-lifetime opportunity. Particularly since, of course, he's a totally deniable – not to mention disposable – asset."

"What's my role supposed to be?"

"You'll be 'Nazeer's' handler. You know how he thinks better than anyone."

"I know nothing about him," she protested. "I thought he

102 C. Michael Forsyth

was Ali Nazeer until five minutes ago."

Mr. Jones smiled.

"You captured him. You out-thought him. There's every chance this con artist will bolt the first chance he gets. You have to prevent that."

Traci's role would be to accompany "Ali Nazeer," Asar, and a third man, whose identity had not yet been revealed to her, after their escape, to the mountains where it was believed The Chief's lair lay. Her cover was to be a member of the Jihadist movement.

"But my Arabic," she protested. "My accent is far from perfect."

"Your cover is that you are a Liberian," explained Mr. Jones. "Their official language is English, so your accent will be perfectly fine unless you run into Henry Higgins. You are also familiar with Pashto and Dari, correct?

"Enough to do some translations for the Bureau, but –"

"That's all we need." Mr. Jones raised a hand, silencing her.

"Now I want you to meet someone." He pressed an intercom button. "Send in the prisoner."

The door opened, and a Marine shoved in a bearded man in handcuffs and leg irons.

For a moment she thought it was X in eyeglasses. He had a similar small, wiry frame and swarthy complexion. But on closer inspection she realized it was a stranger.

"Harry Assad, meet Special Agent Traci King," Mr. Jones said.

"Excuse me for not shaking hands," the guy said with a little smirk that made Traci decide right off the bat she didn't like him.

Mr. Jones explained, "He's been planted among the inmates under the name Moammar el Shabaz. He'll be moved in with 'Ali Nazeer' today."

"You're Saudi intelligence?" Traci suggested.

"Harry's a Lebanese American in the Defense Intelligence Agency," Mr. Jones informed her. "And, like you, now working for the Committee."

"How do we know he's not a mole?" she said sarcastically. "A Muslim fanatic."

"I happen to be a Christian," Harry responded with obvious

irritation.

"Well that's a relief. Hallelujah!"

"Have a seat, Harry," Mr. Jones said with a courteous smile, gesturing to a seat beside Traci. "Harry's a computer whiz. He graduated first in his class at MIT. Made $20 million creating computer games."

"Well that'll come in handy if we run into an army of zombies," she said, using her finger as an imaginary gun to pick off targets. She was liking this less and less.

"We recruited him in 11th grade, and in exchange for a modest sum of start-up capital, he agreed to create programs for us," Jones said. "Some rather nifty ones, I must say – including a virus that's made all of Russia's nuclear missile systems inoperable and some artificial intelligence stuff that would, well, let's just say it would blow your mind."

Traci shrugged.

Mr. Jones opened his mouth to continue his sales pitch, but Harry raised a hand to stay him.

"I sold my company to Microsoft and retired at 23," he said in a somber voice. "But when 9/11 happened, I wanted to do something about it. So I volunteered to be a field agent."

Traci had no snappy comeback to that. Invoking 9/11 was a trump card that had a way of extinguishing debate.

"Harry is an expert marksman. He can match the best of the CIA farm boys shot for shot," said Mr. Jones. "Farm boys" was a euphemism in the intelligence agency for assassins, Traci knew.

"And he has a black belt like you," Mr. Jones went on. "Perhaps you'd like to hold a sparring match some time."

Traci had no interest in Harry's resume, although kicking someone's ass right now held a certain appeal. She had no doubt she could take the little guy.

"So what's the plan, Mr. Smith?"

"Jones."

"Of course."

The spymaster knocked off the friendly host act and got down to business.

"After raiding an Islamist safe house in Berlin, our friends at the BND did some routine neutron bombardment to scan captured documents. They uncovered invisible writing pertaining to The Chief on pages of a Koran," he revealed.

The BND was Germany's intelligence agency, the Bundesnachrichtendienst; Traci knew that much. It literally meant the Federal News Agency, thus a nickname for *their* assassins was "cub reporters."

"The Chief has amassed a war chest of approximately $45 billion," Mr. Jones went on. "We believe he intends to use the money to purchase a WMD from Ukraine. Where the funds are hidden, we don't know."

That got Traci's attention, as talk of nukes generally does with law enforcement officers.

"Nuclear material?"

"We don't know what it is. Our Ali Nazeer and Harry here will penetrate The Chief's hideout and execute a computer theft of those funds."

"Is this con man a computer nerd too?"

"Leave the technical stuff to me," Harry boasted. "All 'Ali Nazeer' has to do is get me to a computer terminal in The Chief's headquarters, or near enough to hack in with a laptop. I'll do the rest."

"Glad it's going to be such a cakewalk," Traci said, crossing her arms with a sour expression. "So, what's next?"

Mr. Jones was beaming again, in full Santa Claus mode.

"First we get you some language tapes to brush up on your dialects," he said. "Then we measure you for a burqa."

Chapter 15
THE GREAT ESCAPE

X ought to have been in better spirits now that he knew he faced no 15th century torture. But it was hard to put out of his mind the little fact that within a matter of hours the Black Plague symptoms would kick in. The disease that had wiped out more than a quarter of Europe's population. So it took all his acting talents to remain jovial when he dined with fawning fellow prisoners in the mess hall.

"We heard how bravely you withstood the torture of the Americans, waterboarding and electric shock and other, unthinkable things," a member of his entourage marveled. "Is it true that they put you on the rack?"

X nodded. "It was nothing. I may get one for my mansion."

His peers roared with laughter.

X grinned and took a bite out of a baloney sandwich (the pork-free variety, of course). At least he could eat without discomfort. Right after his *tete a tete* with Mr. Jones, he'd been wheeled to the office of the prison dentist, where he'd been outfitted with a new filling to replace the one that had been knocked out of his head. X found this random act of kindness on the part of his captors rather bizarre.

He was dragged from his cell for a "torture" session each of the three succeeding days after his initial meeting with Mr. Jones. And the daily two-hour sessions, in which Mr. Jones briefed him on details of the terrorist network he supposedly ran, were somewhat torturous to X. After being forced to repeat back to his mentor intricacies of the Jihadist Brotherhood's chain of command – more mind-numbing than the British monarchy's line of succession – he told Mr. Jones, "Please, don't you have an iron maiden you can shove me in instead of this?"

And of course, he was told about Harry, his new partner in crime.

Back in his cell, he and Asar were trading riddles (Asar seemed to have an encyclopedic knowledge of Arabic ones dating back 1,000 years) when Harry was shoved into their cell.

X greeted the newcomer with exaggerated enthusiasm, embracing him, then clapping his hands on his face and bringing it close to his own.

"Moammar, I thought you were dead," he said excitedly.

"And I you," Harry replied.

X turned. "Asar, this is my friend and ally Moammar. It was he who engineered the destruction of the American consulate in Riyadh."

"I thought that was Al-Qaeda," Asar said, looking puzzled.

"Those rascals try to take credit for everything," X replied without skipping a beat. "No, it was Moammar here and his team, with the aid of Allah. Moammar, I thought you were killed in the firefight by Saudi secret police."

"I escaped in the back of a Red Cross truck that was passing at that very moment," Harry said.

X nudged Asar. "Throw this one in the sea and he'll come up with a fish in his mouth. He's the luckiest devil I know."

Harry laughed. "And you are the cleverest and bravest, my friend."

X placed a hand on Harry's shoulder and announced to Asar, "Moammar is one of my dearest friends. My sister is promised to him."

"Adadwiya, the youngest?"

X nodded. He had described his sister's beauty to the teen so many times, in such vivid detail, he could picture her himself.

"Allah has given Moammar a great gift when it comes to computers," X said. "Many times he has hacked his way into the infidels' computers and retrieved vital intelligence."

For a moment, Asar regarded the two old chums like a jealous lover. Then he stood up and took Harry's hand, shaking it vigorously.

"It is a blessing to meet you," he said. "Ali and I have forged a close bond here. We are like brothers."

X tousled Asar's thick mop of hair.

"This is true. Asar was the personal driver to The Chief, and one of his confidantes. He saved The Chief's life on many an occasion."

"It is an honor to meet you," Harry said, gripping the teen's hand and forearm with conviction.

*   *   *

X's symptoms were beginning to kick in. First an upset stomach, then a hacking cough. He was feeling dizzy when he was led down the hall for yet another interrogation. He was puzzled. The last time, Mr. Jones had wished him a fond farewell, grinning "Break a leg." X hadn't expected to see him again.

When Traci entered the little room, she found X strapped, fittingly enough, to an X shaped steel crucifix. (He'd heard once, by the way, that this was the true shape of the cross on which Christ was put to death.) Presumably for her benefit, he'd been allowed the dignity of underwear.

"Well, well, well," he said. "Don't you keep turning up like a bad penny?" Then he coughed.

"Feeling under the weather?" she said, being sure to keep her distance.

"I'll live – or so I've been told." He added with a smile, "I never got a chance to tell you, you give one hell of a good massage. You still owe me a happy ending, though."

Traci blushed as the whole humiliating episode rushed back into her mind, along with the usual attendant fury.

"I came to let you know that I'll be your handler on this mission," she said evenly. "I'll be watching you every step of the way."

"Like a fairy godmother?"

She leaned forward, but, knowing he was infectious now, resisted the urge to get all up in his face. "Like the Godfather," she hissed. "You try to escape, you do anything to compromise this mission and you'll get –"

"A horse's head in my bed?"

The agent stepped back "Just be a good boy."

*   *   *

By the next morning, the three cellmates had been quarantined in the isolation room of the hospital ward. In the bed next to X, Asar was throwing up voluminously into a metal pan – a spectacular spray of reds, greens, oranges and browns that would put Jackson Pollock to shame. Harry, AKA Moammar, was thrashing about on his cot, strange purple swellings extruding from every inch of exposed skin.

X could not believe the pain in his gut. He was curled up in the fetal position, holding his belly, closing his eyes against the blinding fluorescent light. He was convinced that death was imminent. Try as he might to remember what Mr. Jones had said about the disease being designed to peter out, reason fled and delirium overcame him.

He was a boy again, on the tennis court of his father's mansion in Kuwait, taking lessons from his instructor, a fair-haired young Englishman who smiled patiently as they batted the ball back and forth.

"You know, this never happened," the instructor reminded him in a pleasant Yorkshire accent.

He was a boy again, crawling on an Oriental rug, captivated by the pattern, a toy airplane in his hands. He heard a familiar voice and turned. A woman stood in the doorway, bright light streaming from behind her. He recognized his mother's face, not sad and prematurely aged, but young again, happy. She smiled, surrounded by a corona, like an angel.

He reached for her. "Mommy?" The shadowy figure of a man abruptly appeared behind her. The stranger shut the door, casting X into darkness.

"Mommy!"

His extended hand slammed against wood so hard it hurt. As he groped around in the pitch black, he found to his horror that he was inside a velvet-lined box. A coffin. He beat it frantically. He tried to call out, but no words came.

Suddenly it was bright. He stood under sunny skies in a graveyard next to the coffin, dressed in a black suit and shiny shoes. The coffin was in the grip of a system of pulleys, ready to be lowered into a deep open grave.

The preacher from the sewer, in his filthy priest's robes, stood with a prayer book in hand and listlessly uttered a eulogy.

"He was a man. And what is a man? I am who I am. Who am I? Madam, I'm Adam."

There were no other mourners at the funeral. Didn't the poor guy in the casket have a single soul who cared enough about him to show up? Then X recalled that HE had been in the coffin a moment ago. Was he dead? A ghost? Or buried alive and having an out-of-body experience? X stepped around to see whose name was on the tombstone, fearing that he would see his own. But the tombstone was blank.

What the hell?! He lurched back, covering his mouth.

The Catholic priest opened his prayer book. He began in English, "We pray now for the soul of this sinner, *un homme sans nom, une âme perdue dont l'esprit...*"

The words drifted from French into to Arabic, then meandered into Hindi. Then they dissolved into a pastiche of a dozen different languages. The priest had become a one-man Babel.

The ragged old man nodded and a pair of cemetery workers – who looked a lot like Ali Nazeer's bogus "bodyguards," car washers Babak and... *what was his brother's name*? began to lower the coffin into the ground.

"Stop it," X cried. "I'm not dead!"

The priest regarded him sadly. His lips moved but no words could be heard.

X was back in the coffin, beating on it furiously. "I'm not dead," he screamed.

Then his hands stopped moving as if held by an invisible force. Someone was holding his wrists. He opened his eyes to see Asar restraining him.

"Easy, easy, my friend," Asar said.

"He's coming out of it," Harry announced in relief.

X sank back onto the cot.

"We were worried that the terrible disease would claim you," Asar said, his brow still wrinkled with concern. "But Allah was merciful and spared us all. It is indeed a miracle."

"He must have plans for us," Harry, AKA Moammar,

suggested. "That is the only explanation we can devise."

The belly pain had eased. X could tell he still had a low-grade fever but for the first time in hours – or was it days – he could think clearly. He took in his surroundings. A small room in the prison hospital, empty except for three cots, as white and pristine as an alien holding tank in some science fiction movie.

The plan.

"Are you well enough to speak, my friend?" Harry asked.

X nodded and sat up. He still felt the impact of disease in his bones – as if he'd gone 12 rounds with Mike Tyson.

"It is fortuitous that we find ourselves here," Harry said. "There is – "

"Look at what we have found," Asar interjected excitedly.

He pointed to the ceiling. There was a small grate above them, barely 18 by 18 inches.

X's two companions helped him to his feet and they circled beneath the grate. The identity thief went up on his tiptoes, stretched and reached it.

"There are four screws holding it in place, very tight," he said. "I don't see how we can dislodge it."

"Give me a boost," Asar said to Harry. The older man hoisted the lithe teen by the waist and Asar examined the grate.

"Air is flowing through it," he said excitedly. "I think there's some kind of airshaft."

He tried to twist the screws with his fingers, to no avail.

"If we had something we could use as a screwdriver," Harry said thoughtfully, pushing up his glasses, which had drifted to the bridge of his nose.

"Let's look around," X said, his voice still hoarse. "Leave no stone unturned." He dropped to his knees and made a show of examining the springs of his cot. The solution was pretty obvious – Harry had practically written it out with a bold black Sharpie. But he figured it would be better if Asar found the tool. He waited patiently.

Asar crawled under the bed, probed behind the metal toilet, his buns-baring hospital gown falling open. After 15 minutes, he finally looked at Harry.

"Your glasses!" he exclaimed.

Harry touched his spectacles protectively.

"If we break off one of the arms, and peel it down to the wire, it might work," Asar suggested excitedly.

Jesus, finally! X thought. *The boy is certainly not the MacGyver of terror.*

"How am I going to see?" Harry demanded.

"Afterward, we'll ask for some tape to mend them," Asar suggested, warming to the idea.

"Come, it's a good plan," said X, who'd been looking under his cot on his hands and knees. He climbed to his feet. "And there are no pretty nurses for you to see in here anyway, lover boy. The last one I saw was in a hazmat suit."

Wearing a reluctant expression, Harry took off the glasses and handed them to Asar. The two Americans watched as Asar went about turning the shaft into a tool. At one point, the Afghani caught their admiring gaze.

"When you are a driver in the back country, you must be a mechanic as well," Asar said with a grin. "I have learned to be very handy. We rarely have the proper tool for the job and have to improvise. I can turn a lead pipe into an axle."

As soon as Asar was finished, he asked to be lifted up.

"No, my young friend," X cautioned him. "We must wait for nightfall."

Harry agreed. "Let us return to our beds." Asar pouted, clearly disappointed, but assented.

This proved to be a good decision, because moments later a nurse clad in a hazmat suit as bulky as any astronaut's outfit entered, wheeling a cart.

"I am here to check your vital signs."

X was surprised that his temperature still measured 101. He was feeling pretty good now – was the man-made virus so smart it could fool a thermometer?

When the stocky woman was done, she pulled up their gowns to look at their torsos. Harry loudly protested.

"It is not fitting that a woman look upon the bare flesh of a man."

Through her plastic mask, X could see her smirk.

"You don't have anything I haven't seen before, Short Stuff," she wisecracked. "Only you've got a lot less of it."

When she left, Harry fumed, "These American women are all prostitutes. Yes, I imagine she *has* seen her share of male parts."

*   *   *

It took about half an hour to get the grate off.

"Imagine our luck that Allah placed us here in the prison hospital," Asar mused as he removed the last screw with his makeshift tool. "It is almost too good to be true."

X, holding him up, groaned from the weight and traded glances with Harry. The agent looked a bit frazzled and X winked at him.

"We have been keeping our eyes open for any opportunity to escape," X reminded the teen. "It is said, diligence is the mother of good luck." The other men nodded in agreement.

Asar pried off the grate. They gave his feet a shove and he slithered into the shaft.

"See, I told you I could fit," he said excitedly.

"See where it goes," Harry said. The boy began to worm his way through the shaft.

When the noise of Asar's body banging against the shaft died down, X said to Harry, in English. "So you're the computer geek in this operation?"

Harry flashed him a stern look. "You are to stay in character at all times."

"Oh, come on, he can't hear us."

"That's an order!"

X gave him an earnest Boy Scout salute. "You're doing a top-notch job keeping up the 'rigid jerk' act."

It was about 15 minutes before Asar returned and stuck his head out of the opening, wearing a broad smile.

"The shaft runs for about 30 feet, then there's a large grate. I could feel outside air," he said. "I wasn't strong enough to bust it open but maybe one of you could."

X looked up at the opening dubiously. "I don't know, Asar. My shoulders are wider than yours." Yet another tight place. He wished there were a pill for claustrophobia.

Why couldn't I be afraid of heights or chickens?

Asar clambered down and Harry helped him reach terra firma.

"Come, you can do it my friend," Harry told X. "The Americans have made you skinnier than you know with their accursed Kellogg's Corn Flakes," he said.

X let them boost him up. The shaft was narrow. VERY narrow.

What happened to those airshafts in *Mission Impossible*, wide enough to comfortably accommodate Peter Lupus? He and Harry were quite similar in stature, both short, wiry men, but neither was as slightly built as Asar. X had to stick his arms out straight ahead of him and wriggle forward like a snake.

It took an eternity to reach the end of the shaft. Streaks of moonlight poked through the metal grate and X breathed in fresh air. He shoved hard against the grate. Shoved harder. It didn't give. Finally he gave it a solid punch and it flew off. X reached and grabbed it as it fluttered off into the air. He gave a sigh of relief. He wasn't sure what was out there, but a grate clattering around couldn't be helpful.

He cautiously poked his head out. About 9 feet below was a roof. In the distance he could make out a guard tower and the perimeter wall. There was no room to turn around. He had to worm his way backward now, feet first, until he got back to the cell.

"I've got it open, come on," he whispered.

*   *   *

The drop to the rooftop was not neck-breaking but neither was it easy on the knees. The moon was a quarter full, bright enough to see where they were going without toppling off as they hurried barefoot across the cement surface. The night sky was rich with stars.

X could see a guard tower, and the faint wisp of cigarette smoke trailing from a silhouetted figure. One sound and the Marine in the tower would turn their way. There'd be the glare of the spotlight and a cry to halt. They'd raise their hands – but what if the jarhead was some Audie Murphy wannabe and just opened fire?

The night air was cool, no more than 50 degrees. X could feel the desert breeze hitting his butt through the backless hospital gown, and realized how goofy the trio looked – like The Three Stooges making their escape from an asylum. Maybe the guard would just break out in hysterical laughter.

They reached the ledge. The next building, nearer the perimeter fence, was about 15 feet away. Below there was a drop of 20 feet to the ground.

Asar looked at down and then up at them fearfully. "I don't know if I can make it."

X clapped him on the back. "Of course you can, my young friend. I am nearly twice your age and watch me do it with no problem."

X wasn't much of an athlete. He had vague memories of practicing the broad jump in high school, but counted himself as accomplished in the event as he was an expert discus thrower. Asar was looking at him expectantly and X flashed a confident smile. The identity thief backed up to get a running start.

"What Allah wills," he whispered for Asar's benefit. He took off and hurled himself off the ledge.

He cleared the gap with a few feet to spare, rolling onto the black-tar rooftop.

Harry was next, making it with an even bigger margin and rolling to his feet like the martial arts expert that he was.

"Show off," X whispered.

They looked back at Asar. The teen bolted forward and jumped, his feet kicking in the air like a hanged man. He fell short and his eyes were full of panic as he stretched out his hands toward his companions. Harry and X reached out and each caught a wrist.

They hauled him up onto the roof.

X scolded him. "This is no time for dramatics, Asar."

When they reached the edge of the rooftop they saw that the fence was about 16 feet away. Topped with barbed wire and, X suspected, electrified as well. The spotlight from the guard tower began sweeping the rooftops.

"Look," said Harry.

X turned and a few yards away, dead center on the rooftop

was a hatch. He and Asar knelt and struggled with it, as the spotlight swooped toward them like a bird of prey.

"Hurry, my friends," said Harry.

The hatch popped open. First Asar, then Harry, then X dropped down, pulling the hatch shut after them.

It took a few moments for their eyes to adjust to the dark. The room was illuminated only by moonlight streaming in from the window. Soon X was able to make out rows of metal shelves, crowded with boxes. There were shovels, pickaxes, sledgehammers and other tools leaning against the walls haphazardly.

"This must be where they store their building supplies," X said.

"For what?" asked Harry.

"They're turning the old commanding officer's quarters into a chapel," X explained. "Some of our comrades have had to carry concrete blocks and they told me."

The door had a little latch. Harry unlocked it, cracked the door and looked out. A Marine guard, a rifle slung over his shoulder, was pacing about 25 feet away. He hurriedly shut the door.

"It's patrolled," he said.

"We could ... " Asar suggested, drawing his finger across his throat and contorting his face into a death mask, in a manner that might have been comical under other circumstances.

"And if he screams or squeezes off a round?" said X.

Asar shrugged sheepishly.

Harry went to the window and looked out.

"My friends, come here!" he exclaimed.

They drew up beside him.

"The fence is just over five meters away," he said. "And we have all the tools we need here to dig a tunnel."

X smiled broadly. "Yes, we will use their own tools to defeat the dogs."

Asar stroked his jaw dubiously. "Even five meters will take time. We can't do it in one night or even two."

"We will work every night, while the infidels are sleeping," X explained, waving his hands enthusiastically. "Until we complete the tunnel we must continue to play sick so they keep us in the infirmary."

Harry nodded. "We must be careful to put our tools exactly where we find them."

"What about the dirt?" Asar asked.

A good question. From what X remembered from *The Great Escape*, the POWs brought the dirt out in the cuffs of their trousers and surreptitiously dumped it in the prison garden. But they had no garden, and for that matter, no trousers.

"Here," said Harry, excitedly. He thumped his hand against a huge barrel. He lifted the lid and showed them that it was half filled with cans of wood stain. "There are four of them and none are full," he said.

"Excellent my friend. They won't be using those on the floor until the building is finished and by then we'll be long gone."

The prisoners slid away an empty fuel tank that didn't look as if it had been used in years, and began to chip away at the floor. They worked for five hours that night, agreeing that they couldn't risk staying close to dawn. In that time, they only managed to break through the floor of the store room and dig perhaps two feet into the earth below.

The slow progress perturbed the usually ebullient Asar.

"I do not know if when I see The Chief again I will be in as lofty a position," he said morosely. "He must have another driver by now. I will be back to carrying messages, as I did when I was a boy."

X tousled the teen's corvine hair again. It was a fatherly gesture he remembered seeing on TV. "It is said that it is better to be a free dog than a caged lion," he observed. "First we must get out of this wretched place, then we can worry about our future in the great cause."

An hour later, they stopped work and dragged the empty fuel tank back to its place on top of the hole. Each tool was returned to its proper place.

Then, like vampires retreating before the dawn, they returned the way they came, standing on each others' shoulders to reach the airshaft and squirming through it back to the hospital ward.

*   *   *

Every night they worked on the tunnel. During the day, when the doctor and nurse checked in on them, always in hazmat suits, they faked weakness and pain. The antibiotics they received daily would take some time to cure them, but they would survive, the doctor assured them.

They took turns burrowing in the tunnel, men transformed into moles. The digger passed the dirt back to the others, who placed it in the old barrels.

To allay the monotony they chatted about their personal lives. For some reason, X did not feel comfortable talking about Ali Nazeer's mythical youth in Kuwait with Harry present. Sharing the fantasy with that naive teen, who listened so avidly in the dark, had been moments which, although he'd be loathe to admit it, he'd found somehow magical.

Instead, they talked mostly about women.

Harry bragged about his wife in Riyadh, a strong, devoutly religious woman quite naturally, who maintained strict order in the house. When one of their daughters once brought home a Barbie doll as a gift from a schoolmate, she was severely beaten for accepting the morality-corrupting blond symbol of the West.

"Here, here," X said.

Asar nodded in approval.

Asar told them about the girl to whom he was engaged in an Afghan village near the Khyber Pass. He had never seen her face, or been alone with her, but she had a sweet singing voice and wrote beautiful poetry. They had exchanged many letters before his capture. He was still a virgin, it soon became apparent to X, and was unashamed of it – proud of his purity in the eyes of Allah.

An American his age would be suicidal, the identity thief thought.

"On our wedding night, there will be rose petals on the bed and I will play on the sitar for her before we make love for the first time," Asar said.

The look in his eyes when he spoke of her was priceless. *He looks like the kid who played Romeo in the old Zepherelli movie from the '60s,* X thought. *Or maybe Gidget getting misty-eyed over Moondoggie.*

His idealism was just incredible, X thought as the boy took

Harry's place in the tunnel. *Admirable in a way if you could get past the terrorism and suicide-bombing bit.*

"What about you?" Harry said. "How are those wives of yours, Jasmine and the short one."

X chuckled. "Still fussing at each other like cats and addicted to shopping. Took a trip to Paris and came home with a suitcase full of mink coats. Furs, to wear in Kuwait City!"

The other men laughed.

At that moment, the tunnel collapsed entombing Asar, and dust shot out of the opening. X and Harry dug frantically with their spades. X was surprised to find himself genuinely frightened, his pulse accelerating. He was not used to worrying about other people. It took several moments to reach the boy and they dragged him out by his heels. He was coughing and covered in dust, but uninjured.

The collapse cost them two nights work, but they forged ahead.

It took some doing to keep Asar's spirits up. He had the impatience of most teens and again and again they had to quote from the Koran to keep him going. X was glad that he'd downloaded that collection of Arab proverbs and memorized choice adages on the plane to Las Vegas.

"It is written that men learn little from success, but much from failure," X told Asar after a second collapse two nights later. Harry seconded that, reminding the despondent boy that "Sunshine without rain makes a desert."

The spy had, apparently, spent time on the same Internet site.

When they were, in Harry's estimation, about six feet from the fence – perhaps three night's works – the doctor surprised them with some good news. After carefully examining each of them, he beamed as if he'd just been handed the Nobel Prize for curing cancer and was about to thank the little people.

"You are making remarkable progress," said the doctor, "given that you were at death's door. The latest blood tests show your white count is back to normal. Today's Wednesday. I would say that by tomorrow morning, I will be able to discharge you."

Chapter 16
ON THE ROAD AGAIN

The moment the nurse turned off the light and the door closed behind her, the men sprang into action. They dug furiously until their hands ached. They didn't care what happened to the dirt now; they cast it in a heap on the floor.

"Don't give up, my comrades," X urged, when Asar began to show signs of weariness. "We will prevail, with Allah's help."

In the wee hours of Thursday morning, about 4 a.m. as Harry calculated it, X's fingers breeched the surface. His fingers wiggled in the cold night air.

"We've done it," he exclaimed, turning back to the others. "Three night's work in one!"

In another 15 minutes, the tunnel was wide enough for him to wriggle out, like a zombie rising from a grave. X crawled on all fours on the rocky soil. He could kiss the ground, the feeling of freedom was so exhilarating. He reached back and grabbed Asar's arm and helped the teen out. Together they pried Harry out of the hole.

"We are free men," Harry declared. "We have defeated Satan's minions."

The three men embraced.

"Together, the three of us are unstoppable," X said.

"We're like The Three Musketeers," declared the teen, though perhaps Dumas might roll in his grave. Upbeat as a prisoner, Asar would be insufferably buoyant now, X realized.

Harry pointed the sky. "We will have the cover of darkness for only a short time, my friends," he said. "We must go."

They darted into the night.

"Moammar" had told the others of a safe house less than four miles from the prison. They jogged at a solid clip for a half hour, resting for a few moments every mile. They stopped, panting, at the bombed-out ruins of a barn that was painted a grim tarlike black.

"We should keep going," Asar said, panting.

"No, this is it, the secret place," Harry informed him. Asar surveyed the termite-eaten, broken-down structure, which looked as if it would collapse on anyone foolish enough to enter it. Which, X realized, was doubtless the intention: to ward off nosy intruders.

"It's not the Taj Mahal, my young brother, but it will provide us with a good hiding place," Harry said with a smile. "The Americans must have discovered we're gone by now. Help me with the door, Asar."

They slid across a wooden bar and pulled the huge doors open.

"It's stocked with food and weapons," Harry explained.

"How did you arrange this from the hospital?" Asar asked.

Harry shook his head. "I had my associates put this in place months ago, well before I was captured," he told the teen. "We learned that Abd Al-Rahman Prison was the most likely place we'd be taken."

X tapped his temple. "Moammar is as crafty as a tarantula. He is always two steps ahead of the infidels."

Were tarantulas really crafty? X wasn't sure. He often found himself drawing upon hazily remembered dialog from old movies like *Gunga Din*.

Harry went to a large stack of empty crates and started pulling them off. The other men helped him. Behind the heap of junk, a rusty old Russian-built Tara 138 six by six diesel truck was waiting.

Asar laughed and smacked the side.

"She's no beauty but I can drive her," he said. "She can go up the side of a mountain like a young goat."

Click! From behind them came the unmistakable sound of a gun cocking.

"Do not move," a female voice commanded.

They turned, and a woman stepped out of a dark corner. She was decked out in a *chadaree*, a traditional Afghani garment that covered her from head to toe, along with an embroidered face piece. Not a burqa, but by no means a micro mini either. The lady was pointing the business end of a Kalashnikov rifle at them.

"Who are you?" she demanded.

"I am Ali Nazeer of the Jihadist Brotherhood," X proclaimed, thumping his chest boastfully. "These are my companions Asar and Moammar. We have just escaped from the American prison, Abd Al-Rahman."

She lowered the weapon and gave a gasp of admiration.

"Everyone has heard of the great Ali Nazeer," she said.

"Who are you?" Harry demanded.

"I am Fatima bint Kuttab," she said. "I am from the Islamic Freedom Party of Liberia. Once a month I am to stock this place with fresh food and water. I have been sleeping here for the past two days. I was told by an aide to The Chief that if I encounter any brothers in the Cause who have escaped I am to safeguard them and offer them assistance."

"It is I who made those arrangements," Harry said. "You have done well."

"Do you have civilian clothes for us?" X asked. The backside-baring hospital gowns would hardly make it easy for them to blend in.

The woman nodded and retrieved a wicker basket full of clothes from its hiding place behind a stack of hay.

"There is a set for each of you," she said. To each man she distributed standard Afghan wear: a *tombaan*, a type of pants, a *payraan*, an oversize shirt, boots and a *pakol*, a hat. Then she stepped back and waited. The garments were identical except for color. Harry wore a red shirt, X blue, Asar purple.

"We cannot dress in the presence of a woman," Harry scolded her. "Go to the other side of the truck. The woman nodded meekly and turned to go. Asar suddenly clutched her arm.

"Wait," he said. "How do we know this woman is who she claims she is?"

X stepped in. "My friend, we do not have time for this. The sun is up. The Americans will be coming this way any minute."

"But Ali, I know what this Fatima bint Kuttab looks like," Asar insisted. "I want to be sure it's her."

Well, that's an unexpected development, X thought. *Did Jones forgot to do his homework?*

"Remove your face piece," Asar ordered the woman.

"I will not," she said, crossing her arms defiantly.

"You will do as a man commands you," he insisted. "A woman's duty is to submit."

"To her husband, not to the whim of every strange boy," she retorted. She appealed to X. "Will you allow this pup to shame me? The Koran says that no woman's face is to be seen except by her husband and closest male relatives."

"I've read it," the identity thief replied.

"She speaks the truth," Harry confirmed. "We can not violate holy law because we are afraid."

With speed X wouldn't have thought him capable of, Asar snatched the Kalashnikov out of the woman's hands and pointed it at her.

"We must make sure," he said, reaching for the veil.

"Don't touch me," the female fighter hissed, stepping back in what appeared to be fear. But X had seen enough kung fu movies in his teenage days to know that she was positioning herself to kick the weapon out of the teen's hand.

Asar pointed the rifle between her eyes.

"Asar, think of what The Chief would tell us," X pleaded. "Do you wish to make a mockery of our fight with the infidels?"

In the periphery of his vision, he could see Harry moving quietly behind Asar. If the woman didn't disarm him, the spy would, X thought. But either way they were screwed because only The Chief's teenage driver knew the way to his lair.

Asar hesitated, sweat pouring down his brow, as he weighed X's words. Then, with lightning speed, he reached and jerked away the veil, revealing the face of Traci Kingsmith.

The teen stepped back and immediately dropped the gun.

"A thousand pardons," he said. "I have never felt such shame."

Traci clapped her hand over her nose and mouth, as a Western woman might shield her breasts. But her face was exposed long enough that X saw what appeared to be odd, vertical scars on both her cheeks.

Asar hastily helped her reattach the face piece. "I am so, so, sorry."

"Come, now," Harry said. "You can offer your apologies later. We're wasting time."

The woman retreated to the far side of the truck and the men hastily dressed. It felt wonderful to be in pants and a shirt again, instead of a hospital gown or orange prison jumpsuit. The Afghani getup he'd seen a million times on CNN felt a bit like a Halloween costume. It wasn't exactly an Armani suit, but X felt that he'd instantly reclaimed a measure of human dignity.

They opened the barn doors and started piling into the vehicle. When Traci reached for the driver's side door, Harry interposed his body.

"I will drive," he said sternly. "You should know that it is forbidden for women to drive a motor vehicle."

Traci bowed and surrendered the keys. *I wonder what page of the Koran says that?* X wondered. *Guess I need to bone up.*

Harry took the wheel, while, X, Traci and Asar piled in the back and slammed the door shut. The truck tore off down the road, kicking up dust.

Asar wore a dejected expression.

"I'm sorry, my friends, but I had to be sure. Forgive me." He looked as if he might weep and Traci put a reassuring hand on his shoulder.

X knew by now that proverbs were the best way to comfort him. "My young friend, your zeal is admirable, but you cannot let your emotions get the better of you," he said. "Remember, it is said, 'The most important holy war is the one fought against your own passions.'"

"It is nothing," Traci assured the teen. "When I was crossing the border from Egypt to Gaza, the Jews had me strip naked and bend over so they could inspect my private parts. It was important for you to know you could trust me. You did not behave wrongly."

That was laying it on a bit thick, X thought, but he was grateful to have the visual insinuated into his brain.

She began to hand out *naan*, a traditional Afghan bread, and *quroot*, a sort of dried blend of yogurt and cheese.

"So, when did you two meet?" X asked, with as much nonchalance as he could muster. This he *had* to hear.

"We've never met," Asar replied, taking a huge bite out of the bread.

"You said you saw her before."

"I said I knew what she *looked like*," Asar corrected him. "I had been told Fatima bint Kubbat is a black woman, an African from Liberia, with scars on both her cheeks, where assailants marked her. Few know that."

"Scars?"

Asar gestured at the sides of his face.

X glanced quizzically at Traci, and recalled the faint parentheses that now marred her beauty.

"The men who left them have been cut too," she said quietly. "And they'll do no further harm to women."

Both men winced, then nodded soberly.

So Mr. Jones hadn't slipped up. He'd done his homework on the real bint Kubbat. He thought again that the spymaster would have made a dandy identity thief. Presumably even the Committee wouldn't go so far as to slice up the FBI agent, so she must be wearing makeup. Quite convincing too.

I wouldn't be surprised if Mr. Jones shanghaied some Tinseltown makeup artists into service, X thought. *Are there Hollywood stars working for the Committee too, and stuntmen? Perhaps Angelina Jolie had a hidden motive for adoption jaunts overseas.*

As well as food and water, the back of the truck was stocked with weapons: three more Kalashnikovs, two AK-47s, an M1911 caliber .45, a box of grenades and even a rocket launcher. There was also a spanking new laptop and an ancient boom box type radio. Asar asked for some music and the woman turned it on.

He soon recognized a traditional Afghan song and hummed along with it. X did too, smiling as if he'd heard it a thousand times before. He and Asar exchanged the grin of two high school boys embarking on an excellent adventure.

The music was interrupted by a BBC report.

"U.S. Army Captain Gayle Tofel, a military spokeswoman, confirmed that three prisoners escaped from Abd Al-Rahman Prison – the first escape from any joint U.S.-Afghan detention facility in the country.

"The area around the prison has been cordoned off and roadblocks set up on nearby roads. Photographs of the escaped inmates have been distributed to search teams and local authorities, and landowners near the prison were notified."

The spokesman said that all three were involved in terrorist activity and that they included Ali Nazeer, the notorious playboy-turned-terrorist captured in the U.S. last fall.

An American-accented voice came on. "These men represent a clear and present danger and the military considers their recapture a top priority."

Asar looked a little spooked.

"It sounds like they think we're still on foot," X said. "They don't know we have a vehicle."

The truck screeched to a stop and they were thrown on top of each other. Asar landed atop Traci, his hands, comically, on her breasts, like something that might happen to Leslie Nielson in a *Naked Gun* movie. He rolled off, blushing and aghast.

"So sorry, so sorry," Asar said. "A thousand pardons."

"Something has gone wrong," Traci said.

X heard voices – gruff, distinctly American voices – outside the truck.

"What do we do?" whispered Abu.

"Start screaming," Traci told him. "In pain. Clutch your belly."

"I do not understand," Asar said.

"Do it now," she said.

"I do not take orders from a woman,"

"Do as she says," X barked.

Asar began to shriek in pain – an easy performance because he'd had so much practice feigning illness in the hospital ward.

The back door to the truck was flung open and a pair of GIs stood, one pointing a rifle at them, the other a handgun. One was black, the other white and both were unusually good-looking. Somehow, they reminded X of Sonny and Tubbs in that old show *Miami Vice*. A few yards behind them a third soldier was shoving his automatic rifle in the face of Moammar and gesturing with the weapon for him to lie face-down.

"Get down! Get the fuck down!" the third soldier bellowed.

Harry was gesticulating wildly and jabbering in an obscure Afghan dialect X didn't recognize. "Out of the truck," the black GI ordered them.

"My brother, he is sick," X told them.

"It is true," Traci said. "We are taking him to the hospital."

"Get him off the fucking truck," bellowed the black guy, training the muzzle at X's forehead.

X began to tug the teen out of the back of the truck, but Asar made himself dead weight. Groaning in agony each time, X tried to pull him.

"You must help me," he begged the black soldier.

The GI assessed the situation and reluctantly holstered his weapon. "Cover me. And keep an eye on that bitch – I don't like her eyes," he told his buddy. The white one nodded.

"Get out," Sonny ordered Traci. The woman climbed out of the truck, her hands in the air, palms forward.

"On your knees with your hands on your head," the GI demanded and Traci complied.

As X and Tubbs struggled with Asar's squirming body, he noticed that the confrontation between Harry and the third soldier had escalated, the volume of their voices on the rise. Harry was still standing, though crouching a bit. In another 30 seconds, the soldier would undoubtedly shoot, X realized.

"Get down, get down!" the GI was hollering at the top of his lungs.

Harry got down to one knee, now arguing in what X finally identified as half the Afghan dialect Pashto and half pig-Latin gibberish.

"Just shoot the fucker," the white kid guarding Traci said, turning toward Moammar.

She lunged forward and caught the muzzle of the gun, jerking it into the air. A round discharged. X, who hadn't heard a gunshot in years, jumped at the deafening sound.

Tubbs dropped Asar's feet and leaped out of the truck, drawing his gun like a cowboy, while the GI confronting Harry turned around and aimed at the woman's head.

Before either of them could squeeze off a shot, Harry pulled the .45 from his sleeve. He shot the guy who'd been hectoring him in the back and plugged Tubbs in his chest. The GIs dropped like crows struck by lightning.

Sonny yanked the muzzle of the rifle away from Traci and

whirled toward Harry, raising it to fire.

The woman reached under her skirt, pulled a Beretta 92 Compact out of God knows where and pumped six bullets into his back. Blood shot spectacularly from the exit wound in his chest as the guy crumpled to his knees then sprawled face-forward.

Asar scrambled up and looked shell-shocked as he beheld the carnage.

"Oh, that, that, it all happened so quickly," he stammered. Evidently, despite his terrorist credentials, he didn't see bloodshed all that often.

Harry and X hurriedly loaded the bodies into the back of the Army truck, then dispatched Asar to leave the vehicle over a hilltop and cover it with thick bushes. The teen had enthusiastically volunteered to set the truck ablaze, but the others hastily put the kibosh on the idea, warning that the smoke would signal their pursuers.

While they waited for Asar to return, X whistled. "Well, that was rather impressive. How did you manage to get the blood to do that?"

"Squibs, like the kind they use in Hollywood," Harry explained.

F/X people on call, just as I thought, X marveled. "And you, Traci, you are VERY quick," he said. "A regular Annie Oakley. Where exactly is that holster?"

She smirked. "That's for me to know and you never to find out."

"I never thought I'd envy a gun before."

Harry stepped forward and shoved X in the chest.

"Watch your mouth," he said. "This isn't one of your skanky lap dancers."

X narrowed his eyes and smiled. "I wouldn't do that again if I were you."

"Or what?"

Traci stepped in between them. "I don't need anyone to speak up for me, Harry."

The agent shrugged, sullenly. "Fine. But I thought it was your job to keep him in line."

"Back to business," she said. "It played well, agreed?"

Harry nodded. "I don't think the kid should have any doubts about our loyalty."

"Good. Mr. Jones said those three were the last Committee operatives to help us. We're on our own from here on in."

X laughed. "How are we going to get by? Without all that great aid and comfort he's been giving us so far?"

Harry raised his finger and opened his mouth to scold him.

Traci held up her hand. "Zip it, boys, he's coming back."

Asar was running back over the hill, a wide grin on his face. He came up to them panting. "It is done. It is in a ravine that is difficult to see even by a helicopter."

He turned to Traci. "A second time I must apologize," he said, head hung low. "I should not have questioned your order to scream. I was brought up in a very strict household; I was told that it is the man who is to give the command to the woman."

"It is true what they say: 'What is learned in youth is carved in stone,'" X said. "Next time, don't wait for me to confirm an order."

Harry shook his head. "No, don't listen to him. It is written that obedience to a woman leads to hell."

Asar looked in confusion from man to man, trying to read their earnest expressions.

X laughed and punched Harry in the shoulder. Harry returned the playful gesture – a bit too hard for X's taste – and chuckled as well.

Harry threw Asar the keys. "Good news, my young friend. You can take the wheel for a few hours."

Asar's eyes lit up and he flashed a smile that put the sun to shame.

*   *   *

Two hours later a city came into view, rising like a mirage out of the dusty plain.

"It is the city of Gardez," said Asar. "We will find assistance and fuel. There are many I know there who are loyal to the Cause."

The Cause, thought X. *Wasn't that what the Confederates called their gallant mission too?*

"Praise Allah for protecting us on our journey," said the identity thief, who sat beside Asar and had been keeping him awake with small talk on the ride.

Traci and Harry were dozing in the rear. Or perhaps fine-tuning details of the mission. The equally uptight duo both acted as if they were too dedicated to sleep, X thought. It's a safe bet they weren't making out, although he was beginning to think Harry had a thing for her.

"She's beautiful, is she not?" Asar said abruptly.

"Who?" X craned his neck to see if there was a billboard featuring some Afghani movie star along the road. If the Afghanis were making movies yet. The Taliban had put something of a damper on the industry, if he recalled properly.

"Fatima, of course."

Huh? The woman's face was hidden behind a veil and not an inch of her body was exposed. When she walked, the natural sway of her hips was modestly subdued.

I suppose it's been a long time since he's seen a woman, X thought. *Or at least not one menacing him with attack dogs and mocking his naughty bits.*

Asar nudged him and winked. "Come on, my friend, I have seen you gazing at her too. Those eyes, ah, what do you call that color? Hazel. It is like looking into a peaceful lake."

She did have nice eyes, but X simply didn't look at her that way. Sure, when they were in the hotel and she was posing as a masseuse, wearing that tight mini that showed off her high, round booty, he'd found her sexy. But a lot of water had passed under the bridge since then. Being caught by her and tasered by her henchman after fleeing through miles of sewer; being snarled at by her as he hung half naked from a crucifix – none of that was a particularly potent aphrodisiac.

Asar was waxing poetic now, a dreamy look in his eyes. "Her scent, it is like myrtle – no, rose perfume. They say that African women are passionate lovers. And she has proven herself to be courageous and devout. Islam allows a man to take four wives. Do you not admit she would be a fine wife No. 4 for you?"

It irked X that this teenage simpleton would presume to know who would be the perfect wife for him. The little idiot didn't even know who he was. Maybe it was the heat, maybe it was weeks of being chased and tortured, but he was getting a wee bit p.o.'d and decided to let the kid have a piece of his mind.

"First of all, I do not need a boy half my age to play matchmaker," he chastised Asar, waving a finger in the teen's face. "Second, as I recall you are a virgin and so your thoughts about which nationality of woman – "

A whooshing sound came from overhead. The two men looked up to see a drone in the sky behind them.

"Oh, hell," said X in American-accented English. Whoops. He was pretty sure the young Arab hadn't paid any attention to the slip. He was too busy flooring the accelerator.

Machine-gun fire erupted and bullets peppered the road not five yards in front of them. He assumed these were warning shots. But the next ones probably wouldn't be.

Asar swerved off the road, to the right, around the path of the bullets, then back on it. The machine guns roared to life again and, this time the bullets pounded the highway behind them.

"Buckle your seatbelt, my friend," Asar said. To X's amazement, he saw that the teen was grinning ear to ear. *You've got to be kidding.* Was this fun for The Chief's driver?

The truck sped off and X felt his back pressing against the car seat as if he were aboard a rocket ship. He swore he could feel the muscles of his face pulling back like those of a test pilot pushing a new fighter plane to Mach 4. Had the vehicle been souped up? He didn't put it past Mr. Jones and his real-life Qs to install some kind of turbo drive in the thing.

At any rate, the vehicle seemed almost to be matching speed with the drone. Asar swerved right, then left, weaving like a football player making a broken-field run.

Bullets drilled into the sand and cement on either side, barely missing the vehicle. X had been under the impression that drones carried only bombs, but apparently the latest generation came equipped with a menu of weapons.

What WILL they think of next?

The city was less than a mile away. X could see a checkpoint and the open gates behind it. They would have to crash right through it, braving the potshots of the half-dozen guards. But their more immediate problem was the flying killer robot. A mile was a long, long way to go with a drone firing some kind of high-tech Gatling guns at you.

Bullets ripped through the roof of the truck and into the seat next to them. X screamed as a piece of jagged metal from the roof tore into his thigh.

"F-Fu-!" This time he caught himself. "Bloody hell," he shouted in the British-accented English of Eton, the boarding school the real Ali Nazeer attended. He followed that up by spewing a stream of Arabic obscenities.

As they neared the city gates the sound of the unmanned aircraft became less deafening. The remote-controlled plane was ascending and X prayed that it was going away, although for the life of him he couldn't imagine why.

"I think it's going away," he shouted to Asar. "Maybe the city is too densely populated for them to chase us."

"Perhaps," Asar said. "But I fear it is going to fire a – "

BOOM! The truck tipped over onto two wheels. A huge piece of the road right next to them shot into the air, a flaming chunk of smoky, molten cement. Two missiles left a crater in its place.

The truck skidded precariously along on two wheels, the driver's side tilting in the air. X was sure they were going to flip.

"Lean toward me," Asar shouted, grabbing X's arm.

With considerable effort, the identity thief lurched toward the driver. Whether his trim 150-pound frame (smaller, perhaps courtesy of a prison diet) really made a difference, he didn't know. But the truck slammed down on all four tires and bounced down the road.

The city was less than 50 yards away now and guards had massed at the gates, pointing automatic weapons straight at them.

"Any thoughts?" X said.

Asar smiled as if he were some NASCAR hotshot about to cross the finish line.

"Yes. We improvise, my friend."

X was sure he'd heard that line in some Hollywood buddy movie, but the boy's backsliding into corrupt Western pop culture was the least of his concerns.

Asar swerved off the road and began racing parallel to the city wall. Shots rang out after them and slammed into the back of the truck. For the first time in the chase, X thought fleetingly of Traci, back there bouncing around, and wondered if she was okay. More of the high-caliber bullets had penetrated the back of the truck than the cab.

Asar made a sharp left turn and through the window X saw the drone speed past them.

The boy floored the accelerator and like a charging bull directed the truck at the city wall.

"Are you crazy?" X screamed. "You're going to kill us both!"

"Then we will be martyrs and virgins await us."

"I'll settle for a woman with experience," X snapped. "Stop right now. I'm ordering you."

But Asar didn't stop. X shut his eyes as the truck smashed into the wall at top speed. Only it wasn't wall, he saw as bits of plaster exploded in all directions, coming down in chunks and fine powder, along with pieces of two-by-fours.

The truck turned down a narrow street and continued, still going 90 m.p.h. X was able to confirm with a high degree of certainty that he was still alive: the pain in his thigh was excruciating and the dead were presumably immune to pain.

Asar tapped his forehead.

"I knew there was a gap in the wall created when the old munitions warehouse accidentally blew up. The government promised to stone it back up months ago, but you know how that is."

The drone, useless to their pursuers now, rose and swerved off. But within seconds a green Humvee appeared in the rearview mirror.

"Now the thrilling part begins," Asar said, taking his hands momentarily off the wheel to clap them together.

The Russian truck raced through the narrow streets, not missing a single one of the potholes that dotted the road. One especially deep rut launched the two men so high, their hats struck the ceiling. Venders selling kebabs dived out of the way. It really WAS like something out of a James Bond movie, X thought. All that was missing was a button to pour tacks or an oil slick out the back.

Asar glanced at him and saw how white his face was.

"Do not worry, my good friend. Many times when I was driving The Chief I led the police on chases through Kandahar and this city as well, and didn't put a scratch in his BMW."

"I hope he tipped well," X replied.

"Oh, see if there are any cigarettes in the glove compartment," Asar said casually. "I haven't had one in months."

Through the side mirror X could see three Humvees in pursuit. But Asar didn't seem to be the least bit concerned. It was the first time the young man had seemed competent – something other than a young, misguided fool. Clearly he was in his element.

X popped open the glove compartment and found a dusty pack of cigarettes. There was a picture of genie perched on a flying carpet on the box and a brand name in Turkish. It looked as if they might have been there since the Russian invasion. X shook out one of the three remaining cigarette, blew off the dust and placed it between Asar's lips. He fumbled in the glove box and, amid some papers and petrified condoms, found a lighter and lit the cigarette.

"It's a good thing for you the Russians smoked like chimneys," X said as he watched the teen take a long drag.

"Ahh, Turkish," Asar exhulted. "I've miss this. And tea, how I've missed tea."

As they raced along, X looked out the window. Many of the buildings had been bombed out and rubble littered the streets. It was impossible to tell if it was left over from the Russian invasion, the civil war that followed or the America's turn at bat.

The turns got sharper as they barreled down progressively narrower back streets. The two Humvees separated, presumably to cut them off.

Asar laughed. "They think they know this city better than we do."

"The arrogance of those Americans," X said. But he estimated that inside of a minute they'd find themselves surrounded.

Asar made another razor-sharp turn and sped down a ramp and into a mechanic's shop. A sign over the garage door read "Jamal's Auto" in both English and in Arabic lettering. The garage door rolled down behind them and the truck screeched to a stop. X realized that this was the first time in the chase the boy had applied the brakes.

"Well, we are here," Asar announced cheerily.

As to where "here" was X didn't have a clue. But as he clambered out of the truck, his head aching from being repeatedly bounced against the roof during the pursuit and his thigh gushing blood from the shard of metal, he thought that he'd never been gladder to be any place.

Fatima and Moammar, better known as Traci and Harry, emerged unscathed from the rear of the truck. The interior of the garage was filled with spare parts and an old Jeep sat on blocks, the hood open. But it was quickly apparent that Jamal's Auto was a front.

The fugitives were greeted by a pair of Afghani men who gestured to them to follow. They were both dressed in black. *In vogue on both sides of the War on Terror*, X observed.

"We heard that the mighty Ali Nazeer was on the run from the Americans," the older of the two said. "We are servants of the Warriors of Allah. We hoped that you would grace us with your presence."

"The honor is mine," said X.

He gritted his teeth as one of the men pried the metal shard out of his thigh and hastily applied a bandage.

"Can you walk?" the fighter asked. X nodded.

The fugitives were led through a series of doors and tunnels, a twisting labyrinth in which they changed directions so many times it made X's head spin.

Hopefully I'll never have to find my way back out, he thought. *Where's a ball of yarn when you need one?*

When they emerged, about 200 yards away, it was in a modest family home, adorned with intricately woven carpets and pillows, painted chests and ornate candlesticks. Several women in burqas perched on a kind of daybed, knitting quietly, and an 18-month-old in diapers crawled on the floor pushing a toy fire truck. A teenage girl – it was hard to gauge her age in the head-to-toe covering but X guessed 13 – was washing dishes in the sink. Nothing screamed terrorist safe house.

As soon as they entered the living room, two of the women

jumped to their feet and gestured for the new arrivals to follow them through a beaded curtain. The smaller woman opened a large wooden chest that looked as if it might store Long John Silver's booty. She held up a garment in front of X – a black burqa.

"Hurry, you must wear these," she said.

Asar shook his head violently. "I will not wear a burqa," he declared.

"It is an abomination," agreed Harry adamantly.

"Our first duty is to the Jihad," X pointed out. "We must stay free so that we can fight for our cause. Allah will forgive us, my friends."

Asar looked at Harry, who stroked his jaw thoughtfully then nodded. The men threw off their hats and began to pull the robes over their heads. Traci took a burqa and retreated to a back room to do the same.

Just five minutes later, a trio of Marines kicked in the door. They barged in, M4 carbine assault rifles at the ready. All they met, of course, were women sitting on the daybed knitting, while three others sat at a table, chopping up onions and garlic.

A couple of the younger women hopped up, shrieking at the sight of the guns.

"Hands in the air," one of the Marines barked. Another repeated the order in Pashto. "Drop those knives."

"Sit your asses down," shouted another soldier. "Sit down before I sit you down!"

One dropped to her seat, while the other remained standing. The soldier grabbed her shoulder and roughly pushed her down.

"Where are they, where are they?" demanded a Marine with sergeant's bars.

One of the women stood up, her status as an elder evident from her hunched posture and the raspy voice in which she began scolding them. A Marine sat her down too. The toddler, who'd been in the lap of one of the women, wrenched himself free and crawled to his fire truck. When his mother reached for him, a soldier pointed his rifle at her.

"Move again and I'm going to pop you," he yelled. The tot began to roll the toy around, oblivious to the tension in the room.

X, one of the ladies on the couch, was finding it a bit

difficult to breathe in the burqa. That loose-fitting hospital gown was looking pretty good right about now.

The soldiers pushed through the beaded curtain, kicked in the doors to the bathroom, the bedroom and the nursery in turn, shouting "Clear!" as they ascertained no fighters were present.

Disguising themselves as women was a fairly lame trick, in X's estimation. All that saved them from discovery was that he, Asar and Harry were all of small stature. If one of the trio was a big guy, they'd have been history.

Oh, well, any port in a storm, X thought.

It was at that moment that he noticed that a spot of blood, fresh and glistening stained the carpet where the fire truck had been. His bandage must have leaked! He glanced around to see if anyone else had noticed it yet. Perhaps the elderly woman had. She met his eyes, then looked away. The soldiers hadn't spotted it yet, but they'd have to be blind not to before they left.

The boy cooed and held up the fire truck and a young Marine crouched down, smiling.

"What's that you've got, little guy? I had one of those."

He was going to see the blood in two seconds.

Suddenly the old woman began to screech in her native tongue, "You filthy cat, aren't you old enough to cover yourself properly when your time has come?" She grabbed the 13-year-old by the forearm and dragged her to the center of the room. "Look!" she screamed, pointing at the spot of blood dramatically. "See how you have disgraced your family in front of these foreigners."

The teen bowed her head in shame, saying, "Grandmother, I am sorry," but the old woman boxed her savagely in the ear.

"Hey, hey, knock that off," said the Marine sergeant, grabbing hold of her. The elder lunged at the cowering teen again, beating her with her fists. It took two of the Americans to restrain her. As the adolescent beat a hasty retreat behind the beaded curtain, the sergeant stuck his sidearm in the grandmother's face.

"Leave her alone, you crazy old bat," he snarled.

"You will be beaten when they are gone," she shouted into the next room.

X smiled behind his veil. *Meryl Streep has nothing on this old crone,* he thought. *She deserves Best Supporting Actress for that little performance.*

Finding nothing, the Marines retreated, their frustration evident. One guy tipped over a vase as he left, saying "Ooops!" as it shattered.

Well, that was a bit gratuitous, X thought. As soon as a peek through the window confirmed that the Americans were gone, the three male fugitives threw off their burqas as if they were on fire – Harry with exaggerated disgust.

Asar fumed, "If only I had an AK-47 to hand when these infidels came in and terrorized these honest Muslim women."

"They are cowards,'" sneered Harry. "They would have run from the bang of one child's pop gun."

X turned to the women saying, "May Allah reward you for the good you have done here today."

The eldest woman bowed. "We do not often get genuine heroes as guests," she said. "We will feed you now. Sit, please."

A *dastarkhan* was prepared for them, a large cloth spread over the floor on which the meal was to be served. The four guests sat about it. The teenager presented an *aftabah was lagan*, a copper basin with a pot filled with water.

The teen tiptoed around the *dastarkahn* to each the guests, pouring water over their hands. A sumptuous meal was then laid before them. One woman brought them a basket filled with breads, relishes and fruits. Another brought a platter of *naan torshi*, pickled peaches with lemons, eggplant, vinegar and spices. Plates of *chalow* came next, a traditional Afghan dish composed of white rice, parboiled and baked with oil, butter and salt, served with *quorma*, a kind of stew.

Some was delicious, some merely palatable and some downright disgusting, but on the whole X found the fare a welcome change from the cold mystery-meat sandwiches and flavorless navy beans that typically passed for a dinner in prison. As they sat, the men hashed out their plans as Traci knelt on a cushion beside them, holding her tongue.

"We will take the Khyber Pass?" Harry asked.

"No, it is better we take an old drug smuggler's trail through a smaller pass known as the Forgotten Way. Almost no knows of it." Asar said.

"I suppose they've forgotten it," X wisecracked.

"That's very funny, Ali," said Harry, though the glowering look he gave the identity thief suggested otherwise.

The leader of the cell, one of the two fighters who'd led them to the safe house distributed phony identification papers.

"I hope these will be helpful to you," he said. "We keep such documents at the ready for those who are in the great struggle."

"Do these belong to real people?" X asked.

"One does," Rahim said. "A carpet merchant named Azmaray who betrayed the Cause and ... Allah saw to it that he suffered an accident."

X looked over the fake travel documents, which as a purist, he felt would not stand close scrutiny. He politely told his benefactors the documents were not up to snuff and asked for access to a computer and a digital camera.

Online, within a few minutes he found another Pakistani carpet merchant named Hussein Kulachi modern enough to have a Facebook account. Mining the home page, he was quickly able to gather information about his family, hobbies and other details. He was fond of British TV, liked cricket and often posted comments about astronomical discoveries.

Although the printer wasn't the most up to date, it was good enough to print out documents X created that were similar to the sample, bearing the names, dates of birth and other salient information about Kulachi and three relatives.

He had each of his fellow travelers pose for a photo, took one of himself and uploaded them. Moments later, Asar watched with admiration as X used a razor blade to cut out pictures he'd printed out and paste them carefully onto the fake travel papers.

"Have you done this before, Ali?" he asked.

"I've seen it done," he said. "Is Akeem back with the laminator?"

"Yes, he got one from the print shop."

"Get it from him will you."

Asar nodded and as he rose, he marveled, "You are a man of many hidden talents."

X grinned. "I may take this up as a second career."

Harry glared at X, who responded with a wink.

*   *   *

Harry was to pose as Hussein Kulachi, a carpet merchant returning to Pakistan from business in Kabul. The vehicle was already laden with Oriental rugs, lying over the cache of weapons. Traci was his wife Ghazala, X his brother Asan and Asar his nephew Raheem. The cover story was that they were taking the pass to avoid taxes and, with the small bag of diamonds they'd brought for the occasion, were prepared to pay bribes. Their benefactors also gave them $900 U.S., from a stash of petty cash provided to the cell by the Warriors of Allah.

"I will hold the papers," Harry said, taking them out of X's hands.

Traci surrendered hers obediently.

"I should have made myself the husband," X whispered to her. "I have three specific marital duties I'd like you to perform."

"Keep dreaming," Traci hissed back.

Harry then insisted that they rehearse their roles and, like a schoolmarm, quizzed them on details of their fictitious lives garnered from the social networking site.

"What is your occupation?" he asked X.

"A carpet merchant."

"Where were we married?" he asked Traci.

"In Haripur, Pakistan."

What village are you from?" he demanded of Asar.

"I was born in Girishk," Asar said without hesitation.

Harry consulted the documents. "Wrong, you are from Khalabat."

Asar smacked his forehead. "Ach, that is my parents' REAL home. I am sorry. I am not used to lying. Forgive me."

X rubbed his knee affectionately.

"It is an admirable trait that deceit does not come naturally to you," he said. "I have the same problem."

That prompted Traci to launch into a brief coughing fit. X smiled. He knew it wasn't on purpose; the agent didn't appear to have a sense of humor. But it came off like shtick from a sitcom, which he found somehow endearing.

By now, of course, the Americans and the Afghan army had

encircled the city. Fortunately, the terrorist cell had constructed a tunnel that ran beneath the city wall big enough to run the truck through. A suicide bombing on the other side of town would, hopefully, provide enough of a diversion for them to get away.

X watched as the plucky suicide bomber – or homicide bomber as Fox News preferred to call such workers – hugged his brethren and set off with a backpack.

"I think we are well prepared," Harry announced. "Let us get some rest. The sun will be setting in a few hours and we'll have the cover of darkness."

X looked out the window at the formidable mountains looming in the distance. It was hard to believe vehicles could scale them.

Chapter 17
THE FORGOTTEN WAY

Two days later, they were high in the Sefid Kow mountain range heading through the so-called Forgotten Way toward Pakistan. The truck was surprisingly hardy, making its way through the tight switchbacks and steep inclines with little difficulty. It took X a while to get used to the bumpy ride – it was like being an old sneaker bounced about a dryer.

The pass constantly twisted and turned, arbitrarily cut through the mountain by nature. The 30-foot cliffs on either side of the pass were seemingly impossible to scale. X thought of the countless other men on secret missions who must have passed this way over the centuries: Persians, Mongols, Tartars, Huns, Turks, British and Russian spies in the Crimean War.

The identity thief imagined soldiers of Genghis Khan high above them on the cliffs staging an ambush, raining arrows down on the road. Soviet troops had hunted Afghani freedom fighters here; drug dealers and smugglers had sneaked through with their illicit wares. And now this motley crew of liars: terrorist hunters pretending to be terrorists pretending to be carpet merchants.

They drove until sundown, when the sparse vegetation lining the road became slowly invisible. As darkness fell, it became increasingly difficult to make out the canyon walls on either side of the trail. There was a half moon, but the light was obscured by a dense cloud cover. Clearly, they could go no farther.

They made camp on the side of the road. Their benefactors in Gardez had supplied them with two Russian-era tents presumably snatched from the invaders long ago, one to accommodate Traci, the other for the three men. The trio had to crowd in so close, X found his comrades' body odor unbearable. His wasn't any better, he supposed. None of them had bathed for days; not since a sponge bath by a nurse in the prison hospital.

*   *   *

X was about 150 feet from camp when Harry caught up with him.

"Where the hell do you think you're going?" the computer ace demanded.

"I'm not going anywhere. I'm having a smoke," X replied. He took the pack of Turkish cigarettes from his pocket and held them up.

"Bullshit," Harry hissed. "You're headed back toward Gardez, aren't you?"

"Don't be ridiculous," X said. "Do you have any idea how far that is?"

"Don't get any ideas about going AWOL," Harry snarled. "There's a tracking device planted in your body. We can track you down anywhere in the Middle East."

"You're full of shit. Where?"

"None of your business where. I'm not going to tell you so you can pull it out."

X remembered the filling Mr. Jones had so generously replaced. Nice information to keep under his cap. Harry strode up to him and jabbed his finger in his chest.

"Listen, asswipe, I don't like you and I don't trust you. As far as I'm concerned, you're a cowardly, sniveling piece of shit. If it wouldn't jeopardize the mission I'd shoot you right now."

"I'm hurt that you feel that way," X said. "Because I really like you."

"What's going on?"

They turned and saw Asar, who stood nearby scratching his balls.

"Nothing," said Harry.

"I heard you arguing," the teen insisted.

Harry shook his head, trying to appear clueless, but X leapt in.

"It is just a disagreement between friends," he said. "You know the proverb, 'The wrath of brothers is fierce and devilish.'"

Asar looked from face to face, concerned.

"Beware that you do not utter words you will regret. For it

THE IDENTITY THIEF 143

is also said that 'The wound of words is worse that the wound of a knife.' "

The two men nodded somberly.

"Let us embrace," X said. He grabbed Harry in a bear hug and the spy did an impressive job of faking enthusiasm as he returned the embrace.

The trio returned to the campsite, Asar entertaining them with a traditional Afghani song as they made their way through the dimly lit canyon, the crescent moon over their heads.

The first bandit X spotted was the one holding Traci in a chokehold, the seven others came from behind them, Kalashnikovs pointed at their heads.

"On your knees," barked a tall, gaunt man with a scar stretching from his right eye to his top lip. Harry and X dropped to their knees and a bandit stood behind each of them, rifles pointed to their heads. Asar hesitated. An impatient 6-foot-4 thug grabbed him by the nape of the neck and forced his face into the dirt.

"Search the truck," said Scarface, whom X took to be the leader. Three of the highwaymen held the trio in place while four others searched the truck.

With the captives subdued, the leader strutted back and forth like a rooster newly crowned king of the barnyard.

"You should know you need permission to pass through these mountains. You camp a stone's throw from our base? We will have to teach you respect."

"We are but simple carpet merchants on our way home to Pakistan. That is my brother and his wife, and our nephew," X offered. "We know we have to pay a bribe to pass this way. Here, in my pocket."

The man guarding X dug greedily into his pocket and yanked out the bag. He poured the gems into his hand and whistled.

"There must be $1,000 worth here," he gasped.

Harry shot X a dirty look. "How was that smoke, Aban?" he asked.

"Here!" said the leader. His henchman, somewhat reluctantly, tossed the bag over.

Traci had been rousted from a deep sleep by the bandits about five minutes before X and the others returned to the camp.

She was clad in a white cotton slip that fell nearly to her knees – supremely modest by Western standards – but still felt nearly nude without the veil and heavy garb she'd become accustomed to over the past few days. The guy guarding Traci held her in the chokehold VERY close. To her disgust, she became aware that he'd sprouted an erection, which was now lewdly poking her backside.

The men searching the back of the truck tossed out the carpets, and soon found the Kalashnikovs, the AK-47s, the grenades and the rocket launcher.

"You still claim you are merchants," Scarface said with obvious amusement. "Opium traffickers more likely. Where is your stash? Are you going to tell us or do we have to start checking bungholes?"

"We are in the service of the Warriors of Allah," Asar blurted. "I am the personal driver of The Chief."

"If you are enemies of the Americans, you should aid us," Harry added.

"Well, you see, I'm not very political," Scarface informed them. "I prefer sports. Did you see the game between New Zealand and Brazil? The satellite reception isn't very good here in the mountains, but we saw the second half. A great game."

His men laughed.

"You are a Tajik and that one is a Pashtun," Harry said. "I am a Saudi. But we all have a part in the struggle."

"You fools want to be martyrs, don't you? And receive your 77 virgins?" Scarface said, then spat contemptuously. "You will have your chance to bed your heavenly harem shortly."

The appeal to religious solidarity didn't seem to be working all that well, but Harry carried on undeterred.

"You cannot frighten us. Being killed in the cause of Allah is a great honor," he said. "The Prophet tells us, 'I wish to fight for Allah's cause and be killed, I'll do it again and be killed, and I'll do it again and be killed.' We yearn for this kind of death as much as you yearn to live."

Scarface bowed. "I am glad to be of service, then. I will be happy to grant your fondest wish. But first you'll tell us where the cash is. I know they sent you with some American money in addition to the diamonds."

One of the men jumped off the truck,

"Look what I found," he said, excitedly holding up Harry's laptop.

One of the others leaned over his shoulder and whistled. "It's a beauty!"

Harry tried to struggle to his feet and was promptly shoved back down. That laptop was critical to the mission.

"Be careful with that," he shouted.

"What is this for?" the leader demanded.

"Video games," X said.

Scarface laughed. "You have a good sense of humor. I'll kill you last."

"We use it to communicate with The Chief," Harry explained.

"Thank you for the gift," Scarface said, waving the laptop. He winked at X. "I am partial to Grand Theft Auto myself."

Meanwhile the man holding Traci continued to take liberties. He put his right hand on her breast and began to squeeze it, as if he were testing a tomato for ripeness.

"You are their leader," Traci called to Scarface. "Are you going to let a good Muslim woman be molested by this son of a pig?"

"As I said, you people must learn respect," Scarface replied. "And the first lesson will be how to treat a woman. I'm certain your husband will learn a lot from watching us."

Now having been given the green light so explicitly by his leader, the bandit restraining Traci grew bolder. He stuck his hand between the agent's legs and began groping her.

"Don't worry, you'll have her back when we're done with her," Scarface told Harry. "And there are only eight of us."

"Do you not fear the wrath of Allah?" Asar cried.

Scarface knelt beside the teen. "I am sure that you are a religious man and will do your duty. You will obey Sharia, your holy law, and stone your sister-in-law to death for her sin of 'adultery.'"

Asar struggled in fury, but his huge guardian had him firmly by the neck. Another bandit – a dwarf no taller than three feet – climbed off the truck with the box of cash.

"Got it," he shouted.

"Count it," Scarface commanded.

The little man opened the box and began to count, "$100 … $200 … $300 … "

X thought back to the dwarf who worked as a barker for the Pink Panther. This fellow was even shorter, he thought.

The man behind Traci slid his rough, callused hand up under her skirt and began stroking her inner thigh. She gasped as his middle finger entered her.

"Don't be afraid," he murmured in her ear. "We won't kill you, just the others. I am probably a lot bigger than your little husband, but I will be slow and gentle with you."

"$600 … $700 … $800 … " the pint-size henchman was counting. "$900!"

"Next week, we'll eat steak at the finest restaurant in Kabul, my friends," the bandit leader exclaimed in delight. "And be entertained by the best whores in town." He glanced at Traci and as if loathe to give offense, bowed and corrected himself, "I mean belly dancers."

"Listen," X said. " I am Ali Nazeer, a valued operative of the Jihadist Brotherhood. Deliver us to The Chief and he will reward you handsomely."

Scarface's jaw dropped.

"Hey, we saw a story about this guy on CNN," one of his men said.

"I remember. Well, well, well. That casts a new light on things. What do you mean by 'handsomely'?"

"We are close allies. I am sure he would pay a million for my safe return."

The bandits began to chatter excitedly.

"An interesting proposal," Scarface said. "I wonder how much the Americans would pay?"

"Perhaps more," X said. "But do you want to be known in these mountains as the man who collaborated with the Americans and turned over their worst enemy to them?"

Scarface stroked his chin thoughtfully.

A few feet away, the bandit's thick, dirty finger was stroking in and out of Traci, very rapidly and very deep. Her breaths became heavy. It was the first time she'd been touched by a man down there in over a year.

"Do you feel me behind you?" he whispered, thrusting forward for emphasis. It was a stupid question, because the guy was hung like a donkey. Slowly, she began to rotate her ample behind against him. He gave a grunt of satisfaction.

"I am going to show you how a Pashtun makes love to a woman," Donkey Dick whispered. "How you will cry out with pleasure when I split you in half!"

Traci reached under her slip and placed her hand firmly on his, sinking her nails into his flesh. She moaned audibly.

"She loves it," her captor announced to his associates. "She's wet as a duck in a pond."

The bandits began to chortle.

Asar roared in fury, "Get your hands off her, you pigs. Allah will see that you all burn in the fires of hell."

The man holding him by the nape of the neck shook him with a loud guffaw.

"It's your own tight little ass you have to worry about, pretty boy," the huge bandit said. "We'll make a woman of you next."

It was hard to tell whether this was mere taunting or the big bruiser truly had libidinous intent. In any event, the teen's eyes widened in horror.

X squinted for a better look at Traci and saw that tears were running down her cheeks, which were bright red. Come on, was the uptight FBI agent really getting turned on by the touch of some hairy, one-eyebrowed thug? He'd sensed it had been a long time since she'd gotten laid, but still …

I always suspected you had a freak flag, doll, but what a time to fly it!

The bandit leader strutted over to Harry and patted him on the shoulder.

"It looks like you've married a true slut, my friend," he told the kneeling man. "You haven't been taking care of things at home, eh? Don't worry, we'll handle it from here."

Harry turned away, as if refusing to witness his "wife's" debasement.

Scarface stepped toward Traci. The woman, whose hand was lost under her dress, caressing her captor's hairy wrist, bowed her head in shame. Scarface tipped up her chin to look her in the eyes.

"Are you ready, sweet flower?" Scarface asked, grinning and grabbing his crotch like a gangsta rapper. "You know the leader's turn is always first."

"I'm ready," she whispered. "And you will be first."

The agent pulled the Beretta from its holster strapped to her inner thigh and came up firing. She put the first round in Scarface's heart. With the next five shots she dropped four of the other bandits, each a perfect forehead headshot, and winged the one holding Asar in the shoulder. The big guy was the only one who got even a chance to scream, scrambling to his feet and racing down the road like a jackrabbit.

When she'd emptied the gun, she flipped Donkey Dick over her shoulder and as soon as he crashed into the ground, she brought the butt of the weapon swooping down to cave in his skull.

Harry sank his teeth into the hand of the bandit holding him. As the guy released his hold, the agent executed a textbook judo flip of his own, and then expertly twisted the bandit's neck until it snapped with a sickening *CR--ACK!*

The man holding X keeled over dead, Traci's bullet in his right eye socket. All this took place in the space of less than five seconds.

"Nice performance," X told Traci, standing and brushing dust off his knees. "How will I ever know if you're faking it?"

"He's getting away," Harry said, pointing to the wounded bandit.

Asar scrambled on the ground for a gun. "I will send that sodomite to hell," he cried.

Traci coolly picked up the rocket launcher and aimed it at the cliff which the sole surviving bandit was desperately trying to scale, about 20 yards away. She released the firing mechanism and the missile took off. A second later there was an explosion in the distance and nothing was left of the bandit but smoke.

Asar, kneeling, looked up at her in amazement.

"You are a goddess," the teen gasped reverently.

X stepped beside her and whispered, "Very Sylvester Stallone of you."

*   *   *

They found the bandits' hideout less than 300 yards away. The mouth of the cave was about halfway up a steep incline, concealed by bushes. If it hadn't been for an empty vodka bottle left at the foot of the slope, they would never have seen it.

After a short passage they had to hunch over to squeeze through, the mouth opened up into a huge cavern with a span of more than 200 feet. At the back wall of the cave, a trickle of water flowed down the rocks and dribbled into a little black pool. Their flashlights revealed dozens of carvings, pictograms recounting a forgotten battle waged countless eons ago.

Searching the bandit's stores they found some American-made weapons, an Uzi and crates filled with plastic-wrapped bundles of opium. Roped in a stall were eight donkeys.

"Allah is merciful. We can use the animals from here on," Asar said. "The terrain is becoming difficult to traverse by truck. We would have had to continue on foot."

Next the teen came across a box chock full of pornography that seemed to have originated in India. Bare-breasted, brown-skinned girls with diamond studs decorating their noses leered into the camera as they shed their saris. Asar's eyes bulged. X had the distinct feeling he'd never seen a topless woman before, let alone one naked with her legs akimbo.

Harry took the box from him. "We should burn this trash immediately."

Asar looked mournfully at the stack of porn, then nodded. "We must not let our hearts be contaminated by such filth."

"I'll take first watch," X said.

He sat close to the entrance, a Kalashnikov on his knee, positioned so that he could put a shot in the head of the first uninvited visitor. Of course, he'd never fired a gun in his life – he hadn't even carried one. Con men who did were a disgrace to the profession in his view. Hadn't thrown a punch since seventh grade for that matter. Some boy had said something about his mother.

What had he called her?

Traci settled down beside him, still wearing her face piece. "I thought you were asleep," he said.

"Harry told me you tried to escape last night."

"That's an exaggeration," he replied. "I was taking a walk. A long one."

She shook her head.

"I don't get you. Don't you care about your country? Don't you care about anything other than yourself? If The Chief gets his hands on a nuke, millions of Americans could die. Innocent children in New York, in Los Angeles, in Kansas could be incinerated."

"I guess I'm lucky I'm over here then."

"Why are you so goddamned selfish?"

"Because I'm a criminal,"

"That's no explanation."

"What, do you want my life story now?"

"I want to understand. Explain it to me like I'm a three-year-old."

X sighed. He stood up and leaned the gun against the wall.

"I've been on my own since I was 14 – that was the day my mother offed herself with sleeping pills. I never knew my father. He was some rich bastard who seduced Mother when she was working in his house scrubbing his toilets. She never told me his name. I do know that he was a big shot in the United States government. So do I say the pledge of allegiance to Uncle Sam every morning? No."

Traci had read about the suicide in his file. She could see in him the lost boy who'd just been told he'd never see his mother again. She stood up beside X and touched his hand gently.

"Robbing every rich man in America won't bring your mother back," she said.

"Keep my mother out of this," he said pulling away from her. He cursed himself for bringing Mother up. He'd never told the story to anyone, not a social worker, not a foster parent.

"And there's more to a man's identity than bearing his father's name," Traci went on. "You can define yourself by your actions."

He stared at her fiercely, nostrils flaring, then his face relaxed and he laughed.

"Are you one of those women who feel they have to 'save' a man, save his soul?" he demanded. "Are you some kind of missionary now?"

He smirked. "Or are you more interested in the missionary

position? That's it, isn't it? You want me to fall in love with or maybe just bone you. Gosh, did that little finger-fuck session get you that hot and bothered, honey? I know it's been a while, but try to keep it in your pants, for God's sake. Q needs to equip you girl spies with pens that turn into vibrators or something."

Traci snorted. "Don't flatter yourself, sugar. My flavor is chocolate."

"Really?" he said. "Well, then, why are you blushing?"

"I don't blush," she said.

He tore away her veil. And, sure enough, her face was flushed.

"You, you stinking, arrogant … " she stammered.

He grabbed her waist, pulled her close and planted his lips on hers. She pushed him away – but not far.

"Stop," Traci protested weakly.

He kissed her again, more aggressively now, and her bosom pressed up against his chest.

This is crazy, her robust superego lectured her. But it had been so, so long since she had been with a man, or been kissed by a man, beyond a perfunctory peck on the cheek at the end of a first and last date – or for that matter, had even been touched by a man except in a judo hold.

He pulled away and gave a mischievous grin.

"How do you know I'm not a 'brother,' by the way?"

"Yeah, right."

"Well, maybe part. And I'll be happy to show you which part."

"Hush your mouth."

It seemed like he was going to ruin the moment with more banter, but she used her mouth to shut him up. She slid her tongue into his mouth and wrapped it around his. Her hands found his shoulder blades and pulled him toward her so their groins ground together. She could feel him becoming aroused.

"What the hell do you think you're doing?"

Harry's voice startled them. They broke apart like high-school juniors caught necking in the janitor's closet by the principal.

"What kind of woman are you, that you would throw

yourself at this man so shamelessly?" he snarled. "Cover your face!"

"You're really staying in character as an uptight prick," remarked X, unflustered. "Are you a method actor?"

Harry railed on, as if the other man were invisible. "You're jeopardizing the mission. Asar is 30 feet away!"

Traci was too embarrassed to utter a word in her own defense. But X came to the rescue.

"Is that you talking, or the green-eyed god?" X suggested, casually picking up the rifle and resting it on his shoulder.

"Don't be absurd. I have a wife and three children."

"Methinks the gentleman protests too much," said X. "It looks like we have a love triangle on our hands."

Traci could barely resist a titter. The situation WAS like something out of high school. And Harry couldn't sound more jealous if he tried.

"Please don't fight over me, boys," she said.

"Don't flatter *yourself*," Harry said angrily. Then his expression changed, as if he regretted his choice of words. "I knew Jones was crazy to send a 'breast-fed' cherry on a mission this delicate."

"Excuse me," Traci snarled, facing off with him. "Breast-fed," as Traci knew only too well, was spy slang for a female FBI agent.

"You heard me."

"I will kick your puny unibrow ass from here back to Lebanon."

"That'll be the day."

She stepped close enough to feel his panting breath against her face.

"Listen, John Wayne. I am leading this mission until the minute I am killed or captured. So you will address me at all times with respect."

Harry stepped back. "Respect yourself," he mumbled.

Sobering words. She had indeed allowed herself to be flattered, to enjoy the sense that she was the object of desire, like a doe contested over by two smitten bucks. It was time to reassert her authority.

"Let's call it a night," she said brusquely. "I'll take watch."

She jerked the rifle out of X's hands.

*   *   *

Back in the body of the cavern, wrapped in a blanket beside the still-snoring Asar, X couldn't believe what had just happened. He had never revealed so much of himself to anyone.

His imprisonment had weakened him, he felt. He replayed the entire episode in his mind. He certainly hadn't intended to kiss Traci; he'd acted on impulse – something he rarely did. He'd done it punish her, to unseat her from her high horse. Prove she was no better than him. And it was indeed smug satisfaction he primarily felt as she surrendered to his kiss. At first. Then, as she responded so aggressively and she'd gotten him aroused, well, he felt something else.

He remembered the taste of her lips and the scent of her; no perfume of course – that would be offensive to Allah – but a clean, soapy smell. She hadn't bathed in days, none of them had. How did she manage that?

Feeling himself growing hard again, he shook off the memory. First rule of the game: never, ever fall for a mark.

He wondered, though, how far it might have gone had they not been so rudely interrupted by Harry. What a self-righteous jackass! Something the man had said irked him in particular, though X could not say precisely why.

"Don't flatter *yourself*," Harry had said. He'd echoed Traci's words.

Just how long had he been watching us? X suddenly wondered. *Spying on us.*

Chapter 18
PARANOIA

They continued through the canyon on donkeys. X, fortuitously, had learned to ride while impersonating a polo-playing Andover graduate for a scam. He'd taken riding lessons in New York's Van Cortland Park. Not quite the stable of Arabian stallions he'd told Asar about in prison, but good enough that he was at no risk of tumbling off.

Hooves echoed between the rocks around them as they made their way through the pass in single file. Asar was right; it would have been difficult to negotiate the narrowing ravine in the truck.

"How much farther?" Harry asked.

"Half a day's ride, no more," said the teen. "We are home-free."

A voice came over a bullhorn, echoing through the canyon a half dozen times: "Stop. Put up your hands."

This is getting old, X thought, sighing. The identity thief looked up. Guns were trained down on them from atop the ridges on either side. About 14 men. They wore the uniform of the ISI – the notoriously corrupt and brutal Pakistani security force.

Well, I suppose the good news is we've crossed into Pakistan.

Asar began to go for his rifle, but X grabbed his arm.

"There are too many of them, my young friend," he warned the teen.

"I am not afraid."

X shook his head. "Bravery without wisdom is not bravery."

The travelers tossed their rifles to the ground and held up their hands. A moment later, several of the Pakistanis had scrambled down the slopes and surrounded them. A few remained atop the ridge, still training weapons at them, with sweaty fingers on triggers. They seemed rather jittery to X and it was easy to imagine one of the barely legal young soldiers firing by accident.

Harry told the ISI troopers they were merchants returning from Afghanistan, having sold their wares, and once again the cover story fell flat.

The officer in charge, who identified himself as Captain Hesbani, raised his eyebrows with skepticism and ordered them searched. The Pakistani troopers didn't make the same mistake as the bandits. As well as frisking the men they brusquely searched Traci. She protested, to no avail, when Captain Hesbani personally slid his hand between her thighs.

"Aha!" he exclaimed as he produced the little handgun. "Is this for hunting mountain goats?"

"We're with the Warriors of Allah," Asar volunteered, proudly puffing up his chest. "Our weapons are for fighting the enemies of Islam."

Captain Hesbani expectorated noisily, just as the bandit boss had done.

"My brother was murdered by you fanatics," the officer informed them. He turned to his men. "Chain up these pieces of crap and take them down the road to the trucks."

His men jumped to obey.

"Wait. We're American intelligence officers," X said in perfect English.

Traci turned to him. "Shut up!"

"I'm going to personally kill you," Harry exclaimed.

"It's the only way, Traci," X said. She gasped at his use of her name.

Captain Hesbani raised his eyebrows.

"I suppose you have identification papers to prove this."

"Don't be ridiculous. Suppose we were searched?" X explained.

Traci spoke in Urdu, the national language of Pakistan: "Don't listen to him. He's gone mad from a fever."

"Traci, talk in English," X said. "The game's over." He winked at her.

Traci hesitated. They had nothing to lose at this point. "The rain in Spain falls mainly on the plain," she said in an exasperated voice.

"That was very good," said Captain Hesbani. "It might have fooled another man, but I happen to watch a good number of American DVDs. And I can tell that your very well practiced American accents are phony."

"That was the worst American accent I've ever heard," an underling concurred.

Another piped up, "Mine is better than that. Listen: 'Are you talking to me? Are you talking to me? Well, then, who are you talking to?' "

Another contributed a freakishly high-pitched impression of Chris Tucker in *Rush Hour:* "Can you hear the words that are coming out of my mouth?"

"That's more than enough," Captain Hesbani said, wearily running his hand through his hair.

"Wait a minute," said X, stepping forward. "Let me speak to you alone for a minute."

Captain Hesbani frowned, then gestured for his men to keep a close eye on the others. He walked with X a few yards from the soldiers, till the two were just out of earshot.

"Okay, you have outwitted us," X said. "We're not CIA. We're with the Jihadist Brotherhood and the Warriors of Allah, which as you must know are in close alliance. If you let us go free, we have a little gift for you."

"Go on."

"Over that hill, in a cave about two kilometers away, we've stashed five kilos of opium. Enough to get a few platoons high. Worth more than $500,000."

Captain Hesbani frowned dubiously. It was well known that the insurgents trafficked in opium to finance their operations, while vehemently condemning the use of drugs and alcohol as an offense to Allah.

"Take me there."

"Promise you'll set us free. All of us."

"Done. Let's go."

"Let my friends go first. "

Captain Hesbani laughed. "I don't think so. First the drugs."

"If I'm lying you can shoot me."

"What makes you think that I won't shoot you when I have the drugs?"

"You have an honest face."

Captain Hesbani smirked and they returned to the group. He announced that the others would be allowed to ride off on their donkeys, but X would remain.

"We're not leaving without him," Asar protested.

"Shut up and get lost before I change my mind and have you shot."

Harry whispered something in the teen's ear that convinced him it would be all right. X watched as the others, who'd been given back their weapons, mounted the donkeys. The captain gave Traci's horse a slap on the rump that conveyed an admixture of lechery and contempt.

The two men watched as the animals trotted down the road, past his men. X didn't trust the Pakistani officer as far as he could throw him. It was certainly possible he'd order his men to track his companions down and round them up in a few moments. All he could hope for was to give the others a decent headstart.

Captain Hesbani told his men to stay put. Then he ordered X into the back of his Jeep, nestled around the bend. A driver hopped in and they drove in the direction from which the travelers had come.

"So this is how The Chief and his cronies fund their glorious Jihad, selling opium, eh?" the Pakistani officer snickered. "This man of God is a filthy drug dealer."

"Be careful of how you speak of The Chief," X warned.

"I'll be careful of nothing, Mr. Nobody and Mr. Everybody," said the captain.

In 10 minutes' time they had reached the bandits' cave. X and Captain Hesbani climbed the steep slope, leaving the driver in the Jeep. X got to the opening first and reached to help the Pakistani up. They descended into the cavern.

"A bit Spartan," Captain Hesbani remarked with a sneer, at the sight of the cots and makeshift furniture. Egg crates served as chairs. A rickety wooden bookshelf did double duty as a pantry and grenade rack.

"Creature comforts mean little to me now," said X. "I've

found a cause to live for. You should do the same."

The officer grinned unpleasantly. "When you have the gun, I'll take advice from you." He gestured toward the crates with his pistol. "Where are the drugs?"

X knelt before one of the crates and, with some effort, pried it open. Captain Hesbani looked at the stash, his black eyes glistening like pearls.

"I didn't believe you," he said, marveling, as he held up a bag of opium.

"You should have greater faith in your fellow man," replied X.

"I must thank you for making me a very rich man." Captain Hesbani pointed the pistol at the American's head. "Since I know you are a religious man, I will let you say a prayer. You have one minute."

"You promised you would let me live."

"Your minute is flying by."

X dropped to his knees and feverishly began to utter a Muslim prayer. The scam artist had memorized a "stalling verse" for just such an eventuality – the longest he could find in the Koran. While he rambled on, the Pakistani lit a cigarette and stood calmly savoring it by the cave entrance.

"I've always wanted to retire to Venice," the officer said, his eyes growing misty. "To see all that magnificent artwork. I studied to be a painter, you know. But my father insisted that I drop out and take a 'real' job in his brother's factory. It's only by accident that I found myself in the military."

When X finished the first prayer, he segued quickly to another, continuing to improvise and embellish as long as he could.

"And may Allah watch over my children and my mother and my nephews and my nieces … "

Captain Hesbani had finished his cigarette and emerged from his reverie. "Wrap it up," the officer said. He ground the cigarette into the dirt with the heel of his boot.

"I'm not finished," X protested.

"In fact you are," said the Pakistani.

"Look, wait, wait," X said. He stumbled to his feet. "I really *am* an American. Not CIA. DEA. Drug Enforcement Agency, working undercover. My name is Jeremy Blinkhoff."

"It really doesn't matter to me if you are an American secret agent, a drug smuggler, a jihadist warrior or the King of Siam," Captain Hesbani said. "You've given me what I want and you have nothing to bargain with."

He pointed the gun at X's left eye.

"That's where you are mistaken, my friend," X pressed on. "There is more, much more opium than this nearby. Five drop-off points along a trail extending from here to Kabul. We're talking in the neighborhood of $15 million. I can take you to them one by one."

Captain Hesbani shook his head. "Tut. Tut. Tut. You should have let your last words been a prayer, not a lie."

X closed his eyes and a deafening gunshot echoed off the walls.

When he opened his eyes, he was relieved to find himself alive and the Pakistani officer lying dead on the cavern floor. A bullet hole bisected his brow. Harry stepped into the light, a wisp of smoke trailing from the .45 in his hand.

I didn't know you cared," X said.

"Don't get any ideas," said Harry. "You're key to this mission."

"How did you get back here?"

He pointed up.

"I came on horseback along the ridge. The others are waiting for us up ahead."

"What about the driver?"

"I've already taken care of him."

"Well, I owe you one, sport."

"Whatever. I'm sure you wouldn't have pulled that stunt if you weren't pretty sure I'd come for you. Let's get out of here before those goons come looking for their commanding officer."

X stepped over Captain Hesbani's body and headed to the cave entrance.

Looks like you'll ncver see Venice, he thought.

*   *   *

Back on the donkeys, the party continued down canyon.

Asar, riding beside X, remarked, "For what it is worth, I think your American accent was very good. It was worth a try."

X punched him in the shoulder with good humor.

"It's no compliment to say I've mastered the Great Satan's tongue," he said. "Let us pray that the day will soon come when English is no longer spoken in the Persian Gulf."

*   *   *

By late morning they had emerged from the canyon and vistas beyond the walls of the pass soon came into view. Snow-capped peaks soared beyond rolling hills. Below the trail there was a narrow strip of green surrounding a river that meandered through the rocks into a sprawling valley. The rich green stood in stark contrast to the shades of brown they'd left behind. In the middle of the valley stood a small town.

"The town of Jafuzi," Asar told the others. "The people here are friends of the Cause."

They rode down the winding path toward the village. As they approached the town, they saw young men on horseback playing Buzkashi, popular among the tribes on both sides of the border. Similar to polo, it's played by horsemen each trying to grab a goat carcass and use it to score a goal.

When the men saw the four strangers approach, they continued to play, but one veered off and raced toward the village. He returned a moment later with a man who was, presumably, a village elder. The somber-looking fellow wore a black turban adorned with gold. When he recognized Asar, a broad smile spread across his face. The two men dismounted and embraced.

"Young warrior, I did not think I would ever see your face again," the elder said.

"It is good to see you again, noble Fawad," the teen replied. "I will never forget that it was you who recruited me into the Jihad."

Asar introduced the others, paying special attention to X.

"Fawad, this is the man responsible for my escape, with the

help of Allah. Ali Nazeer."

The tribal chief shook Ali's hand vigorously.

"I have heard all about you," he said. "The CIA tried to suppress the news of your escape – how you made fools of the Americans. But it is all over Al Jazeera."

X bowed humbly. "It is you who fight unobserved who are the engine of the Jihad," he said. False humility seemed to work wonders with these folks; Fawad beamed with pride.

"Come, follow me to my house," he said. "You will be my personal guests tonight."

*   *   *

Though the exterior was as humble as all the rest in the village, Fawad's house was well appointed. Vases lined the shelves; Oriental rugs that would go for 10,000 bucks in the U.S. adorned the floors. There was, much to X's delight, even a toilet, albeit in another small building apart from the main dwelling.

They sat around a table, dining on traditional foods. On the menu was *paloa*, a rice dish given a rich brown color by caramelized sugar, *nadroo*, an onion-based stew with yogurt, roots, *dolma*, stuffed grape leaves and *londi*, a kind of spiced jerky.

X had difficulty stomaching the londi, and barely managed to avoid puking, but dutifully complimented Fawad's wife. Traci eagerly asked for recipes and the burqa-shrouded woman was clearly ecstatic about the attention.

The discussion turned from food to politics, a topic X would have preferred to avoid. Mr. Jones had briefed him on the intricate relationships between the governments of Pakistan and Afghanistan, and he'd pretended to listen, but those kinds of details always bored him. He had consistently received C's in social studies in high school.

Fawad was intrigued by "Ali Nazeer's" background of wealth and privilege.

"Your family is so close to the royal family of Kuwait," he observed. "Do they approve of your involvement in the Brotherhood?"

X shook his head. He *did* recall that Mr. Jones had briefed him on the bitter feud between the real Nazeer and his brothers.

"They have pressured me to cease my efforts," he explained. "Their companies did a lot of business with the royal family, but because of my activities, the king has cut them off. They sent me my uncles, my nieces, even my mother a dozen times asking me to stop and return to Kuwait and make an agreement that would keep me a free man."

"You could be living like a king," Fawad marveled. "Enjoying fast cars, yachts, all the trappings of wealth. Instead you choose to fight alongside us in these mountains, like bin Laden himself. You are truly like a martyr of old."

"Hopefully not a martyr anytime soon," X joked.

His host laughed. "Agreed."

Then, more solemnly X went on. "How can I enjoy luxuries when my brothers are oppressed by the Americans, the Zionists and their lapdogs?"

Harry stood up. "Speaking of luxuries, I think I'll take advantage of the modern plumbing."

Slinging the knapsack bearing his laptop over his shoulder, he slipped out of the room.

They continued talking about politics for a moment, Fawad railing about the latest outrages of the Israelis in what he called "occupied Palestine."

After enduring the tirade for a few moments, X excused himself, quietly beckoning Traci to follow him.

X reached the little building that housed the toilet, looked around to make sure no villagers were watching, then grabbed the door and wrenched it open. Harry sat on the john, his trousers around his ankles and his laptop on his knees. He looked up in shock at X.

"What is wrong with you?" he demanded, falling into English. "Can't you see I'm taking a dump?"

X grabbed his feet and dragged him off the commode.

"What the fuck?! Are you insane?" Harry shouted.

When he saw Traci standing there, he tried to cover his privates with one hand, while clutching the laptop with the other. "Can't a man have some privacy when he surfs for porn?"

X yanked the laptop from him. "Nice try, Harry, but you're

not a hard enough man to pull that one off."

He handed the laptop to Traci and pointed to an outgoing email. She couldn't make out the words, which appeared to be in code, but the names of the villages they'd passed through were there, along with a map.

"He's been updating them on our location every step of the way," X said triumphantly.

Traci stood back and stared, stunned, at Harry, who was hastily pulling up his pants.

"Christ," she gasped. "He's a triple agent."

"That's ridiculous!" Harry sputtered. "A triple agent? Why not a quadruple agent – that would make me back on your side, wouldn't it? Honestly, you're being paranoid."

"Paranoid?" Traci shot back. "There's an agency so secret the President doesn't even know about it, and we're working for it – at least *I'm* working for it. So paranoid makes a whole lot of sense right now."

"I've had enough of this," Harry said. He reached for the laptop and tried to touch the power button.

"Touch that computer and I'll put a bullet through your brain," Traci said, pulling her Beretta and pointing at him. "Keep your hands where I can see them."

"For God's sake, woman, they could come around that corner any minute," Harry said, holding out his hands palm up and to his sides. "Stop pointing that thing at me." He added, "I know an FBI agent isn't going to shoot me in the head."

She lowered the gun.

"A bullet in your testicles, then."

"Let me see the screen," said X. She passed him the laptop.

"All that superpatriotic B.S.," Traci muttered, shaking her head in disbelief.

"What are you talking about?" Harry asked, doing his best to look bewildered.

X began to laugh, till tears ran down his cheeks.

"Let us all in on the joke," Traci said, her weapon pointing unwaveringly at Harry.

"Those are Hebrew words," X said. "Holy smokes, you're Mossad."

"That's nonsense. Now I insist –" Harry began.

Traci cut him off. "You're in no position to insist on anything."

"This is crazy," Harry whined. "When Mr. Jones hears about –"

"Oh, knock it off, you're busted," X said. "Do you want us to be at this all night?"

Harry sighed. "Yes, of course I'm Israeli intelligence."

"Well, *shalom,*" said X, bowing.

Traci returned her weapon to her holster, flashing a generous helping of brown thigh in the process.

"Jones said you were recruited by the CIA in high school," she said, shaking her head in bewilderment.

"I'm second generation," Harry explained. "Israel recruited my parents in college. They changed their background from Jewish to Lebanese Christian back in the '70s."

Traci was dumbfounded. "I knew the Russians did that kind of thing, but the Israelis?"

"I knew something wasn't kosher about this guy," said X. "So to speak."

"What's your mission?" Traci demanded.

"Simply to observe and report."

"I vote we plug him now," X said.

"This isn't a democracy," Traci snapped.

"Can we talk alone?" Harry said to Traci. "Without this idiot? He can't be trusted."

"Oh, you're funny," Traci said, bitterly. "Give me one reason why I shouldn't waste you right now?"

"I'll give you two. Number one, you need me to complete the mission – unless you're a computer expert, which isn't in your file."

It irked Traci that he'd been given access to her 203 file, while she hadn't been allowed to see his.

"Number two, we're allies. Israel and the U.S. have a special friendship that dates back more than 50 years."

"With friends like these …" X muttered.

"Last time I checked, espionage was still a capital offense," said Traci.

But Harry, emboldened, put down his hands. "This is

getting boring," he said smugly. "Either shoot me or let me file my report."

"How about neither of the above," Traci shot back. "We go forward with the mission, and when it's complete, and we're back in Washington, *then* Uncle Sam will decide if you get to report back to your boss in Tel Aviv – or go to prison."

"Yeah, maybe you'll end up sharing a cell with Jackson Pollock," X added, crossing his arms.

"That's Jonathan Pollard, moron." Harry said. "Jackson Pollock is the artist."

"Right ... well both of you are drips," X said, the best comeback he could muster.

"Fine, I accept the terms of the agreement. May I have my laptop back, please?"

"It's not an agreement, it's an order," Traci said. She gestured to X. "And he'll hold onto the laptop until I say so."

X took the laptop. "And be sure to wash your hands, Harry," he said. X and Traci turned to go – and received an unpleasant surprise when they bumped into Asar coming around the corner.

How much did he hear? X wondered.

"You can't fool me any longer. I know exactly what's going on," Asar announced.

Harry tensed. Out of the corner of his eye, X could see him positioning himself for an attack. He remembered how swiftly the Israeli agent had snapped that bandit's neck. The thought of that happening to Asar dismayed him.

Traci was already reaching for her holster. X stepped between them and the teen.

"Oh, really," the identity thief said, his voice betraying nothing but amusement. "And what is that, my friend?"

"The two of you have been quarreling over the woman."

The two men traded glances, then in unison nodded sheepishly.

The youth lectured them. "I know it is natural for us to be attracted to one who is so beautiful and brave and virtuous as this," he said. "But we cannot let emotions harm our cause. "Recall the proverb, 'Love makes a man both blind and deaf.' "

Harry's body relaxed.

X ruffled Asar's hair yet again. "Don't worry about the two of us," he said. "We have no intention of killing one another – yet. They say sometimes even the intestine and the stomach disagree."

*   *   *

Lying on her tummy on Copacabana Beach in Rio de Janiero, flaunting her slimmed down tush in a thong, Samantha Adamson was updating her Facebook page. Not hers, exactly, but a creation of hers named Cassandra. Unlike Samantha, Cassandra had always been slim and sexy and had been a cheerleader in high school as well as homecoming queen. She worked as a consultant and had a pet dog.

Sam was almost broke now, having burned through the $100,000 in cash she managed to flee the apartment with. Trying to access the nest egg in the Caymans with all this federal heat would be foolhardy. But she was content. She had found a kid who was handy with electronics to make a gadget to attach to gas station card readers and ATMs for "skimming." When a user swiped their debit or credit card, her own reader would snatch banking information off the magnetic strip. It was a ruse she and her former partner had been using just before the Ali Nazeer fiasco.

One of X's brainstorms was to extend the concept to the airport kiosks you use for getting boarding passes. She was hoping to try the idea out at Rio's main airport. Technically, it would present little problem. The thing was working up the nerve to plant the scanner in an area teeming with cameras and airport police. In theory, it would be easy to appear to fumble with her credit card at the kiosk to cover the placement, but in practice it would be tricky. It would be a few months before all the details were worked out and money would start rolling in.

Yet her heart was content, thanks to her Brazilian boyfriend – her "Aztec Prince" as she gushed to her Facebook friends (off by a few thousand miles, but love has poor geography). Santiago was not only a better lover than her ex, he treated her like a queen – even before she lost weight he told her she was beautiful.

When the "Dear Honey Hips" email arrived, Sam was stunned to see who it was from. Incensed, in a way, that he had reentered her world. She knew the writer's true name – or rather, thought that she did – but in her mind now he was simply The Soulless Black Hole. Bad memories from what she dubbed her "old fat days" when she, frankly, hated herself came rushing back.

But when she saw how much money he was offering for a "little favor," as he but it, her green eyes brightened and felt a familiar sensation between her legs, as hot as the Brazilian sand.

She looked out at the ocean as Santiago emerged from the sea, a bare-chested Adonis. He flashed his gleaming teeth and she smiled back.

Chapter 19
DOWN THE RABBIT HOLE

The next morning, Harry and X saddled the donkeys in Fawad's barn. Traci was over at the well, filling a water bucket for the animals, while Asar chatted with Fawad nearby. The pair embraced, then Asar strolled over to them, an odd smile on his face that X found disconcerting.

"Asar, come help us pack the donkeys," said Harry, who seemed not to notice the boy's creepy expression. "We need food and water for the rest of our journey."

Asar shook his head. "There will be no need for that."

X and Harry exchanged glances, perplexed.

Was he saying this was the end of the road? Had all that stuff about thinking his companions were caught up in a love triangle been a clever ruse? Does this mean he's blown the whistle on us to Fawad and we're all about to get shot?

"What do you mean, we do not need food or water?" X asked. "Is The Chief's stronghold that close?"

Asar gave a mischievous grin.

"The end of your journey is closer than you would ever imagine, boss. Come, follow me. Bring only your weapons and the computer."

The men slid their rifles off the donkeys. X loaded the knapsack bearing the laptop onto his back.

"Walk this way," Asar instructed them.

"What about the woman?" Harry asked.

"Women are forbidden," Asar told them.

When they reached the well, the teen explained that to Traci.

Traci frowned and told them, "My assignment was to escort you safely to the headquarters."

"Then your mission is at an end," Asar assured her. "I will never forget your courage."

"We will part company then," said Traci. "I will return to Afghanistan and report to my superiors."

She bowed to Harry and then to X. It seemed that something more was called for. A hug, at the least. But X gave Traci only a salute.

"I will tell The Chief how well you have served the Cause," he said.

Traci turned and headed back to Fawad's house. X watched her go, suddenly filled with an ill-defined yearning. The plan called for them to separate, but he had become accustomed to having her around. As much as he hated to admit it, he would miss her.

The men followed Asar to the small mosque at the center of the village. Along the way, they passed villagers rolling carts full of grain; a one-legged old man hobbling with a cane. The peasants nodded in greeting.

Their path took them by squealing children playing Aqaab, a version of tag where "It" was an eagle and the others pigeons he preyed upon. X was no believer in omens, but to his discomfort, he could not help thinking that in the parlance of old-school con artists, a "pigeon" was a mark who was easily fooled. Were the two of them being duped and about to be pounced upon?

"Are we going to pray?" Harry asked. But X had an inkling about what they'd meet behind the mosque doors.

Inside the modest temple, candles were lit and the walls were full of religious markings, swirling wheels within wheels. There were no paintings of Allah or Mohammed. Islam forbids such images as idolatry; that much X knew about the religion. There was no one else around but a prayer rug lay in place as if any minute a devout Muslim was about to kneel toward Mecca and pray. X and Harry looked around, mystified.

"Well," Asar challenged them. "Do you see it?"

X had a pretty good idea, but he humored Asar and shook his head. The teen knelt and pulled away the prayer rug, revealing a wooden trap door.

"The Americans have been in this mosque a half dozen times and never found this," Asar said.

X found this a bit surprising. It would have been the first place he looked. But then again, hiding money and other items was one of his specialties.

"After you, my young friend," he told Asar.

The three men descended a rickety staircase into blackness. X had by no means overcome his claustrophobia, but this was a good deal better than squeezing through their escape tunnel. For some reason, he was reminded of *Alice in Wonderland*. And he had a feeling The Chief's headquarters would be as topsy-turvy a universe as the Mad Hatter's.

About 18 feet down, they reached a tunnel. A huge high-intensity flashlight was hanging from a hook and Asar grasped it and flicked it on. The passageway was surprisingly wide, enough to accommodate all three men abreast, although they had to hunch over as they walked.

"The Warriors of Allah carved these tunnels out?" Harry asked in wonderment.

"The caves are natural but the passages were widened and many of the chambers expanded," Asar explained. "Bin Laden himself assisted us. He flew in heavy equipment from his father's construction empire. It is said he drove one of the bulldozers himself."

X pictured the legendary master of disaster piloting a bulldozer with a John Deere cap in place of his turban and found the image so comical – like Eddie Albert manning a tractor in a banker's suit in *Green Acres* – that he had to choke down a hysterical giggle.

They walked nearly 100 yards before they reached a checkpoint. There, two guards hurriedly got to their feet and shoved AK-47s in their faces.

"We are servants of The Chief," Asar told them.

"Yes, I recognize you. You are Asar, The Chief's old driver. Don't you recognize me? Omar."

Asar unslung his rifle and dropped it, then hugged the other man.

"Still, we need the password," said Guard No. 2.

"Peace," replied Asar without hesitation.

"And we must search you," Omar reminded the teen

somewhat apologetically.

"Of course."

They surrendered their weapons and allowed themselves to be frisked. Then they marched behind Omar down the passageway and entered a cavern.

X had imagined something more spectacular. Perhaps it was childish, but he'd literally pictured the bat cave, complete with giant computer mainframes. Still, the complex was extensive. They passed through a warehouse for military supplies including huge stockpiles of guns and ammunition, bazookas, artillery shells, rocket-propelled grenades, mines and stolen U.S., Afghan and Pakistani army uniforms. In another room, caches of water and food were stored. Next they passed through barracks with pillows and blankets scattered on the ground where dozens of men, presumably resting from their duties of killing and maiming, peacefully dozed.

"We have a state-of-the-art ventilation system and our own hydroelectric generators – three of them," Omar bragged as if he'd built them himself. "They run off an underground river."

"How many men?" Harry asked.

"1,200 fighters."

"1,203 now," Asar pointed out, and his old friend grinned.

After another 300 yards or so, Omar announced that they had reached the offices of The Chief. X held his breath. According to Mr. Jones, he and the real Ali Nazeer had never met. But the Committee had only just discovered that Ali was anything more than a reckless, selfish playboy. Who knew for sure?

The Chief emerged from behind the door. He was far older than in the file photos Mr. Jones had shared with him. But then, X supposed, that famous picture on the FBI's Most Wanted poster must be 10 years old. Apparently, he'd decided to age gracefully and not dye his beard like bin Laden.

"Where is my dear friend?" the old man demanded when he saw the newcomers.

Oh, drat, X thought. *Busted.*

But when The Chief spotted X, he shuffled hurriedly over and embraced him in delight, kissing the visitor on both cheeks for good measure.

"You are taller than I recalled," The Chief said. "But I saw you only from afar at the gathering in Kandahar."

At least 80, and decked out in what appeared to be pajamas, The Chief looked like the grandfather of a 7-Eleven clerk more than the head honcho of the world's biggest terrorist organization. In the Arab press, he was portrayed as a cross between Batman and Robin Hood. X had not expected someone so frail. Instead of the signature camouflage jacket, in which The Chief delivered his many video performances, he wore a red bathrobe. He reminded X of Hugh Hefner in his declining years.

"Your escape has been a great propaganda victory," The Chief declared. "You showed that despite all their millions of dollars in weapons, all their satellites and spies and drones, the infidels can be defeated."

He hugged Asar. "And you brought this brave one who is like a son back to me."

The Chief introduced a tall, gaunt, bespectacled man. The guy held his lips pursed in a manner that reminded X of a spinster librarian in a *Little Rascals* episode.

"This is Dr. Zawari, my second-in-command."

"I've heard many good things about you," X lied. "And this is my dear friend, Moammar, who aided us in our escape."

Dr. Zawari scrutinized them with an intensity that suggested X-ray vision. "Many have tried before to escape from Abd Al-Rahman Prison," he observed. "It sounded miraculous, indeed – almost too good to be true."

Harry began to explain, "Well, Allah was merciful … "

The Chief waved him away and chuckled. "Don't worry. Our sources in the prison confirmed all the details reported by Al Jazeera. Forgive my aide. Dr. Zawari was in the camp of el-Safvadi when the man was murdered by assassins posing as journalists. Having been bitten by a snake, he's afraid of a rope."

"I remember that incident well and understand," nodded X, who had no idea what the old man was talking about. "We must all be on our guard against deception."

"Dr. Zawari, please escort Asar to the dormitory and Moammar to the guest quarters," said The Chief. "Come walk with me, Ali."

X wouldn't have minded going to the guest quarters too.

But he obligingly accompanied the tottering terrorist bigwig into his office suite, noticing for the first time that The Chief wore fluffy bedroom slippers.

In the first of three rooms was a large table on which was laid out a huge topographic map of Afghanistan. Dozens of pushpins every color of the rainbow dotted the military map representing, X assumed, where The Chief's forces and those of his adversaries were stationed. X had only seen something like it in World War II movies.

I suppose if I were one of those spies with a photographic memory, I could commit it to memory, he mused.

Ushered into the next room, X beheld a small greenhouse lit by fluorescents. The identity thief inhaled the fragrances of dozens of unfamiliar flowers.

"This greenhouse is my pride and joy," The Chief said. "We grow many exotic plants here, some that the London Botanical Gardens would have cause to envy. Here, look at my blue forsythias."

"They are beautiful. What an accomplishment to cultivate such a garden underground," X marveled. But he was thinking, *a nine-foot-tall, man-eating Venus flytrap would suit you better. You're like a James Bond villain, but senile.*

The next door led to the terrorist leader's private study. There was a photo of The Chief posing arm in arm with his underling Bin Laden, and another between a pair of prominent Iranian mullahs. On his large, ornate mahogany desk a TV was tuned to Fox News, where an anchor was feverishly updating the public on the details of a celebrity's shoplifting trial.

His shelves boasted an impressive collection of books – perhaps 200 – and the variety surprised X: tomes on gardening, architecture, anatomy, Biblical archaeology, even home decor.

"It is as I have heard. You are truly Renaissance man," X said. The Chief beamed at that.

Whew! Wasn't sure the Renaissance was a good thing to you folks. Thought maybe the Dark Ages was more up your alley.

The terrorist leader proudly pointed to a row of six large tomes, set aside from the others on their own shelf. "Those are the ones I've written."

X examined the titles. *Poems for a New Afghanistan* was the name of one collection. *I Sing of Freedom* was another. *Thought the identity thief, You have to give the old coot credit for being upbeat.*

The old man took the book from X and thumbed through it until he reached a page bookmarked with a news clipping about a U.N. bombing in Libya. He handed the book back to "Ali Nazeer," gesturing with seeming diffidence that he should read it. The American, who was still more adept at speaking Arabic than reading it, slowly recited:

"My love for you is like a cloud from Heaven
That makes the desert bloom. Your fragrance is like
A mixture of lavender and honey,
And your touch is as pure as raindrops
That tap upon my skin."

It went on in that vein for another 40 stanzas. *A love poem,* X was startled to realize.

"Are you familiar with the works of Jalal al-Din Muhammad Balkhi?" his host inquired.

"Well, I've read a few of his works," the identity thief lied through his teeth.

"He is my model. Though of course my words are like the scribblings of a child next to such a master."

"I hope that years in the future, your books will sit on a shelf next to his," X said.

"You are gracious, but it is only a hobby," the old man said, returning the book to the shelf. "We hold *mushha'ra* competitions every Tuesday night. You are welcome to participate. You can get pen and ink from my secretary."

"You are most generous, Chief."

Great, a poetry jam with a bunch of Islamofascist lunatics, X thought. *Well, that should be entertaining. What's Wednesday's activity – Twister?*

The Chief guided him to a small desk in the corner on which a yellow legal pad rested. "This is what I'm working on now. I would be honored if you would take a look at it."

The simplicity of the language threw X a curve ball. But by the bottom of the first page, it became clear what he was looking at.

"Is this … "

"Yes, a children's book," The Chief said, with some excitement. "My first."

Skimming the text and the attendant stick-figure illustrations, X quickly gleaned that the villain was a Jewish golem who preyed upon the people of a village and ate them. The children defeat the monster by pelting him with magic stones.

"It is an allegory," he said.

"Very perceptive," smiled The Chief, clapping him on the back. "It instructs children about the wickedness of the Zionists at an early age. Forgive my primitive artwork. I will of course hire a professional illustrator."

Okay, that's just about enough bonding for one day, X felt. *Now it's time for the setup.*

"I bring a warning," X told The Chief. "The Americans have used all their means to seize some of my assets in the Caymans. I have had to transfer all that remains to a hiding place."

The Chief frowned and nodded sympathetically.

"I am concerned that they may use their cunning to go after the assets of the Warriors of Allah as well," X continued. "The CIA hacked into our computers to locate our funds and could easily do the same to you."

The Chief chuckled. "You have no reason to worry, my son. These walls are shielded by many feet of rock and we have sophisticated security safeguards and firewalls. Our assets are safe."

X frowned dubiously. "Well, that is welcome news. But always keep in mind the proverb, 'You cannot store milk in a sieve and complain of bad luck.' "

The Chief laughed. "This is true, my brother. Very true."

"It is my suggestion that you convert your funds to gold bullion so that the enemies of Islam cannot seize them with the touch of a button. Hide the gold where the Americans cannot find it. My organization has a facility in Uzbekistan where you could be safely store it."

The terror boss stroked his beard thoughtfully. "That is one possibility. Tell me, where is it that you have moved your own funds?"

X shook his head. "I am sorry, my honored friend. Even to you I cannot divulge that information."

The Chief looked a bit taken aback. Then he nodded. "I understand. Do not fret. You are my brother whom I trust and love." He hugged X.

After what X found to be an awkwardly long embrace, the old man released him. X pointed to the rock walls.

"How do you communicate with your followers? With all the shielding and the rocks? Surely cell phones don't work down here."

The Chief opened what appeared to be a cigar box on his desk and showed him a phone, plugged into a charger.

"It communicates with a relay box that is hardwired to antennae outside," he explained. "The signal bounces off four satellites so the Americans can't trace it. Or something like that, I'm not sure of the technical details. The point is that it allows me to communicate with my commanders in the field. One of my aides got the idea from a spy novel. Now, I have a surprise for you."

As noted earlier, X was not fond of surprises. And under these circumstances especially so. What other hobbies did this demented old murderer have? Water colors, perhaps or crochet? Perhaps he was about to be invited to a friendly game of Battleships.

"Your brother-in-law is here," The Chief said, beaming. "I have heard that the two of you have had many grand adventures together."

X felt his heart skip a beat.

"What? In the cave complex?"

"In the country. He will be here tomorrow."

"So soon?" X resisted the urge to gulp. "Truly, that is wonderful good news, Chief."

The pace of their mission would have to be accelerated. A lot.

*   *   *

X and Harry had been given a private room a stone's throw from The Chief's office – a considerable honor, they were given to understand – while Asar bunked in Dormitory Number 3.

When X told the Israeli spy about the imminent arrival of Ali Nazeer's brother-in- law, Haseem bin Aleel, he became anxious.

"You need to convince The Chief to transfer those funds,"

he demanded.

"You can't push a mark too hard or he'll back off," X pointed out.

"Mark? Stop thinking like a goddamned thief and start thinking like a spy," Harry fumed.

"Stop thinking like a spy and start thinking like a thief," X retorted. "Because that's what we're doing. Stealing stuff."

"So what's your plan?"

"I'm working on that."

"And what about the laptop? I need it."

X took it out of the backpack and held it in front of the Israeli, who sat on one of the two beds.

"You won't be able to get a signal out of here, so there's no harm you can do," he said.

"Harm *I* can do?"

"Just keep it under the bed," X told him. "I want to be able to check it and keep tabs on you, make sure you're not up to something outside the mission."

Harry fumed. "*Me* up to something? I'm not the criminal."

"You're not getting the laptop till you agree."

"Fine," snarled "Moammar" and yanked the computer out of X's hands.

Chapter 20
IN-LAW TROUBLES

That evening, he dined with The Chief, Dr. Zawari and two of his top aides. The Chief meandered back and forth between geopolitics, religion and popular culture. He decried as obscene the sensuality of films produced in both Hollywood and Bollywood, finding kissing scenes the most objectionable. Oddly enough, he seemed to have a soft spot in his heart for the actress Reese Witherspoon, whom he referred to reverently as "angelic."

Dr. Zawari gently interrupted the rambling monologue.

"Sir, we had scheduled a brainstorming session for tonight," he reminded The Chief.

"Yes, yes, you are quite right," said the octogenarian terror boss.

"Fareek, you are up first," Dr. Zawari said, turning to a young aide.

Fareek had a large hooked nose and oddly sensual lips that reminded X uncomfortably of a vagina.

He cleared his throat nervously and began, "My idea is that we infect prostitutes in Saudi Arabia, where the Americans have many bases, with the AIDS virus. When the U.S. soldiers sleep with them, they will catch the virus and die."

The physician sighed. "Anyone have an idea that isn't foolish?"

Fareek sank back in his chair, demolished.

Another aide, no more than 25, raised his hand timidly. He was the first terrorist X had encountered who was obese, probably tipping the scales at close to 300 pounds.

"Hamid?"

"Well, FAA regulations state that one is not allowed to bring more than four ounces of liquid on board a plane," he started out.

"Yes, yes, we all know that," Dr. Zawari said impatiently.

"Okay, so, so, so, s-s-s-s-s-s ... " Hamid launched into a bout of stuttering that lasted easily 45 seconds. The others waited patiently for it to end, Fareek politely making notes on a pad. Only Dr. Zawari rolled his eyes.

When the porky terrorist was finally able to continue, he said, "I apologize. So, my thought is that perhaps what we could do is place 10 men on the plane, each with three ounces of nitroglycerin, or something. Each one goes into the bathroom and pours his vial into the toilet. When the last man flushes ... "

"Kaboom!" said Dr. Zawari, clapping his hands in delight. "Not bad at all. You are finally learning to think, Hamid. Write that down, Fareek."

The full-lipped aide hastily jotted down the notion.

Dr. Zawari continued. "It needs some fine-tuning, of course. Our scientists need to devise the right explosive. Now, I have been working on a little scheme of my own ... "

The healer opened a folder and handed out copies of a six-page typed document full of diagrams and aerial photographs.

"Wait, I want to hear what Ali has to say," The Chief said. He hardly seemed to have been listening up to this point. Dr. Zawari looked positively apoplectic as all heads turned to X.

The identity thief hadn't expected to bring any fiendish grand designs to the table. But while the others ran their ideas up the flagpole, he had hastily gathered his thoughts.

"We all know that the Americans rely heavily on racial profiling to prevent attacks on airplanes," he said. "What if we begin a program of recruiting and training blond, blue-eyed Muslims from Bosnia to be martyrs?"

The others murmured in agreement.

"You are a genius!" cried The Chief.

Even Dr. Zawari grudgingly admitted that the idea had potential.

"It would be very expensive, of course, mounting such a recruiting campaign," he said. "But certainly, we should look into it. Now, my idea is – "

The Chief cut him off, abruptly changing the subject.

"I want all of you to hear the next speech I plan to make

in response to the American president's address at the U.N. condemning so-called terrorism," he said. "I feel his lies must not go unanswered."

Dr. Zawari opened his mouth to protest.

X didn't let him get a word in edgewise. "I would be so honored to hear it."

Dr. Zawari's eyes blazed with fury but he held his tongue. As his chief adviser sulked, the Chief stood up and embarked on his diatribe:

"Throughout history, America has never differentiated between soldiers and civilians," he pronounced. "Not even between adults and children. It was the United States, remember, who dropped the atomic bomb on Hiroshima. Consider the genocide they perpetrated against the Native Americans. They are the inventors of germ warfare. They used smallpox in blankets to exterminate their Indians.

"Their president condemns us as terrorists. But it is the Americans who are the true terrorists. They do not grant mercy to civilians. Therefore, nor should we. All of them, men, women, children, are legitimate targets, subject to the fatwa our religious leaders in their wisdom, have issued."

The aides nodded and raised their glasses in agreement; clearly the old man was preaching to the converted.

But the whole spiel sounded vaguely familiar. Suddenly X recalled that he'd seen virtually these same words on the screen in the Pink Panther strip club, in The Chief's last video. *Has this guy actually forgotten he'd said all this before?*

"What do you think, Ali?" The Chief asked.

X nodded gravely and said, "It is all well said. We must continue this battle, God permitting, until victory or until we meet God."

The Chief smiled. "That is very good. I must use that line too, if you don't mind my borrowing it. Make a note of that, Dr. Zawari."

The bespectacled physician, clearly miffed at being demoted to the role of secretary, looked as if his pen might snap in his hands. But obligingly, he took a small spiral notebook out of his breast pocket and took down X's line.

Or perhaps "FUCK YOU" in Arabic, X thought.

"The Russians in Afghanistan are the most wicked of the infidels, and though their might is great, the will of Allah is greater still," The Chief continued. "So decadent, with their vodka and their prostitutes. Their lack of morality will be their downfall."

X saw The Chief's aides eyeing each other uneasily and he realized that the old man had misspoken. He meant the Americans. Hamid raised a finger as if preparing to correct the aged leader, but Fareek shook his head.

Surprisingly, The Chief caught himself.

"I mean the Americans, of course. I am getting old," he conceded. "One day soon the Cause will need a new leader. Someone with courage and charisma. A young man with vigor like you, Ali."

Dr. Zawari did not look pleased. He was, X surmised, supposed to be next in line.

"I could never hope to fill your shoes, master," X protested.

"You will have others to give you guidance on tactics, like my loyal friend Dr. Zawari. You have become a folk hero. You will inspire many to take up arms against the Great Satan."

"I am but a tool of Allah," X said with a humble bow. "I will serve him in any capacity I am needed."

"You are much too modest," Dr. Zawari said. But he looked like he wanted to toss acid in X's face.

The good doctor was doubtless even more perturbed when the leader invited X back to his study for tea. With time growing short, the identity thief tried to turn the discussion back to money. His first few bids failed.

The Chief was more interested in hearing his thoughts on the newswoman Katie Couric, who, he was quite convinced, should interview him. Getting her to agree to cover her face for the on-camera chat might be a sticking point, The Chief fretted. X assured him that Miss Couric seemed quite reasonable and, after some negotiation, would probably agree to the condition. After all, The Chief was an important world figure whose opinions people around the globe would be anxious to hear.

Then he took another crack at it.

"You have built quite a war chest," X said. "We hear that

you have $45 billion."

"Money can build roads in the sea," The Chief said. "It has taken a long time to accumulate those funds – a lot of pleading with those stingy clerics in Jordan and Saudi Arabia. But it will allow us to accomplish a grand goal."

"My sources say you are close to obtaining a weapon to use against the infidels," X pressed on. "A biological agent?"

"Much more potent than that, my friend," The Chief said with a mischievous wink Tom Sawyer might have given Huck Finn. "You see, we do not seek to make war, but to make peace."

X frowned. "They say true peace is possible only after war."

"For one so young, you are full of wisdom," The Chief said. He gestured for X to sit down on the loveseat and poured him a cup of tea, then settled down beside him, so close their hips were touching.

"Have you ever heard of Weapon Z?" The Chief asked in a confidential whisper.

X shook his head. It sounded like something Spiderman might have to defuse.

"When the Americans developed the original atomic bomb," The Chief began, "before they tested it, the Manhattan Project scientists calculated that there was a one in 100,000 chance that splitting the atom in such a way would spark a chain reaction that would destroy the solar system."

X nodded attentively. He'd heard some story vaguely along those lines in high school and long ago discounted it as apocryphal.

"Well, in the 1970s, the Russians developed such a weapon," said The Chief. "It was a sort of doomsday device they could hold over the heads of the Americans as the ultimate deterrent to a nuclear war. And it indeed worked. That is why the world was spared a nuclear holocaust at the peak of the Cold War."

X could barely repress laughter. The whole thing was ludicrous on its face. Wasn't that doomsday device out of *Dr. Strangelove* or a *Get Smart* episode? Some fast-talking arms merchant was about to soak this crazy old goat for $45 billion!

"Think of it," The Chief said with growing enthusiasm. "With such an instrument in our hands, America will fall to her knees before us. All infidels can be compelled to convert. It is the dream of the Prophet Mohammed, blessed be his name, fulfilled."

Pax Islamica now? The same old crazy dream: world domination. X was reminded of a saying from the proverb Web site: "The same donkey, but with a new saddle."

Needless to say, he didn't quote it. But he must have looked unhappy, because The Chief said, "You hesitate to praise the plan. Are you so unable to picture an Islamic America?"

Paris Hilton in a burqa. Yeah, a wee bit difficult to picture.

"I wonder if it would not be better to let the Americans continue their own ways, though we don't agree with them," he ventured. "Let them choose the joys of Paradise or the fires of hell."

The Chief nodded. "Ah, maybe you are thinking of one of the old sayings you are so fond of quoting. 'The mud of one country is the medicine of another.' "

"Perhaps."

"My young friend, our call is the one that was revealed to Mohammed. It is a call to all mankind. We have been entrusted with a sacred mission, to follow in the footsteps of the Messenger and to spread his wisdom to all people. It is an invitation that we extend to all the nations to embrace Islam, the religion that calls for justice, mercy and fraternity, not differentiating between race or gender. That is why the West must be converted. Spain will return to Islam, as it was in the 14th century. France, Denmark, England, all of Europe as well."

He continued, "Afghanistan will once again submit to Sharia law and women will no longer walk the streets brazenly, with their arms and even faces shamelessly bared."

"I see. And those Afghanis who collaborated with the Americans, those in the puppet government, will they be … ?" X drew his finger grimly across his throat.

"No, my young friend, for forgiveness is the choicest flower of victory," The Chief said. "Those sheep who return to the fold will not be slaughtered. We will show mercy that curs of the West have never shown to us."

*   *   *

If the imminent destruction of the solar system were not bad news enough, X was told by a messenger that his brother-in-law Haseem had arrived in the cave complex and was anxious to meet him. Haseem was waiting, so he was told, outside the prayer hall. X told the messenger to assure his beloved in-law that he'd be there shortly and to wait. As soon as the young man was out of sight, X hightailed it in the opposite direction.

I suppose this place is big enough that I can duck the guy for a day, he thought. *After that …*

Back in their room, X told Harry about his discussion with The Chief about Weapon Z.

"It's a garden-variety scam," X told him. "Unbelievable that someone as supposedly crafty as The Chief could fall for it. I guess it's yet another sign the old duffer has dementia. Reminds me of a little trick my mentor told me he pulled on an IRA stooge back in the '80s. Got him to pay 50 grand for a trunk of C-4 – the main ingredient of which happened to be baking soda."

To his surprise, he saw that Harry was white as a Klansman's sheet.

"We've heard chatter about Weapon Z being on the market," he said in an anxious voice. "Some former KGB agents smuggled it out of the Ukraine."

"You've got to be kidding," X laughed. "It's the stuff of an Austin Powers movie."

"I wish I was kidding," said Harry. "A weapon like that in the wrong hands …"

"Whose hands would be the right ones for something that blows up the solar system?" X said, by no means convinced.

"You have a point. But the stakes in this game just went up about a thousandfold. You've got to put the pressure on The Chief. You have to get me to his computer terminal."

"You haven't been able to hack in with your laptop?"

Harry shook his head. "Too many layers of security."

"Even for you, the Lesbian Bill Gates?"

"Lebanese."

"Israeli, unless of course that's another cover story. What are you really, Swedish? Try to keep it straight."

The agent stood up and repeatedly jabbed his index finger in

X's chest. "You worry about keeping your own part straight. I heard about the brilliant terror plots you pitched to The Chief. Nice job. Could almost make a person wonder whose side you're on. You sure got palsy walsy with those murderers at Abd Al-Rahman. Just get me to that damn terminal."

X glanced down. "I spoke to you once about touching me," he said coolly. "You don't want to find that finger broken off and midway up your alimentary canal."

"When this is over, we'll see what's up whose ass."

X gave him a bemused look. "Is that a threat or a promise? Why, Harry, you old devil, you really do care."

*   *   *

X hurried down the hallway to meet The Chief, mentally rehearsing the exact words he'd use to convince the old man to make the transfer. The guy was clearly senile; surely he could be defeated in a battle of wits. Unless the treachery center of the brain somehow remained intact, while everything else turned to Swiss cheese.

He heard Asar's voice calling his name excitedly.

"Ali, I've been looking all over for you," he cried. X turned to see the teen with a tall, bearded man clad in a surprisingly bright purple and orange shirt. It was far from loud, but compared to what X had been accustomed to the past week, the guy might as well have been wearing a Hawaiian shirt.

The man strode toward him, a smile expanding on his face. He was carrying a red gift box. "My brother, I have spent half a day looking for you in this maze," he said. "If I didn't know better, I would think you were ducking me. Do you owe me some money I've forgotten about? They told me this young man could lead me to you."

As Haseem neared X, his jocular manner changed and his eyes narrowed in confusion.

"Ali, this man is an imposter," X declared. "Quickly, draw your weapon."

Asar, who'd been doing guard duty at the entrance, pulled the rifle slung over his shoulder and pointed it at Haseem. Just as fast, Haseem drew a handgun from a holster at his hip.

"This is not Ali Nazeer," Haseem declared. "Do not be deceived by his lies."

Asar looked back and forth between the two men in obvious confusion.

"Asar shoot him," X said. "He is a puppet of the infidels."

"Don't be a fool, boy," Haseem said. "I know my own brother-in-law and this isn't him."

"Your brother-in-law is a pig, your sister is a pig and you are a pig," X said. "And you are not Haseem."

Haseem stepped toward Asar. "Put down your weapon, boy. Don't make me harm you."

Asar hesitated, the gun trembling in his hand. He glanced uncertainly at the two men.

"This man is my friend," he declared. "He told me everything about his boyhood, the names of each horse in his father's stable and the one he rode as a young boy, Iron Heel."

"Ali is terrified of riding horses," Haseem said. "All lies."

"Shoot this son of a pig," X said. "Don't let this Satan confuse you."

There were the sounds of footsteps running. Their voices must have echoed down the tunnel.

"Let The Chief decide who is telling the truth and who is the imposter," Haseem said with confidence. "We can make a phone call to my sister in Kuwait. I think she can tell who is her real brother and who is not her real husband."

The long shadows of men with rifles appeared along the wall of the tunnel. They were just around the bend. X was unarmed, but he reached into his vest as if for a weapon in a shoulder holster.

Haseem spun to shoot him and Asar pulled the trigger. Haseem returned fire, pumping two slugs into the boy's chest. Ali Nazeer's brother-in-law keeled over, clutching his throat as blood gushed from a smoking black hole. The box, which had been tucked under his left armpit, fell to the ground. It popped open and a dozen chocolate-covered strawberries spilled out.

X knelt beside Asar, who lay slumped against the wall, a red stain spreading out across his shirt.

"You'll be okay," he said. "Men are coming, they will take you to the infirmary."

Asar shook his head. He tore open his shirt to reveal a gunshot wound squarely at his heart.

"I am finished," he said.

Jesus Christ. He's going to die. And he's only a boy, X thought. He realized he'd never asked Asar exactly how old he was.

"I am frightened," Asar cried out.

"You are dying a hero," X assured him. "You are going to Allah's side a martyr. You will be entertained by 77 virgins. More beautiful than any girls you've ever seen. Their voices will be a heavenly choir more captivating than any siren's song."

Asar clutched his arm. "Are you sure? Who knows what really awaits us after death?"

"I am sure," X said emphatically. "Heaven is waiting for you, I promise."

Asar smiled. It was the biggest whopper X had ever told and he had told many. But he couldn't bear to see the terror in the boy's eyes and his words seem to quiet his fear.

"Ali, my father was a brute who beat me and abandoned me," the dying youth whispered. "You, Ali –"

"Hush," X said, covering the boy's mouth. "Don't say it."

"You are my true father."

Three armed fighters came alongside X, including one he recognized as Omar.

"What happened here?" demanded a man who boasted the physique of a Vin Diesel.

"He was a traitor," Asar gasped. "He fired upon me."

"Is this true?" said Omar, aghast.

X nodded. "An imposter."

"One of my men vouched for him, said he recognized him," said the pumped-up guard, apparently in charge.

"The infidels are using lookalikes now," X warned him. "Instruct your men to be more wary. Interrogate newcomers intensely; take nothing for granted."

The security chief nodded, chastened.

"The cunning of the infidels knows no bounds," said Omar, kneeling beside his fallen friend. "Their deceit is infinite. They are truly monsters. Their wickedness –"

"Oh shut the hell up," X growled, running his hand through

his hair. Omar looked at him, taken aback.

"Forgive his anger," said the beefy security boss. "He is overcome with grief."

"Hold me, brother," Asar whispered. X put his arm around the dying young man.

"I am so cold," Asar said.

"It's okay. It's all right, I'm here with you. I won't leave you."

He rocked the teen in his arms, as the three guards looked on, awkwardly. After about four minutes, the light went out of the boy's eyes.

"May Allah have mercy on him," Omar said, bowing his head and beginning to utter a prayer.

X realized he was crying. Except that one time being abused by the prison guards, this was something he hadn't done in 20 years. Not since his mother died. And this wasn't a solitary tear that rolled down his cheek. It was a torrent that went on at least ten minutes.

Asar died for me. Or for someone. A phantom, a man who did not exist.

Chapter 21
BETRAYAL

X could not shake his depression over the death of Asar. Try as he might, he could not convince himself that he was guiltless in the boy's death. He told himself it was Mr. Jones's fault for springing the youth from the prison and sending him here. Or it was Fawad's fault for recruiting him into the terrorist underworld to begin with. When those lines of reasoning failed him, he resorted to the argument that the teen deserved to die because he was a terrorist.

If he had lived, who knows how many Americans he would have killed, X reminded himself. He deserved a medal, if anything, for actions that led to Asar's death.

But he was your friend was the nagging thought he kept hearing like a bee buzzing in his ear.

He felt like a battleship, once thought impregnable, whose hull had been breached by a torpedo. Now, like a seaman desperately welding metal plates over a hole to keep the ship from sinking, he steeled himself.

I can NOT let myself have feelings for a mark ever again, X told himself with conviction. And so, after an hour, the identity thief was at last himself again.

On the upside, the news that an enemy agent had penetrated the headquarters' layers of security played to X's advantage. A thorough sweep was done of the cavern for listening devices, especially in every place that Haseem had set foot. X was summoned to The Chief's office. He, Dr. Zawari and the other top aides sat at a conference table.

"Someone has tried to hack into our computer system," The Chief said gravely. "Just as you warned us. Fortunately the system put in place by Dr. Zawari blocked the attempt."

"Praise Allah for that," X said. "Your work will earn you a place in paradise, Dr. Zawari."

Dr. Zawari gave an unpleasant smile. The gaunt man handed X a paper. "We received a very interesting email."

X read it aloud. "'Beware of a man named Moammar Sharif. He is an Israeli intelligence agent.' Who sent this message?"

"It is anonymous," The Chief said. "The sender's name is, oh, I can't pronounce it, a Hindi word meaning 'friend.' What do you say about this?"

X frowned. "It seems impossible. I have met his family, they all seemed devout Muslims. And yet, who knows the cunning of the Jews, what they are capable of. You say the message came from India?"

Dr. Zawari said, "What proof do you have that you are not in league with this Moammar?

X ignored him and turned to The Chief.

"We must examine that laptop of his immediately. The hacker who attempted to find your assets may well be within these walls."

Hamid snapped his fingers. "That would explain why the cavern walls didn't shield against it."

"You did not answer my question, Brother Nazeer," Dr. Zawari said.

"Sometimes the right answer to a fool is silence," X said coldly.

Hamid pounded the table. "Better a thousand enemies outside your tent than one inside. Who-who-who-who-who-who-who-who-who knows what damage the Zionist has already done?"

"At the very least, the enemy knows the location of our base," agreed Fareek. "If he sent a message."

"How?" asked Hamid.

"Through his laptop."

"It's being checked, as we speak," Dr, Zawari said. "Taken apart piece by piece."

"What has he said?" X asked.

"He denies everything," said Hamid.

"Has he been tortured?"

"Don't worry. We won't waterboard your dear friend," Dr. Zawari said with a sneer. "That would violate the Geneva Conventions."

Hamid and Fareek laughed, elbowing each other, at the little joke.

"Let me interrogate him," X said. "What harsh means might not be able to gather from a hardened Mossad agent, wit perhaps can."

The Chief nodded. Dr. Zawari leaped to his feet.

"I wonder if it is wise, Chief," the good doctor objected. "He was the one who brought him here. He who has approved of wrongdoing is as guilty as he who has committed it."

The Chief stilled him with a raised hand. "Shall the gosling teach the goose to swim? I have been at this since before you could walk."

Dr Zawari sat down, wearing a sheepish expression.

But X said magnanimously, "Dr. Zawari is right. I have brought suspicion upon myself. I will send an order giving your contacts full access to all my files, to every contact in Kuwait, to my entire network. If you conclude that Ali Nazeer is in league with the Americans, I will personally supervise my own beheading."

This did not, X realized, entirely make sense, but it seemed to impress his host.

"Let it be so," The Chief said. "Come with me and you may use the phone in my office."

X turned to the other aides. "Once I have given this order, I will concern myself with this Jewish interloper. Bring me your cruelest instruments of torture. I want this spy who betrayed me to know that his suffering will be great if he does not cooperate."

*   *   *

As X watched coolly, The Chief opened the cigar box on his chest, where his phone was secured, and picked up the modified smart phone. X turned his back politely as The Chief punched in a four-digit security code. *Beep. Beep. Beep. Beep.*

After speaking to a number of Ali Nazeer's subordinates, who verified that they were speaking to The Chief himself, he was put on the line with Ali Nazeer's chief aide in Kuwait. He then handed the phone to "Ali Nazeer."

X confirmed that he was indeed in The Chief's compound

and ordered that agents of The Chief be given authority to probe all of the Jihadist Brotherhood's computer hard drives and allowed to grill its members. Their grilling, X suspected, might not be pleasant.

"I hope no unflattering memos about you are discovered," X joked after pressing the end call key.

The Chief rubbed his shoulder affectionately.

"This is only a precaution, my friend. By tomorrow we should have an answer."

"In the meantime, it is vital that we find out what the Jew knows," X said.

The Chief concurred.

*   *   *

When X entered Harry's cell, he found his comrade stripped to his underwear, hands and feet bound. His body was covered head to toe in bruises and he bore an oozing wound over his eyebrow. One eye was black. On the whole, not as bad as X expected.

"Why haven't they locked you up?" Harry demanded.

"Because they think you 'betrayed' me," X said.

"I'm sure you didn't do anything to give them that idea, to save your own chicken-shit neck," the Israeli spy said bitterly.

"We don't have much time," X said. "They know they've been hacked, and if I play it right they're going to let me into the system to transfer the funds. But I need the code to access the Committee account, and you need to tell me exactly what to do."

Harry shook his head. "No way. Only I'm supposed to make the transfer. Those are our orders."

"One thing you'll learn about a swindle is that you have to improvise when circumstances change," X said. "And from the looks of things, your circumstances have changed."

Harry remained dubious.

"How do I know you didn't send that email implicating me? You had access to my laptop."

"Now who's being paranoid?"

"Who else knows I'm Mossad?"

"How should I know? Maybe there's a mole in the

Mossad."

"There are no moles in the Mossad," Harry growled angrily "We have the best intelligence agency in the world."

"Still, you're in here, trussed up like a Hanukkah turkey," X noted. "Haven't you broken your agency's Eleventh Commandment? I believe in Hebrew it's "Thou shall not get caught."

"You're not getting those codes."

"If you don't give me the codes, the mission is over. And the Warriors of Allah will have the dough for Weapon Z, or if that doesn't exist – and I still don't believe it does, for the record – at the very least a small tactical nuke. Now I wonder who they'll use it on? Mnn… Lithuania? French Polynesia maybe?"

Harry mulled that one over for about 20 seconds, then gave him the codes.

Chapter 22
THE STING

"Your funds are not secure," X informed The Chief. "The Americans have located them and they are going to seize them sometime within the next 72 hours. He also told me the Americans are coming. This cave will be overrun by Special Forces with two days."

"We must evacuate," Hamid said.

"We can fight them," Fareek argued fiercely.

"They tried that at Tora Bora."

"We will evacuate," The Chief decided.

Fareek tried to protest and The Chief silenced the hothead with a raised hand.

"He who fights and runs away may live to fight another day," he said. He winked at X. "You might appreciate that old English saying, given your fondness for proverbs."

Well, it was inevitable that sooner or later someone would pick up on the fact that 75 percent of the words that came out of X's mouth were aphorisms. Thank goodness this old duffer took it as a verbal tic.

Dr. Zawari paced up and down the room. "How do we know this is true?" he demanded. "The captive might be spewing lies to save his skin."

X nodded. "Dr. Zawari is correct. We could leave the funds where they are and hope for the best."

Dr. Zawari glared at X, though The Chief seemed oblivious to his sarcasm.

The Chief stroked his beard. "It has taken 10 years to accumulate that money. We cannot risk it. Fareek, initiate emergency protocol 18."

Fareek nodded and hurried out of the room.

"How did you get the Jew to talk?" Hamid queried. "Those

Mossad are said to be tough. Did you use ph-ph-ph-ph-ph-ph-ph-physical torture?"

The Mossad was the envy of spy agencies worldwide for its training in SERE – survival, evasion, resistance and escape – so it was a reasonable question.

"Let us just say he knows he's been interrogated," X said with the appropriate wicked grin. That garnered an appreciative chuckle from the tubby terrorist.

"No, let us hear," Dr. Zawari pressed him. "How did you learn in a single hour what our trained interrogators could not extract from him in five?"

"I told him simply that we had his wife and children and they would be executed if he did not cooperate. Sometimes a warrior must use brain, not brawn."

"And this worked?" Dr. Zawari said, raising one eyebrow. "With a Mossad agent?"

X smiled. "Just enough to gauge his reaction and assure me that he valued his family. Then I sprang on him the truth: That I had proof that he had committed the sin of sodomy while in prison."

Hamid covered his mouth in horror. "But he seemed so m-m-m-m-m-m-m-m-m-m-m–"

This time Dr. Zawari interrupted him impatiently.

"Masculine. And what was this proof?"

"A photo taken by one of my moles in the prison, showing him in the act with an older detainee from Yemin, a former wrestling champ."

The Chief was appalled. "You mean …"

X nodded grimly. "Yes, he assumed the female role in the acts. Once he knew that proof of his disgrace would be circulated on all our Internet site, he began to sing like a Moroccan mockingbird."

"Well done!" exclaimed the Chief.

Dr. Zawari stroked his beard. "Something about this …"

"Of course, under the circumstances, I gladly will provide you with proof of this," X assured them. "I will have the photos sent here, that clearly show the Jew being penetrated as well as – "

Dr. Zawari turned green. "No, er. That, er, won't be –"

The Chief stood up. "We must move our funds immediately." Clearly he understood the urgency of the situation.

He was decked out in sweat clothes instead of pajamas.

Dr. Zawari reluctantly nodded. "At this point, we have no choice. Temporarily. Then we will put the money in a place of our own choosing."

"Very well," said X. "The funds can be electronically withdrawn from a branch of your bank in Tashkent, Uzbekistan in the form of a purchase of gold bullion. I can arrange to have the gold transported by gold by truck to a mountain cave there that the American dogs will never find. It will then be a simple matter to use the gold to pay those from whom you wish to buy that wondrous weapon."

"Yes, gold," said Hamid, his eyes glistening. "How fitting that we keep our treasure in a solid form, so it can be touched and held as it was in the days of the Prophet."

"Good," said X, clapping his hands. "Now all we have to do is – "

"Not so fast," Dr. Zawari said. "There is another place where the funds can be stored safely. The same place where you store your own assets."

X gulped. "I beg your pardon?"

"You bragged to The Chief that you have a secret place where your funds are concealed," the second-in-command said with sly smile. "Surely if it is good enough for you it is good enough for the Warriors of Allah?"

X turned to The Chief in annoyance. "We do not have time for this."

But he saw that the terror chief was staring at him solemnly.

"Dr. Zawari and I discussed our options at length the very first you arrived and mentioned our funds were at risk," The Chief said sternly. "I must now ask you to tell us where you are hiding your assets."

"My dear friend, I have told you that is impossible."

The Chief turned to Hamid and nodded. The henchman dug into his pocket.

"You are not the only one who knows the value a man puts on the lives of his family," the Chief said, finally adopting that arch tone X associated with movie villains. The gentle grandpa act appeared to be over.

X paled. "What are you saying?"

Hamid took out his cell phone and showed X a blurry image. An elderly woman and two younger ones huddled together in a corner, masked men surrounding them.

"If you cooperate, we swear no harm will come to them," Hamid said.

X turned to The Chief. "My mother? My wives? You would do such a thing to a brother in the Great Cause?"

"We must do what we must do, we must pay any price and bear any burden for the Jihad," The Chief intoned.

The last person you'd expect this maniac to steal lines from is JFK, X thought.

"But they are in a secure location," he said, affecting a bewildered expression. "How …?"

"You gave us full access to your people and your files," Dr. Zawari reminded him.

"And this is how you repay me – with such a grave betrayal?" X said bitterly.

The Chief patted his shoulder soothingly.

"They are safe and I will give the order to release them as soon as you do me this favor. Your funds will not be touched, you have my word of honor."

X paced about the room uncertainly. Then he threw up his arms in the air. "Very well, you win."

"Grand, grand," said The Chief. "Where are you hiding your assets?"

"Zimbabwe."

"Zimbabwe?" The Chief said, taken aback.

"Yes, I have made arrangements with the director of the national bank."

"Clever indeed, clever indeed." He turned his henchmen. "Dr. Zawari, why didn't you think of this? Who'd ever look in Zimbabwe?"

"I … I … er …"

"We have no time to place blame," Hamid pointed out.

X agreed. "Every player sometimes drops the ball. All I will need is a computer and access to your account. And as soon as it is done, I must be allowed to speak to my wives on the phone."

*   *   *

They reached the small unmarked room that housed the computer. Entry had required two keys, one turned by Dr. Zawari and the other by The Chief. As Dr. Zawari turned the second key and prepared to open the door, a pair of aides came running down the hall. The spokesman wore Coke-bottom-bottle glasses that looked as if they could barbecue a 400-pound hog under the sunlight. Unlike everyone else here in terrorist Wonderland, he didn't wear a turban, but rather an American-style baseball cap with a Batman insignia.

"We did as you said, Dr. Zawari. Took the laptop apart piece by piece, examined every piece of data even recovering all information on the hard drive someone had attempted to erase."

His voice was monotonic, reminding X of an after-school special he'd seen ages ago about Asperger's syndrome. *Perhaps he's an idiot savant computer genius,* X speculated. *That's why they tolerate eccentricities like the silly hat.*

Dr. Zawari turned from the door and looked at X.

"I don't imagine you anticipated that we would have a forensic computer team down here?"

"No, I am indeed impressed," X replied. "I am eager to hear what you found."

The terrorist Rain Man showed them a tiny chip smaller than a ladybug.

"This is a tracking device," he said in that disconcertingly robotic voice. "We also found evidence of multiple attempts to hack our computers. There were also encrypted messages sent. We have been able to unlock only one. It is in Hebrew, but coded.

"Six message we have traced to an IP address in Tel Aviv. There is one other we have traced to an IP address in Brazil."

"Brazil?" Dr. Zawari said, his brows knitting.

X nodded. "I've heard that the Israelis have bases in both Brazil and Argentina. They started out as safe houses for Nazi hunters."

Dr. Zawari snatched the tracking device and angrily crushed it under his heel.

"I'm afraid it's a bit late for that," X pointed out. "We must accomplish our task before this place is reduced to rubble."

*   *   *

The Chief, Dr. Zawari and Fareek clustered around X as he sat at a terminal in the cramped confines of the computer room. The identity thief prayed they couldn't see the sweat trickling down his forehead. His partner Samantha always handled the computer work. He was far from computer illiterate, but beyond a little phishing, he was a rank amateur.

The Chief told him how to access the funds of the Warriors of Allah. They were racking up interest in a Swiss bank account. X was a bit surprised. He didn't think evildoers trusted the Swiss anymore. Hadn't they given up their criminal clients and corrupt rulers under pressure from international investigators and gone straight?

The Swiss must be up to their old tricks. I should have known they wouldn't go back to making cuckoo clocks.

"The account number?" he asked The Chief.

"It's 8502-384-95871-9687," the elderly man said, referring to a slip of paper in his hand, as X punched in the numbers.

"And the password?"

The Chief hesitated. X shifted in his seat uneasily. Was the oldster finally growing suspicious? Surely 20 years of running a terrorist organization must have given him heightened survival instincts.

"The password, sir?" X repeated in as even a tone as he could muster.

"Give me a moment," The Chief said. The Chief's eyes narrowed and he seemed to be scrutinizing X.

The party's over, the conman thought. *Unless … you've got to be kidding me. The old duffer really is going senile. He's forgotten the number!*

"Your child's birthday?" Dr. Zawari suggested.

The Chief seemed offended. "I would never choose something so obvious."

"The Chief is far wiser than that," Fareek scolded the physician.

"Perhaps a line from one of your favorite poets?" X suggested.

"Of course," The Chief said, clapping his hands in delight.

"It is 'Xanadu.' "

First X remembered this as the title of a dreadful '80s roller-skating musical starring Olivia Newton John. Then the opening of Coleridge's poem, last read in high school, came back to him.

In Xanadu did Kubla Khan a sacred pleasure dome decree …

X found it puzzling that The Chief had chosen an English poet. But he typed in X-A-N-A-D-U and sure enough the account popped open.

$45,401,033,656.07

X stared at the figure and resisted the urge to whistle. He'd never seen so many digits. He was literally salivating and wondered if dollar signs were flashing in his irises like in a Bugs Bunny cartoon.

Leaving that account open on the screen, X visited the site of the "National Bank of Zimbabwe" and accessed an account held under the name of the International Crusade to End World Hunger. The Web site displayed the bank's logo, featuring the country's flag. The account held $20 million.

Dr. Zawari raised an eyebrow. "Only $20 million? I thought your fortune was far greater than that, Mr. Nazeer."

The Chief chuckled, "That from a country doctor who made $20,000 a year treating farmers for sores on their penises."

The aide blushed. "I was only saying …"

Dr. Zawari, a urologist before signing up, was sensitive about money matters. He'd never raked in as much as his father, one of King Abdullah's personal physicians.

"These are emergency funds," X explained. "I have accounts in eight other countries. I don't believe in putting all my eggs in one basket."

"We should diversify too," Fareek said. "I've always said so."

The Chief nodded. "This is true, but for now, we must concentrate on keeping our funds safe from the Americans. Transfer the funds to your account."

X shook his head. "It is written that wise men live together like brothers and do business like strangers. Let us do this in such a way that no one can be accused of chicanery. When I transfer your funds to the Zimbabwe bank, let us give you a new password so that no one except you will be able to access the account, not even myself."

"Is there time for all this?" The Chief asked. "The Americans…"

"Oh yes," Dr. Zawari jumped in, clapping a hand firmly on X's shoulder. "Trust me, there is most certainly time. I insist."

"I would feel more comfortable doing it this way," X said. The Chief nodded. "Let it be so."

X's fingers flew over the keyboard deleting the old password. A screen popped up asking for the entry of a new password. He swiveled around so that his back was turned as The Chief typed in a complex phrase. It had at least 20 letters and the odds he'd forget it by the afternoon seemed high.

"Finished," said the old man at last.

"Now we can transfer the funds," said X, the cursor poised over the "Confirm" button.

At that moment, Hamid burst into the room and all the men turned to him.

"The information has come from our agents in Kuwait," he said, hyperventilating. "Their investigation of Ali Nazeer has borne fruit."

"You could not have arrived at a more auspicious moment," Dr. Zawari said.

"Our agents have discovered th-th-th-th-th-th-th-th-th-th-th-th-th--"

X's hands hovered over the keyboard as the men waited for Fareek with bated breath. It took half a minute for the young aide to put the brakes on his stuttering.

"Our agents have discovered that Ali Nazeer is clean of any involvement with the infidels," Hamid declared. "His entire organization is devoted to the Cause."

X's fingers unfroze.

The Chief smiled broadly. "Of this I had no serious doubt," he said. "Transfer the funds."

X punched a key and up came the prompt. "Well, Chief, are you sure you want to execute this transaction? Speak now or forever hold your peace."

The Chief nodded and X clicked on "Confirm."

It took a moment for the transfer to take place, a green

bar creeping snail-like across a little rectangle in the middle of the screen. Ten percent … 20 percent … 40 percent …

As was said at the outset, X found occasions like this rather nerve-wracking. But trying to play it off, he leaned back in the swivel chair with his fingers interlaced behind his head.

"After this I must have some of your fine tea and read that children's story in its entirety," X said. "Once I have confirmed that my family is safe, of course."

"You deserve much more that that for your service," The Chief said, beaming. "When it is complete, I will send you a signed first edition."

"That I would surely treasure."

Dr. Zawari rolled his eyes.

On the right side of the screen the number $45,401,033,656.07 showed up in the Zimbabwe account, while on the left side of the balance of The Chief's account read zero.

The Chief gave a sigh of relief. "It is done."

"The CIA has no knowledge of this bank in Zimbabwe," X said. "But you must remain vigilant and be prepared to move the funds again in the future."

"Glory be to Allah," Hamid said.

The Chief embraced X. "You have done a wonderful thing, my young friend."

"There is no power nor strength except Allah," X said.

"True, but there has never lived a man who has given more to the cause of the Jihad," Dr. Zawari said, surprising X with this tip of the hat. "If the Americans had seized those funds, all our years of planning …"

"You give me too much credit," said X. He slumped on the chair. He didn't have to fake exhaustion. The stress had nearly killed him.

The Chief gestured for him to rise. "Now you may have some of my tea," he said.

The leader of the Warriors of Allah smiled and led X to his study. He allowed his valuable ally the honor of sitting at his mahogany desk and poured him a cup of tea.

"I am sure that as an Eton man, you will appreciate this," he said. "It is a special blend from Salisbury."

He phoned his men at Ali Nazeer's mansion and gave them the order to set the hostages free. Then he handed the phone to X.

"Ascertain for yourself that they are safe," he said. "Pass on to them my humble apologies."

"I will tell them that they were in no danger, that it was all in the service of the Jihad," X replied.

"Good man."

X delivered that terse message to the billionaire's still distraught, weeping wife and assured her they would speak again soon. He returned the phone to the Chief, who put it back in the box.

"Relax a few minutes and enjoy, my friend," the leader said, beaming. "You have earned it."

There was a bowl of candies on the desk, including mints, chocolates and Jolly Ranchers. X saw a yellow hard candy on top.

"May I?"

The Chief gave the kind of smile a dad might give a son who'd just batted in a homerun in Little League. "Of course."

X popped the lemon candy in his mouth.

"I would join you for some tea and a discussion of the book, for I value your suggestions," the Chief said. "But I must supervise the evacuation."

X couldn't imagine the logistics in getting that many men and, presumably, their weapons out of the caverns, but it was obvious the terrorists had drilled for such an eventuality.

The Chief looked around the library wistfully.

"In a few minutes someone will come for the books. I wish I could take them all but my old Britannicas will have to stay. I shall have them burned rather than be soiled by the infidels. Have you heard that the company has ceased to publish the print addition? Philistines!"

As he left, X sat back in the leather-backed Captain Kirk chair, savoring the citrus taste. *So this is what it feels like to command a terror network,* he thought.

*   *   *

Traci was in bed in her private quarters at Fort Freedom, located at the base of a mountain in Afghanistan near the Pakistan border, when a knock came on the door.

"You have a phone call, Miss Washington," the young officer said. It had taken nearly a week, but she now responded to the false name without hesitation. (She wasn't all that happy with the Committee's choice, by the way. Why does every black person have to be a Washington?)

"I'll take it my office."

She had been airlifted to the secret base by chopper from the extraction point, after radioing in. (Where exactly on her person that tiny transmitter was hidden will remain her little secret.) She hated being reduced to overseeing the operation from afar – "playing Zeppo" as intelligence officers often called those who remained behind the scenes manning recording devices.

The agent sat at the desk in the cluttered office – from which a captain had been booted, much to his chagrin – and was surprised when she heard Mr. Jones's distinct voice on the line. She had expected to receive notice via an encrypted email.

"The funds have been received," the spymaster told her. "It's a go."

"I thought you were going to send a coded message through the Riyadh office," she said.

"There's been a change of plans, obviously," he informed her impatiently. "Now will you kindly stop asking questions and get your ass in gear."

"Yes sir.'

"And Traci, you've done a good job."

Traci lowered the phone. It had actually worked. That scam artist and that computer nerd had actually pulled it off. She had been 90 percent sure The Chief would smell a rat and have them beheaded. To be frank, she hadn't slept a wink since she'd parted company with the duo. With X. Grinning, she picked up the phone again.

"Initiate Operation Terminex," she said. "Get those birds in the air. And tell the extraction team to move."

Chapter 23
CASABLANCA

Less than 30 minutes later, 15,000-pound daisy cutters dropped by B-52s began to pepper the ground beneath which the cavern lay, throwing flames hundreds of yards into the air. In the village, a quarter mile a way, concussion waves toppled buildings and knocked men carting goods on donkeys off their mounts.

X was in his room, kneeling in prayer, when Hamid burst in.

"Why are you still here?" the young aide asked, bewildered. "Don't you hear the bombs?"

"I called my family to make sure they are safe," he said, rising from the prayer mat. "The Chief honored his word, as I knew he would. I am thanking Allah for watching over them."

"We must go. The Americans are c-c-c-c-c-coming. Our spies at Fort Freedom say the helicopters will reach here within m-m-m-m-m-m-m-m-m-m minutes and raiding parties will come pouring in every entrance. We are all to evacuate."

"Through the mosque?"

"No, we have secret escape tunnels leading to the valley. Built for just this eventuality."

X started out with Hamid, then stopped in his tracks. "What about the prisoner, the Jewish spy?"

"In 20 minutes, nerve gas will fill this place," the overweight terrorist replied with a grin that revealed a lifetime without dental work. "It's a little surprise The Chief cooked up for the Americans. That will take care of the conniving bastard."

X shook his head. "I want to take care of him myself. It was I who brought him into this haven; it is I who must finish him."

This appeared to make perfect sense to Hamid. "Hurry, meet us at the rear of the hydroelectric generator room. May Allah protect you."

They embraced.

Gosh, they're a touchy-feely bunch, X thought.

The Chief's escape plan was far from foolproof. While the majority of his men were able to make their way out through a plethora of hidden exits dug into the mountainside, Hamid and Fareek were not so lucky. Marines with the help of infrared probes had located one of the tunnels and were working their way through it, armed with Armalite M16 assault rifles plus Sig 9mm pistols as backup.

Fareek, leading a dozen fighters, toppled as his head exploded. He was wearing body armor, but the Americans, anticipating just such a precaution, took down their foes with head shots.

The Marines, firing special ceramic ammunition that shattered on impact to avoid ricochet injuries, poured round after round into the dark. Barely audible beneath the deafening gunfire were the shouts of confusion and fear from the fleeing terrorists as the Americans calmly cut down them down.

When the Marines, emboldened, pressed on into the tunnel, the Warriors of Allah fared better in the fierce hand-to-hand battle that ensued. The jihadists slashed throats with kukris, the traditional curved Gurkha knives, while the Americans struck back with commando knives nicknamed K-Bars.

Against all odds, Hamid fought his way past the Marines and out into the open.

Unfortunately for The Chief's loyal aide, he ran into the path of a 7.62 mm round that literally cut him in half.

"Allah, receive your serv-v-v-v-v-v-v--!" the fat man screamed, firing his AK-47 at the U.S. soldiers as he bit the dust.

*   *   *

As X expected, no one was guarding Harry's cell. The two fighters previously posted there had already made their way to the tunnels.

"I didn't think you would …" Harry began.

"Come back for you? I'm hurt," said X as he knelt and began untying the spy. "What sort of fellow do you think I am? We con artists have a motto: 'Never leave a comrade behind.' "

"I thought that was the Marines."

"Right. Ours is: 'There's no honor among thieves.' Should I go?"

"That's okay, carry on."

The knots were trickier than X had hoped. Precious moments flew by as he fumbled with the ropes.

"Whoever did these must have been an Eagle Scout," he said.

"Not likely."

After finally undoing the last and most vexing knot, he helped Harry to his feet. A massive explosion shook the ceiling above their heads, almost throwing them down.

"What the hell was that?" X exclaimed.

"A daisy cutter," Harry said. "Over 12,000 pounds. Our boys are already bombing the place."

"Well, perhaps we'd better leave, then."

"For once we agree."

He helped Harry into the hall and they made their way slowly through the passageways. The lights were flickering. At least one of the generators was kaput and the identity thief had no doubt the other two would go within a few minutes.

When they reached the tunnel leading to the generator room – and presumably the secret exit – they were greeted by the rat-a-tat-tat of automatic gunfire.

"Well, that's out," X said. "We'll have to go out the way we came in, the mosque."

"We don't have much time, five minutes tops," Harry said. "The guards told me about the nerve gas. One said, 'I hope you Jews can hold your breath.' The cocksucker. "

"A bad apple, for sure."

They moved swiftly through the passage toward the mosque, hoping their sense of direction hadn't failed them. It was a good thing X had spent so many hours eluding his "brother-in-law." He was well enough acquainted with the labyrinth to know a shortcut to the mosque entrance.

"This way."

As they turned the corner, they were greeted by the unwelcome sight of Dr. Zawari pointing a handgun at them. It was a gold-plated vintage Luger, X was surprised to see, presumably a souvenir from some anti-Semitic fan of the Warriors of Allah. It made him look remarkably like a Nazi officer in a black and white World War II movie he'd watched on TV on the couch next to Mother late one Saturday night.

Casablanca?

"I thought the Jew would be useful to us," X informed him. "A hostage we can trade."

"I don't think so," said the urologist-turned-terrorist. "Hands up."

X raised his hands, as did Harry.

"I solved the puzzle too late," Dr. Zawari said with a less than entirely chummy smile. "The email warning us about the hacking. It was you, wasn't it?

"Don't be absurd, Doctor," X said. "We've got to get out of this place. The Americans are bombing. And the gas —"

"The new account in Zimbabwe, it is a fiction, is it not? The Chief's 'code' useless. Where did that money really go? Into the U.S. treasury? Or some anti-terrorist slush fund like the one that your President Reagan used to pay the Contras?"

The No. 2 man of the Warriors of Allah took a step toward them and pointed the gun directly between X's eyes.

I really wish people would stop sticking guns in my face, X thought.

"Now you will die," Dr. Zawari snarled.

"Wait," said X. "Listen, it is true, I am not really Ali Nazeer. If you give me but a moment I can explain who I really am."

The physician hesitated. "I'm all ears."

"The Chief is a traitor, in league with the Americans. He has been on the CIA payroll for decades. My true name is Wahid al Khayr. I have been sent by a secret committee of imams in Saudi Arabia to bring him down. The Americans believe that I am a lookalike they coerced into working for them, but the truth is I infiltrated them deliberately."

Harry stared at him, stunned. "What????!!!" he exclaimed.

X smirked and tapped his head. "It's called planning, my Jewish friend. This man here is indeed a Mossad agent and when we get to safety, I will tell you what I have in store for him. It will not be pleasant."

His accent had shifted now. It was not the cultured lilt of a man raised in luxury in Kuwait and trained in gentlemanly speech by tutors but unmistakably and beyond the shadow of any doubt the guttural growl of a Bedouin.

"You have been selected to replace The Chief," the man revealed to Dr. Zawari.

A smile played upon the lips of the physician as the truth seeped in. "Me?"

"You filthy son of a bitch," Harry said. "I actually thought for a minute you had an ounce of compassion in you."

"You thought what I wanted you to think," X said coldly, lowering his hands. His entire manner had changed – the sly, sardonic man was gone and a hardened leader stood in his place. Harry watched in disbelief as even the impersonator's eyes transformed. A new kind of evil glowed in them now, no longer the casual moral idiocy of a sociopath, but something far more frightening.

Dr. Zawari stared at his compatriot, still wavering.

"Yes, they see what they want them to see," he murmured.

"You will be given authority over all operations in Afghanistan and Pakistan," the man who had identified himself as Wahid al Khayr informed the second-in-command authoritatively. "You will report directly to Iman –"

"Shut up, shut up," Dr. Zawari blurted, abruptly sticking a finger in one ear. "Your days of telling lies and lies within lies are over. It is time to die, both you and your Zionist master."

He shot Harry, who dropped like a stone. Then he pointed the gun at X's chest.

"I wish I had a scalpel so I could cut out your organs one by one as you watch," he said. "A bullet is far too merciful for you."

The explosion came without warning and threw X to the ground. He looked up to see the roof had caved in, burying Dr. Zawari under a mountain of rubble.

"Now that was a timely interruption," X said, clambering to his hands and knees. How much time had that little *tete a tete* eaten up? They probably had two minutes to get to the ladder to the mosque. He heard the Israeli agent groaning and crawled toward him.

"Fuck, fuck, fuck," Harry was moaning. "This hurts like hell."

"Stop whining," X said. "I can see it's only a flesh wound in your shoulder. The guy was a terrible shot. I thought they sent those fellas through some kind of boot camp. Hopefully he was more on target with his prostate exams."

"Not the gunshot, idiot. My leg."

To the identity thief's dismay, he saw that rubble had buried Harry's left leg. The Israeli spy was trying to shove the rocks off himself, to no avail. X knelt beside him and started pulling the heavy stones off.

"Next time be more careful," he suggested. He thought, *if I start running right now, I'm sure I can make it.* X had been on the track team in high school and was surprisingly fast for an athlete with relatively short legs.

"Swell performance, by the way," Harry said.

"Likewise," X said. "You do righteous indignation very well."

It took a full minute to free his comrade. X helped the injured man to his feet.

"Can you walk?"

Harry shook his head.

"Here, put your arm around me," said X.

Awkwardly, they moved through the narrow passage, Harry groaning as he hobbled along on his busted leg. To make matters worse, the lights finally went and they were forced to forge ahead in total darkness. X recalled the sewer through which he'd fled the federal agents.

"Here we go again," he mumbled.

"Stop," Harry said. "Look, you'd better go on. That gas will be released any minute."

It was certainly tempting. Running at top speed he still could reach the ladder in time. And with Harry out of the way, well, things would be simpler. A LOT simpler.

What do I owe this rude, self-righteous son of a bitch? What do I owe anyone?

"Oh, damn it all," X said. He grabbed Harry and threw him over his shoulder fireman style. They were nearly identical in height and weight, so it took considerable effort.

"Put me …" Harry said. "You're not strong enough …"

X staggered down the passageway. Another explosion came, almost knocking him from his feet. He hadn't carried another person since he gave a piggyback ride to a girlfriend four years earlier (one a good deal more svelte than Samantha) and he was soon struggling under the burden.

Yet somehow a minute later, X bumped into the ladder with a clang.

"Upsy-daisy," he said. Harry began to climb.

Am I hallucinating or is that green mist wafting down the tunnel toward us? It was hard to believe you could see nerve gas. Still, the stuff looked ominous.

"Pick up the pace, if you don't mind," he shouted up to Harry.

"My leg is broken, remember," Harry yelled down.

"Bad contusion more likely."

X started up the ladder. He remembered how interminable the climb down had been, like Alice descending into the rabbit hole. Their ascent seemed to take even longer. He could definitely smell something now and his eyes were beginning to sting. Becoming woozy, he stopped climbing and hung there confused, suddenly unable to recall if he was supposed to be going up or down.

His finger tips began to tingle, and he felt paralysis creeping through his muscles. His joints began to ache and his legs went numb.

So this is how it ends? Better than that sewer, I suppose.

Above him, a burst of light and a rush of fresh air flooded in as Harry flung open the trap door. The Israeli agent thrust down his hand.

"Come on!"

As soon as Harry hauled him up through the opening, X slammed the door shut. It was doubtful it was airtight, but he didn't want to take another breath of that foul gas if he could help it. He helped Harry limp out of the mosque.

People were evacuating the town on horseback, in Jeeps, on motorcycles and even bicycles. Over the village square, an AH-64D Apache Longbow helicopter was hovering, a machine gun poking out of an open door.

"Looks like our ride's here," X told his companion, "right on schedule."

X used his arms to form a triangle, the signal Traci had instructed them to make. Dressed like everyone else, they would otherwise have been impossible to pick out. The pilot caught the gesture and the chopper descended noisily into the village square, kicking up choking dust. As the two men stumbled toward it, X felt as if he was in some old Chuck Norris movie, a POW belatedly rescued from Vietnam.

A pair of Marines in desert fatigues helped them aboard and the helicopter zipped away into the sky.

Below, the people of the village scattered, looking like insects escaping a flooded nest. Some carried small arms, grenade launchers and SAMS. One plucky villager fired an AK-47 at the chopper and bullets tore through the fuselage, narrowly missing the agents as the chopper went aloft. The machine gunner beside them returned fire and the townsman dropped dead.

"Get Lady Hawk on the line," Harry said.

"Yes, sir," the pilot replied.

"Well, we did it," X said. "Do you fellows have cigars? Or champagne? This really calls for a toast."

"We'll be putting you down in Kabul, is that right?" Harry said.

"That's the agreement."

"And you'll disappear into the crowd, a free man."

"It's not that I don't trust the government, but I really prefer that we part with no strings attached."

"Meanwhile, The Chief's money is safely in the hands of the U.S. government," Harry said.

"Yes, indeed," X replied. "To build schools and bridges, I'm sure."

"Or is it?" Harry said. X turned to see a stern look on his companion's face. He looked like a school proctor who'd caught a student cheating on the SATs.

Oops.

X gave him a "who, me?" look. "Beg pardon?"

"What account number did you give them?"

"The one you gave me, of course."

"Bullshit. You transferred it to your own account, didn't you? All $45 billion. Where is it? In the Caymans? Switzerland?"

X sighed. He was hoping that Harry wouldn't put two and two together until they reached Kabul and he was able to slip free. The account in which he'd deposited The Chief's nest egg was actually in Denmark; he'd set it up months ago when they were planning the ill-fated sting on Ali Nazeer.

"Look, the terrorists don't have it," X said. "That's what's important, right?"

"That money is the property of the U.S. government." Harry fumed.

"Technically, it's The Chief's money. And what do you care? Aren't you Mossad? Or are you secretly working for Outer Mongolia?"

"Where is the goddamned money?" Harry screamed.

"All right, so you got me. Of course I have the money. I'm afraid a take of $45 billion was irresistible. And now, of course, that'll be just $22.5 billion."

"Meaning?"

"Fifty-fifty, right down the middle."

Harry, kneeling and ignoring the pain in his leg, grabbed X by the collar.

"Not everyone is a greedy, rotten bastard," he snarled.

"Sir, we have Lady Hawk," the co-pilot announced.

Harry snatched the microphone.

"This is Bluebird," he said.

"Harry, are you guys all right?" Traci's voice came over the radio.

"Yes, but tell the Marines to retreat from the caves. The Chief flooded it with some kind of gas. It's not sarin. I don't know what it is."

"Roger that. I'll bring them out."

They heard her barking orders in the background.

"Why did you order the attack?" he asked.

"We received the transfer."

"You got a confirmation on that?"

"I got a call from Mr. Jones himself."

"A call. Let me guess. A cell phone call."

"Well, yes."

"Contact Jones. I guarantee you the money isn't there."

More than 100 miles away, in the command center outside Gardez, Traci blanched. It had SOUNDED like Jones. But X was a master mimic, wasn't he?

Harry turned to X. "How did you make the call?"

The identity thief sighed. "The Chief has a cell phone he leaves charging in his office. He left me at his desk for five minutes. There was a security code, but of course in my line you get a lot of practice listening to keypads. "

Harry shook his head in disbelief.

"And you sent that email blowing my cover, using my own laptop, didn't you? So you would be the one at The Chief's terminal, not me like we planned."

X couldn't think of a comeback.

Harry was red in the face, shaking with rage.

"They beat the shit out of me, threatened to castrate me, you asshole," he shouted.

"I apologize. Didn't know about any ball-cutting."

"When we get back to the U.S., I'll see to it that you rot in jail for the rest of your stinking life," Harry shouted at the top of his lungs. "And believe me, you WILL cough up the location of that mon –"

Before he could finish the sentence, a rocket slammed into the helicopter blowing right through the floor, through the roof and into the rotors. As Harry, X and the gunner tumbled about in the cabin the way beans might knock around in a maraca, the aircraft swirled around like a dragonfly with a missing wing.

"Mayday, mayday," the pilot hollered as the chopper careened toward the mountainside.

At the base, Traci heard the horrific sound of an explosion.

"Harry! Harry! Harry!" Traci shouted into the phone. But the radio was dead.

Chapter 24
REQUIUM FOR A BELOVED ROGUE

It was Mr. Jones – the real Mr. Jones – who relayed the news to Traci.

"Only one person survived the wreck. Our man Harry Assad, or as we now know, the Israeli's man Harry Weinstein, son of Malik and Alia Assad of Lebanon, or, in actuality Noah and Rachel Weinstein of Michigan. He was airlifted to Landstuhl Regional Medical Center hospital in Germany."

"X?" she said hopefully.

"The radio signal from that tooth implant was detected among charred remains in the wreckage. The retrieval team had to leave the bodies behind because they were coming under enemy fire."

"It's not possible ...?"

"No, I had the Office of Security requisition the fingerprints taken for Harry's original FBI background check. The OOS received them from the Bureau and relayed them to me this morning. It's Harry all right, 100 percent match."

Traci didn't want Jones to hear her sigh, but he did.

"I suppose a Christian burial wouldn't be too important to X," Traci said.

"No, I don't suppose so."

"How's Harry?"

"Half the bones in his body were broken and he was badly burned. He'll be undergoing facial reconstructive surgery and they have some of the best people in the world for that at LRMC. We supplied file photos of Harry's face and they'll come close. I've seen them work miracles on soldiers who were horribly disfigured by IEDs."

"What will happen to him, now that we know he's a mole?"

"We'll flip him, of course. He'll be sent back to Israel as a reverse double agent."

Traci thought about Harry's rigidness and generally ornery disposition. "You think it will be that easy to flip him?"

Mr. Jones chuckled. "Of course not. He'll continue to spy for Israel."

"So ... you can feed them disinformation."

"You're getting the hang of this. Yes, and moles within the Mossad will pass on the false information back to their handlers in Iran."

"Isn't that exactly what they'd expect us to do?"

Mr. Jones hesitated, then laughed. "Why, Agent Kingsmith, don't tell me you're developing a sense of humor."

"What about The Chief? Was he caught?"

"Slipped away. Wily devil has nine lives. But now at least he's broke and won't be able to do much damage for a while. The mission was a complete success."

"Except for X dying. And the missing money."

"Oh, we'll track that down. If your identity thief comrade were still alive, he'd probably keep moving it like a game of three-card monte, but sitting in an account, we'll trace it within a few months."

Traci fell silent, contemplating the fates of the two men under her command.

"You are to be commended, Agent Kingsmith," Mr. Jones told her, in a surprisingly soothing tone. "You've earned the respect of the Committee. We'll be calling on you again."

"Thanks," Traci replied. "I think."

*   *   *

She visited the Israeli spy in Germany on a stopover back to the States. Although he was in traction his face and head were bandaged, mummy-style, she recognized Harry's familiar, irritating voice at once.

"I hear Uncle Sam won't be prosecuting you for espionage," she said.

"Yes, luckily for me no one wants this fiasco to ever see the light of day. Imagine the blowback? As soon as I recover, they'll be putting me on a plane to Israel with nothing but a clean suit and a one-way ticket."

"Maybe we'll work together again some day. After all, our countries really *are* allies. What did Netanyahu say? 'We are you and you are us'? "

"Well, it's a small world," Harry agreed.

She nodded.

"Any luck tracking down the $45 billion?" he inquired.

"Frankly, I don't think we'll ever recover that money, though Mr. Jones is optimistic. Wherever X stashed it, he stashed it good. Not in a Swiss bank – or one in Zimbabwe, that's for sure."

"Well, at least those Islamofascist sons of bitches won't get their hands on it," Harry said. There was a bowl of candies next to the bed and Traci took one. She sucked on it thoughtfully.

"He was a strange guy, wasn't he?" she said. "His actions probably saved millions of lives, who knows, maybe the solar system, if The Chief wasn't totally demented. But I don't know if he ever really understood right from wrong."

"He wasn't much of an enigma to me," Harry growled. "He was a greedy, calculating snake."

"Maybe, but I think in the end he became a hero, didn't he? I mean, he did go back for you. He saved your life. He didn't have to do that."

"I don't know why he went back. Probably had some self-serving motive we don't know about, some reason the sociopath needed me alive for his crooked scheme."

She waved her hand as if shooing the notion away. "I believe there was something decent in him and in the end he found it."

"Christ, you talk like you had a crush on him."

She shook her head.

"Come on now, admit it."

Traci relented and smiled. "I guess us girls have a weakness for bad boys."

"Well, I have a bit of bad boy in me," the injured man said. "Maybe when I have my face back, we can have a drink or something. They say I won't look like the Elephant Man, just different. Maybe they can give me Cary Grant."

Traci smiled at his attempt at humor. He'd never tried to be funny before. Perhaps there *was* a hidden side of Harry she hadn't seen before.

"Maybe," she said. "Yes, I'd like that." She gave him a peck on her cheek, and as she leaned in, he took the opportunity to pat her ass. She didn't complain. She figured he'd earned it.

The patient watched the woman exit the hospital room, leaned back and sighed. He reached into the jar on the nightstand and selected a candy. Lemon had always been his favorite.

He thought, *Sri Lanka is supposed to be beautiful this time of year.*

THE END

ABOUT THE AUTHOR

C. Michael Forsyth was born in New York City. He is a Yale graduate with an MFA in film from NYU. For 10 years he was senior writer for *Weekly World News,* the outrageous satirical tabloid. Many of those stories can be found in a collection titled *Batboy Lives.* He is the author of *Hour of the Beast, The Blood of Titans* and the children's book *Brothers.* Forsyth taught film and journalism at Coker College in Hartsville, SC. More about him can be found at http://freedomshammer.com.

Made in the USA
Charleston, SC
23 May 2016